Live, Laugh, Lattes

Cougar Tails Book 1

S.L. MACY

Cougar Tails

Cover Design by Self Pub Book Covers, Heather McNeal

Editing by Trish Kuper

Interior design by Angela McLaurin, Fictional formats

Live, Laugh, Lattes

Cougar Tails Book 1

For my Brynlie Belle

I love you more than all the words in the world.

Thank you for being my heart, my pride and my biggest fan.

Always believe.

XO

Live, Laugh, Lattes

Madi Kennedy is 40, fabulous and has it all, an exciting career as an ER Nurse at Bridgewater Memorial, a charming home in a suburb of Phoenix, loving and supportive parents, the best group of girlfriends any woman could ask for and the pride and joy of her life, her beautiful 9 year old daughter, Claire.

What else could Madi possibly need?

Maybe something that doesn't require 2 'C' batteries and likes to cuddle?

Insert Declan Hillier, Vanilla Ice, and a treadmill here.

Declan is very tall, very hot, very Southern, and very 29.

When Madi meets Declan she falls for him, literally.

Can someone who knows the cultural significance of the telephone number 867-5309 make a relationship work with someone who doesn't know life without MTV?

Madi loved New Coke and Jake Ryan.

Declan doesn't know what "Where's the beef?" means.

Madi loved Xanadu and wanted to be Julie McCoy, Cruise Director.

Declan loved Fight Club and wanted to be Stifler.

Can they overlook and overcome their differences?

Will the Cougar make a catch?

Chapter 1

SEAGULLS CRY OUT overhead as we stroll along the water's edge, listening to soft rhythmic whoosh of the ocean. He slowly grabs my hand, and looks at me out of the corner of his eye, I assume to gauge my reaction to his gesture. This man is beautiful. I mean, it's almost gross how hot he is… and HE is holding MY hand. I give him a shy smile; after all, I don't want him to think that just because he is getting a little hand holding action that it entitles him to anything else. But let's be real, he totally is. I at least have to try and play shy. I don't want him thinking I am some sort of epic whore bag.

As we walk down the beach, the sea spray starts to kick up and suddenly I have warm salty water being sprayed into my face… like a hose.

What the fu…

"MADI! MADI! Earth to MADI! I think he's good. You can stop with the ambu-bag now. Dr. Kelly called it 2 minutes ago. He's not a Macy's Day balloon. You can stop pumping him full of air."

Looking up, I see my friend Savannah holding a now empty syringe of saline—I'm assuming the very same warm salty water I now have all over my face.

Yep, it was too good to be true. This is what happens when you work the night shift in the ER.

I sigh deeply. Back to reality, Madi. You're not walking on the beach with a hot ass guy, you're standing in ER Triage 3 at Bridgewater General Hospital, over a dead body, while your friends and coworkers find entertaining ways to torture you. I really shouldn't complain. After all, it could be worse. I could be lying here like this guy.

"What on earth were you thinking about, Madi? Jesus, Mary Mother and Joseph, you were in another world, weren't you?"

I give a pathetic nod to Savannah. Yep, I was in a land far, far away where 20 minutes ago I didn't fall ass over tea kettle trying to dodge the epic fight that broke out between 2 drunk guys brought in by the police after a bar fight. Apparently they still wanted to rumble. This hospital looks just like the skeezy bar they were pulled from. Granted, yes, there are people puking and there are bodily fluids on the floor, but for vastly different reasons. And when we say we are giving you a cocktail, it doesn't come in a PBR can or with a fancy umbrella. It's usually shoved into your arm with a gigantic needle to shut you the fuck up so you stop screaming, "I'm dying! I'm dying!" Heads up—no one, and I mean NO ONE, has ever dropped dead in an ER because they broke their ankle falling off of their stripper shoes. Just sayin.

Savannah and I start the lovely task of cleaning up "Bernie", the now dead man lying in front of us. We call him Bernie because we don't know his real name—all unknown dead guys that come in are Bernie to us. Yes, it's crude, but don't lie, you laughed a little as flashbacks of *Weekend at Bernie's* went through your head, didn't you? Granted, we didn't try and reanimate this guy for our own shits and giggles, but Bernie fits.

I feel badly for his family and friends. Does he have family and friends? Will anyone notice that this man isn't on the golf course tomorrow? Does anyone care that he had a massive heart attack in his driveway this morning, going to get his newspaper? I assume the woman out for her morning walk who came across him on the sidewalk cares. After all, she did call 911, so that shows some form of empathy. But how long will she care?

Would anyone notice if I didn't show up in the ER for work tomorrow? Would anyone care? Oh, who am I kidding—of course they would. That would mean more work for those bitches if I wasn't here. They would hunt me down if I didn't show up. And if I WAS dead, they would in fact reanimate my corpse for their own shits and giggles.

I guess I am lucky enough to have an amazing circle of friends, and by amazing I mean judgmental, bitchy, catty, a tad whorish and all around awesome. I love those bitches!

Savannah is one of such bitches. "I'm about ready to blow this joint and my husband! I have done my 12 hours!" Jesus, she's blunt.

"Thanks, Savannah, way to rub it in. I get to go home and do laundry, and the only blowing I will be doing is with my hair dryer after my shower. Jealous much?" I say, with a batting of my eyelashes and a flounce in my step as I walk over and pull up the sheet over Bernie.

"I told you, we need to find you a man. It's been way too

long since you have gotten laid and that is not OK. You and Andy split up what, like 6 years ago? He's already married to that skank he fucked while you two were married."

"Wow, that's not at all painful to be reminded of. Thanks."

It's true. Andy Kennedy and I were married and had a beautiful baby girl we named Claire. Life was perfect, until (cue evil bitch music) Sindee the Slut happened upon our perfect little life. OK, I may have oversold the perfect life thing just a tad. But Sindee *is* a slut. I mean, really? Who names their kid Sindee, spells it that way, and doesn't expect them to be a slut? That's like naming your kid Cinnamon or Sapphire and not expecting them to spin on a silver pole bobbing for dollars.

Sorry, Savannah! I should mention that Savannah paid her way through nursing school by spinning on said pole. But she didn't wreck any homes, as far as I know. Now she uses the skills she learned having George Washington's face shoved in her panties by teaching Pole Dancing classes on the side. One of these days I may take her up on the class, but to be honest I am too chicken shit and she won't let me forget it. Bitch!

"Yes, Vannah, I know, but I have been busy working and taking care of Claire. The last thing I need to be doing is barhopping. How pathetic does it look for a 40 year old single mother to be trolling a bar for a guy? I can't compete with these 24 year old skanks, with their perky boobs, no stretch-marked skin, and fresh faces that aren't sleep deprived. I have bags under my eyes so big they ask me at the grocery store if I'd like to just take my shit home in them!"

"Oh my God. Shut the hell up, Madi. You are hot and you need a man STAT!" Yes, we throw around medical terminology in our day to day conversation. It's what we do.

"We need a GNO! You know, a girl's night out! All of us—you, me, Lynn, Grace and Taylor. No excuses! You need to get drunk and dry hump some hot piece of ass while you're gettin' your swerve on," she says with a laugh, shaking her ass.

"I will give you $1000 to never ever say the words 'dry hump' to me again."

I'm afraid if I try to 'get my swerve on' I may need one of those 'I've fallen and I can't get up' things.

Do I have it in me to troll the bars? Is it sad and gross? Will people look at me like I am some sort of icky cougar? I can't think of anything worse than being called a cougar. Well, maybe Savannah saying the words 'dry hump' again.

"OK, Vannah. Yes, girl's night. How about Saturday night in 2 weeks? But I'm telling you right now. If the word 'cougar' or 'dry hump' comes up, I am taking my ancient ass home to Ben and Jerry."

I heart Ben and Jerry, they do God's work. I don't need a man—I have Chunky Monkey and Phish Food. They never let me down, I never have to worry about the toilet seat being left up, and they don't hog the blankets or remote. They don't ask questions and they don't judge. They are just there, and it's a beautiful thing.

"You're thinking about ice cream, aren't you? You're going to go home and watch *Antiques Roadshow* and eat ice cream. Jesus, you need help, Eunice."

I begin to laugh. "No, I am not going home to eat ice cream. It's 7:20 in the morning and we just worked 12 hours in hell. I think I am going to hit the gym on the way home since Claire is at Andy's until tomorrow. What are you going to do?"

"I told you. Go home and fuck my hot husband," she says

as she climbs into her gigundous truck. Seriously—it's fucking huge, like I need a step stool to climb in it huge. If I didn't know any better I would think Savannah was overcompensating for a small dick.

Did you hear that? Did you hear my eyes roll into the back of my head? Because it was pretty loud. That girl has more sex than anyone I know. But then again, I guess if I had a 6'4", hot, tattooed, cowboy slash firefighter for a husband I would too. But noooo, I had to marry and divorce a 5'9" Italian salesman with the words *Summers Eve* stamped on his forehead. Strong work, Madi. Strong work.

"Bye, Vannah. Have fun dry humping Luke!" I shout with a wave over my shoulder.

"Oh, there will be nothing dry about it!! Later, hooker!" she shouts as she cranks the engine on her overly obnoxious phallic truck. I love her but she pisses me off sometimes.

As I walk over to my car and unlock the doors, I take yet another moment to indulge in buyer's remorse. What was I thinking, buying this thing? Good God, I thought it was SO cute and I would look adorable in the Gucci Edition Fiat.

Really, Madi?

You have an 8 year old and 2 huge dogs. What business did you have buying Gucci anything, much less a tiny freaking clown car? That's what I get for going car shopping hungover and possibly still drunk the morning after my 40th birthday. The salesman said I looked hot in it. He might have oversold it just a tad. It would do me good to remember in the future that they work on commission. Asshat. I should have gotten personalized plates that said *Midlife Crisis*, but that's too many letters. Maybe *LAME* would be better.

Pulling up to the gym, I take a moment to say goodbye to

my dignity before I attempt to work out. You see, I am not the most graceful person out there and have been known to forget that there are others around when I am working out. On more than one occasion, I have been humiliated to see several sets of eyes on me while I bust a move or hum a little too loud while on the treadmill.

"Hi, Taylor. How are you?" I say and wave as I walk into… are you ready… *The Jungle Gym.*

Yes, I currently have a membership to an establishment called The Jungle Gym. And no, it's not at all stupid that the employees walk around wearing animal print shirts that say 'welcome to the jungle'. I mean, really? Ripping off an 80's classic for financial gain? I guess it could be worse—the shirts could say 'let's get physical'. Good luck getting those words out of your head and not picturing Olivia Newton John in shiny spandex, leg warmers and a headband. Why did headbands ever go out of style? I think it was Richard Simmons. He ruined it for everyone. Sorry, off topic.

Taylor Allen is the owner of The Jungle Gym. Jesus, I hate saying that. I met Taylor a few years ago when she came into the ER after getting hit in the head by one of the people she was training. We've been best buds ever since. Taylor is not your typical gym rat; she is one of those classy bitches who would never call anyone a classy bitch because she's too classy of a bitch to do that.

She is always put together and immaculate in her appearance. I should remember that just because you work out in a gym doesn't always mean you are going to be tall and beautiful like Taylor. No matter how many miles I log on the treadmill, I will never grow 7 inches in height and have her beautiful bone structure. I decided to join her gym after stitching her up and seeing what amazing shape she was in. I had put on a few pounds after Andy and I split as I chose to find comfort in the arms of Ben and Jerry while he found comfort in the crotch of a whore.

Taylor has always been extremely athletic and bought the gym after she came into an ass load of money several years ago. She has never spoken about how she made her money so it must be something good, like selling organs on the black market, or maybe she helped a Nigerian Prince move his money to an American bank and to repay her he split his fortune with her. Ooooooohhhh that's cool!

"Hi, Madi. How are you? Are you going to do more than walk on the treadmill today?" Taylor asks as I walk in the door.

"No, just gonna feel the burn for a bit before I head home," I reply as I head towards the locker room to change out of my Bernie-covered scrubs.

"You know, Madi, you pay me a ridiculous amount of money every month to use this gym and all you ever do is walk on the treadmill. I'm not one to turn away money"… *I bet it was the Nigerian Prince thing…* "but you do know that you can walk outside for free, right?"

"You're right, Taylor, and I would if we didn't live in Hell's armpit. I can't walk outside in this heat—no one can except camels and Sindee, the troll. And that's only because trolls love the heat."

"You're an idiot, Madi, but I love you. Go do your thing and get the hell out. I know you're dying to go home and eat ice cream and watch *Antiques Roadshow,*" she says with a chuckle.

"Bitch! Love you!" I shout as I walk into the locker room.

After about an hour on the treadmill, I decide it's time to head home. It was a pretty long shift in the ER and I am exhausted. "Bye, Taylor. I'm headed home. I need to get some sleep."

"Hey, don't forget that it's Girls Night In at your place tonight!" Taylor shouts as I head towards the door.

Oh shit, I forgot! It's my week to host our monthly 'Stitch and Bitch' but to be completely honest, there is no stitching, just a whole lot of bitching, eating, and wine drinking.

"Aww crap. I forgot! OK, I will see you guys at 7. Don't forget to bring the wine!!" I toss back as I head out the door. Great, now I have to go home and bake a cake for tonight. Ugh *(face plant palm to forehead)*.

Why do I do this to myself? Maybe I'll try out my new s'mores cake on the girls. What's the worst that could happen? They all croak right in front of me after eating the cake? Would that be so bad?

I wouldn't have to listen to Savannah bitch and moan about me getting laid and Taylor wouldn't harass me about utilizing a personal trainer at her gym. Elise and Grace? Well, the hospital would be very quiet without them, and Lynn? Let's just say I wouldn't have to worry about getting arrested when I spend time with her.

"Ahh, home sweet home," I say as I pull up in front of my house. I love my house. I bought it after Andy and I divorced. It's my dream home, really. It has a huge kitchen and family room which was so important to me. All Claire cared about was that it was a 2 story house. What is it with kids and stairs? I think she will feel differently in a few years when I make her haul her own laundry up and down 2 flights.

The neighborhood is very quiet, mostly young families

with kids around Claire's age. The streets are lined with Jacaranda trees, covered in beautiful purple flowers. The front porches have rocking chairs, even though it's hotter than a swamp rat's ass in Arizona. We only get to use our porch swings and chairs a few months of the year, but they sure do add a homey feel. To be honest, the neighborhood is very charming. I'm waiting for Beaver Cleaver to skateboard past my driveway any minute, and I can hear the theme song playing in my head when I drive down the street.

Walking in the house, I am nearly knocked over by Zoe and Athena, my two huge mutts, also lovingly referred to as Moose and Cow. I swear they eat their body weight in food every week and it's not OK, because as we all know, what goes in has to come out. I could fertilize crops with the amount of shit they put out. I won the dogs in the divorce, along with the furniture and everything else in my former house with the exception of the BBQ grill and surround sound system. Men do have their priorities. See, that's what happens when you cheat and put your penis into a nasty troglodyte. Your ex-wife gets all the good stuff.

I jump in the shower quickly and rinse off the Bernie juice and Jungle Gym sweat of my day. Changing into a night shirt, I decide to take a quick power nap before I have to get up and start making a fucking cake for my fucking friends who are invading my fucking house tonight.

I wake up around 5:00 to the sound of my cell phone beeping with incoming messages. Nope, that's not at all annoying. Time to make the whores some s'mores.

I love to bake and who better to test out my recipe ideas on than my friends? They love me no matter what, even when I accidently make a cheesecake with salt rather than sugar and they all dry heave in my living room. I warned them that I had just pulled a double shift in the ER and was too tired to bake, but no, Lynn wanted cheesecake. Well, she got it—a lovely salty as hell cheesecake. Ooops! To be honest, I was mildly amused to see their gagging faces; it reminded me of the blow job class Savannah tried to give all of us. I swear to God that girl is hornier than anyone else I know. How does she walk and not limp? Thanks to a few too many glasses of wine, an impromptu sleep over on their couch, and an unlocked bathroom door, I've seen Luke; I know he's not normal. She must have some type of cavernous coochie.

MAN, THE HOUSE smells good. I love the smell of a baking cake. Sometimes when I think about my life I wonder if I should have gone to pastry school rather than nursing school. I love to bake and decorate cakes. Anything that has to do with flour, eggs, sugar, vanilla, chocolate and lard is just good stuff to me. Everyone is happy to see you when you walk into the room with an ooey gooey sweet concoction. People are less than pleased to see you when you walk into a room with an enema bag and rectal tip. But then, I remind myself that if I hadn't gone to nursing school, I wouldn't have met Elise, who got me the job at Bridgewater. And Bridgewater is where I met Grace, Savannah, Taylor and, of course, Andy. And if I hadn't met Andy, I wouldn't have Claire, which led me to meet Lynn. And I wouldn't be where I am in life right now or be the person I am today. And how does that all tie back into Kevin Bacon? Yeah, it doesn't.

I could have opened my own bakery, weigh 400 pounds, actually watch *Antiques Roadshow* and eat ice cream all day. No one would give me shit about it except the 14 cats I would have that I call my babies and dress in clothes.

Oh, God. Thank you for nursing school and Claire, Savannah, Grace, Taylor, Lynn, Elise, the gym and my allergy to cats. I shudder to think where I could be right now. Well, that was sobering.

It's about 7ish when the first hag arrives. Lo and behold, it's Taylor. She is never late—she is always 5 minutes ahead of everyone else and always dressed to the nines. She walks in and places her pricey quilted Chanel bag on my sofa table. Dear baby Jesus, please don't let my dogs drool on that bag. I don't make enough in a year to repair or replace it. Maybe I need to find a Nigerian Prince who needs to move some cash to the U.S. and share with me.

"House smells great like always, Madi. What did you make this time?" I take the bottle of wine she brought and walk into the kitchen.

"Chocolate s'mores cake. Wine?"

"No, I don't want any wine. I came here for the witty conversation and insightful banter. Of course I want wine, you moron! Pop that open and give me a straw!"

I laugh and open the bottle of Chardonnay. As I hand her the glass, the doorbell rings. Guess who? Yep, it's Savannah, and I could be wrong but she appears to be limping a little. Maybe Luke finally fucked an organ loose.

"Hey, Vannah, come on in. Taylor is in the kitchen sucking down the Chardonnay."

"Bitch, save me some!' Savannah shouts on her way into the kitchen.

"Where is Elise? Is she coming? I didn't hear from her today," I ask Vannah.

"No, she can't make it. She's working tonight. Someone called out in LDR and they had 5 women waiting to push kids out of their vaginas all at once so she stayed to help out."

"I never get to see her anymore," I reply sadly. Elise McCaffery is one of my oldest and best friends. She is a Labor/Delivery/Recovery nurse at our hospital and the one who helped me get my job at Bridgewater. How she works with screaming babies—and even worse, screaming mothers—all day is beyond me. I have the luxury of turning up the morphine drip if someone is bitching too much; she, however, can't. I admire her for what she does. God knows I couldn't do it. I would go ape shit on some woman who was screaming at the top of her lungs to get her an epidural and ice chips. Bitch, you are dilated to 3, get your own damn ice chips. You can walk.

I walked into the hospital with a smile on my face and dilated to 7 with Claire. True story. Walked in and said, "hi, I think I'm in labor." 15 minutes later, they checked me and I was 7 centimeters. 3 hours later she was born. No epidural! BAM! That's how it's done, bitches! OK, sorry. Back to the story.

Elise and I met in nursing school. She worked at Bridgewater in transport while she was in school so when we graduated she had an instant job, and apparently sang my praises so they offered me one as well. YAY US!

We started working in the same unit together as new grads. Let me just tell you, the night shift in Med/ Surg is no fun, but it did give us experience and seniority. Elise married Eamon after they met through mutual friends. Eamon is a great guy and they are such a cute couple. He's a computer wizard, not to be confused with a pinball wizard. He has the luxury of working from home so that he can be there before and after school for their 8 year old daughter Phaedra. I know, right? Irish much? Elise, Eamon and Phaedra McCaffery. I can practically see pink hearts, yellow moons, orange stars, green clovers and blue diamonds floating above their heads.

Phaedra and Claire are besties and have known each other since they were born. They are only 10 months apart and have grown up together. Elise and Eamon were my lifeline when Andy and I were separating. They helped me with Claire when I would get called into work at the last minute and Andy wouldn't show to pick her up. They helped me when we moved and were just there for moral support. I could always count on Eamon to greet me with a freshly made cocktail in hand when I would arrive and they always knew when I needed one. Elise is also a baker like me and can I just say her carrot cake is the best I have ever had, better than mine. There, I said it.

Just as I am about the close the door, I see Lynn and Grace coming up the walkway. They must have pulled up at the same time. "Hey, BITCHES!" I shout to the last 2 to arrive. "Come on in! Taylor and Vannah are sucking down wine in the kitchen," I give air cheek kisses to the girls as they come in, cuz you know it's fancy and that's how we roll.

"Quit pretending that you're an actual hostess and get in here and have some wine with us, Madi!" Savannah yells from the other room. Grace walks into the kitchen with Lynn and shouts, "HEY, FUCKERS! The party can start, I'm here! Whoop! Whoop!"

Did she just say 'whoop whoop' and do that 'raise the

roof' thing with her hands? Really? Have some decorum, Grace. You're a doctor, for fuck's sake.

Oh, Grace. Also known as Dr. Grace Kelly, ER doctor extraordinaire, and yes, her name really is Grace Kelly. She just dropped the F-bomb in my kitchen in pure Grace style—she's pretty special that way. Dr. Grace Kelly is kind of the shit, though. She is the best ER doctor on the face of the earth and makes going to work every day worth it. For comic value alone it's worth taking a shift with her.

I was lucky enough to meet her at the hospital when she was doing her residency and we clicked instantly. It could be the fact that she threw a scalpel at my foot to get my attention during a trauma code, but it worked, and we became fast friends. Most people would be offended that a sharp as hell blade was thrown at them, but I know she was just trying to "teach me"—teach me what, I have no idea. Perhaps how to dodge knives, which could come in handy if the whole nurse thing doesn't pan out. I can always be a carnie, travel the country with toothless hicks and live out of a van…

WAIT! Never mind, I am TERRIFIED of vans! *Cue slasher music 'Re Re Re Re Re Re'.*

At any rate, I now have mad fast feet and can Riverdance my way around the ER. I won't lie, it's impressive.

She is a petite spitball of fire with great hair and I love her to death, but to be honest, she is the most foul mouthed, vagina obsessed woman I know. She's worse than Savannah and I didn't think that was possible.

"Hey, what happened to you after you called the TOD on Bernie at shift change today?" I ask Grace.

"Oh, um, I had some charts to sign off on," she replies with a shit eating grin.

"Are you serious, Gracie? Who the hell do you think you're kidding? You were messing around with Kai in the resident's room again, weren't you? Charts, my ass," I mumble.

Oh my God, I am surrounded by whores! What is wrong with me? Why do I do this to myself? I haven't had sex in almost 2 years and these women can't go 12 hours without an orgasm. Jesus. Is it really SO great that you have to have it every day? I mean, I am living proof that you CAN function like a normal human being without regular orgasms. I wonder if I even remember how to have an orgasm. Is it like riding a bike? Do you just… get on and instantly remember?

I picture my vajayjay, dusty and knitting a quilt, surrounded by cats, watching *Antiques Roadshow.* I'm 40 but I'm pretty sure my vagina is 85.

"Hey, it's not my fault I married a fine piece of Hawaiian Irish ass!" Grace says proudly.

It's true. Her husband Kai is a nurse in the PICU. Yes, he's a nurse who is hot and works with critical babies—he's the whole package. He probably knits shoes for orphan kids and reads to the deaf too. The beauty of their relationship is that they are OK with the fact that Grace earns 4 times his salary and is 5 years older. I think it's because she puts out at work. I could be wrong, but doubtful.

"Let's get down to grass tacks here," Lynn says. "When was the last time YOU had sex, Madi? And I mean real sex, not 'Charlie the Wonder Toy' sex."

"Oh my God Lynn! It's BRASS tacks, not grass tacks, you idiot. If you are going to insult me, at least be grammatically correct!"

The girls all bust up laughing as Grace pipes up. "It's been

2 years. 2 YEARS since she had a penis-induced orgasm and you know what, that shit's NOT OK, Madi. It's not natural. Your hoo-ha has needs and it's crying out for you to feed it! It's like that plant from *Little Shop of Horrors*. FEED ME, MADI, FEEEEED ME!"

The room fills with laughter again, and in true Savannah style she spits wine all over the back of Lynn's head.

"Really? Really, Savannah? You just spit Chardonnay all over the back of me! What the hell is wrong with you?" Lynn shouts.

"That is a waste of good wine, and I call party foul!" Taylor pipes up, and we all know what that means. It's a long standing tradition of ours that whoever commits the party foul has to bring the wine next time. But I have a feeling we won't be having wine. Knowing Savannah, she will tap a keg filled with Bud Light and expect us all to do keg stands in her living room. Gotta love my Texas girl.

After hours of hoo-ha talk and the round table discussion on my lack of sex life, the night winds down. We start to clean up the epic mess that is now my living room—scattered Chinese takeout containers, empty wine bottles and cake plates. As we gather in the kitchen with our handfuls of trash and dishes, Lynn makes a comment on the s'mores cake I made tonight. "You know, Madi, the party planning business is really picking up. I had to take on a partner and I think your cakes would be a perfect addition to the business. I can plan the parties and you can supply the baked goods for the client. We can call it Madi's Morsels or Madi Cakes. What do you think?"

Lynn is amazing. She started a party planning business called Bubbles & Fizz out of her home and it has now become an empire. The things she can do with crepe paper and a glue gun knows no bounds. Martha Stewart's got nothing on her. I met Lynn when I hired her to plan Claire's first birthday party. She did an amazing job, and during the arduous process we learned we had a lot in common and became fast friends. Lynn has a keen eye for detail and apparently and even keener eye for bullshit. She's the one who pointed out to me that something was fishy between Andy and Sindee.

Lynn has been asking me for a while now if I would make cakes for her clients. Baking has always been something I did as a hobby and for those around me that I love, but I don't know if I could do it for strangers. What if they didn't like my work? What if the cake was burned and we didn't know until it was cut into? I can handle my friends talking shit about me, it's done on a daily basis, but I don't know if I could handle strangers talking about me behind my back.

"I don't know, Lynn. It sounds like a great idea, but I'm afraid with my shifts at the hospital and taking care of Claire I might not have time. Besides, what if I do a bad job and your clients hate it? I wouldn't want it to affect your business in any way."

Lynn rolls her eyes at me "Trust me, Madi, I wouldn't have asked if I thought you weren't up to the challenge. I have eaten countless cakes, cookies and ass-widening concoctions of yours and have yet to be disappointed. Just say you'll think about it… again."

I smile and nod, to appease her for now. It's always been a deep-seated dream of mine to open a bakery… could this be the beginning of it? Doubtful.

After I walk the last of the girls out I decide it's time to head to bed. I have the next few days off and my baby girl Claire is coming home after spending a few days with her father and the troglodyte. I always feel the need to scrub off the first layer of her epidermis with bleach when she comes home from their house. I am sure their house is clean and lovely; I mean, after all, pharmaceutical sales reps and trolls make decent money, right? It's just the idea of my baby girl having any of their ick on her.

I finish closing up the house, turn down all the lights, blow out the last of the candles and make my way upstairs to my room. Can I just say that I love my room? It's so cozy and inviting, inviting to who I have no idea, but I just love the Tiffany blue and grey color scheme I chose. My favorite part is my fluffy cloud four poster bed with its 147 pillows. It's just divine. OK, 147 pillows is a slight exaggeration, but there are a lot.

As I climb in, I say a silent prayer, hoping maybe I can pick up where I left off on that beach earlier today with Mr. Fine-as-hell and see where it goes.

Deep sigh.

Chapter 2

OH MY GOD, his tongue is so warm and soft. The things Mr. Fine-as-hell can do with that tongue are amazing; he is such a great kisser. Ooooh, I wonder what else he can do with that tongue… mmmm…

Wait… why is he licking my face? That's odd, I can't say I have ever had a guy lick my face before. Maybe he thinks it's a turn on? Some people are into weird things, you learn that real quick working in the ER.

Wait, why does his breath smell like kibble? And ass? What the fu…

"ATHENA! Get off me, stop licking my face! AACCKKK!" Yes, for the record, I did just sound like Lucy from Charlie Brown. You know, Mr. Fine-as-hell and I are never going to get to second base at this rate.

I guess the slobbery kisses and tail thumping against the wall are my cue to get up for the day. Who doesn't want to start their day off at 5:12am by having asshole kisses placed all over their face? Good morning.

I might as well make use of my time before Andy drops Claire off at 10, which I should clarify in Andy time means 11ish. I guess I will head to the gym and try to run away from my thoughts of Mr. Fine-as-hell licking my face smelling of ass.

I pull up in front of the Jungle Gym a little after 7 to see Taylor's Mercedes is already here. That woman is always at the gym. I wonder how she finds the time to run the gym, spend time with her husband Garrett and run the charity she founded. Taylor has a soft spot for the elderly; she started an organization feeding senior citizens who are on fixed or low incomes. She really is a wonderful person, but I still hate her sometimes.

"Morning, Taylor!" I wave as I come in. "Morning, Madi, here to 'work out'?" she says with air quotes. Really, I expected more of Taylor than air quotes. This isn't 1995.

I smile. "Yep, just a little work out before Andy drops Claire off today. Looking like THIS" -I give her a little shimmy—"doesn't come easy," I finish.

"Yeah, neither do you," Taylor says with a wink. I think that bitch just insulted me!

Off to the treadmill. Perhaps I will kick it up a notch today and do a fast walk—not run, mind you, but more of a rapid saunter. You see, I don't run. Unless I am being chased by a van (*Re Re Re Re Re Re*) or a clown who wants to harvest my essence, I DO NOT RUN. Well, maybe for a good sale at Nordstrom's or on Black Friday but those are the only reasons.

About 30 minutes into my work out, I am minding my own business and sweating to the oldies when I spot HIM. Oh my God in heaven, he is beautiful. I didn't know they made them like that in real life. I look up towards the heavens and internally chat with God. "Well done, sir, or madam, or whoever."

Glancing back down, I attempt to not look at him but I can't help it. You don't want look but you just have to, like an eclipse or when I run—it's a feast for the eyes of anyone who can see me. It's hard for them to look away from the epic tragedy occurring before them.

He is amazing and he's smiling at me AND making eye contact. Really? Me? Is this happening right now? Am I being Punked? Is Ashton Kutcher going to jump out any second, laughing and pointing at me? Get a grip, Madi.

I look around. There surely must be some Gymbo, AKA gym bimbo, nearby, with her ass hanging out of her spandex onesie, her boobs at full and upright attention with nary a hair out of place. Maybe I just got caught in the flirting crossfire. I'M HIT! Ego Down!

Nope, no one but me.

No way this fine specimen is looking and smiling at me. I decide to put my big girl panties on and smile back. What's the worst that could happen? I shouldn't have asked.

As I give him my best flirty smile with a slight giggle, I feel a hand tap me on the shoulder. It's Taylor. I remove my ear buds and ask "What?" in a curt tone. I am more than a little annoyed that she busted my flirt groove. I see he's still smiling. I think he's checking me out!

"Shut the hell up. No one wants to hear your rendition of *Ice Ice Baby*. No one wants to stop or collaborate and listen to you," Taylor says with an eye roll before walking away.

Oh. Em. Gee. That's why Mr. HotTottie was smiling at me. I just made a complete asshole out of myself and he had a front row seat. Of course he did, because life is just that cruel sometimes.

Dear baby Jesus, I don't ask you for a lot but if you could create a giant sinkhole that would swallow me up, treadmill included, I would be much obliged.

Well this is clearly my cue to tuck my tail between my legs, put on my sunglasses and make my exit, stage left. I think I'm going to have to check with Taylor to see if the contract I have with this gym has a moron clause that would allow me to break my membership without some epic financial penalty, because clearly I can't show my face here ever again.

Alright, how do I do this? Treadmill stopped-check.

Face pointed firmly towards the floor-check.

Gym towel pulled far up around my neck-check.

Time to bolt-check.

As I round the corner, headed towards the lobby, I take one last fleeting peek at Mr. HotPants. Jesus, he's fine. As I speed walk past the front desk, Taylor attempts to say something to me but I feel like I'm just a blur at this point. Sprinting for the car, I suddenly realize my purse and car keys are locked up… in the locker room … inside the gym I just bolted from.

"SERIOUSLY?" I shout. I take my phone out of my armband and text Taylor.

–Can you please get my purse from the locker and bring it to me. :) Smooches–

–Come in and get it yourself. Chicken.–

–Bok Bok. Please T, I am mortified.–

–Fine. Baby–

–Locker 5, Combo 4238 XO–

After what seems like an eternity, Taylor meets me at my car. She hands me my purse and says, "Nice work, genius. That was quite a show you put on in there. I should charge an entertainment fee for that." She's laughing as I unlock the door and quickly start the engine.

This calls for a Starbucks iced venti nonfat 7 pump light ice chai latte. Yes, it takes me longer to order it than drink it. I decide to call my girls. I need back up, moral support and a cinnamon scone. I just humiliated myself on a grand scale. I feel that caffeine and dense English pastries are needed STAT. Maybe Savannah could start an IV on me in the lobby and I could just main line my latte. Perhaps I could talk Grace into writing me a prescription for some anti-humiliation tablet. Ooh, maybe Eamon has one of those flashy mind erasing things like in the movies. He has all kinds of gadgets.

About 30 minutes after placing my "MAN DOWN" text to the girls, Savannah and Grace arrive. And none too soon—I was about to drown my pathetic existence in another cinnamon scone. They are delicious and if you have the means, I highly recommend you pick up one… or seven.

"What the hell did you do?" Grace asks as she walks in to find me slumped in a chair in the corner of our favorite Starbucks.

"I was singing on the treadmill and the most beautiful creature I have ever seen caught me and was laughing at me."

"Oh for Christ's sake, Madi, is that all?" Savannah pipes up.

"Is that all? Are you kidding me with this? I just made a total asshole out of myself in front of some hot guy and, well, whoever else might have been paying attention!"

"I told you to knock that shit off on the treadmill, Mads. I knew you were either going to sing yourself into humiliation or dance your ass right off the belt and face plant. I was, of course, hoping for the latter and that I would be nearby with a video recorder," Savannah says with a smile. God, I hate her sometimes.

"Go get your drinks and shut up." Back to my scone.

Just then a text comes in from Lynn.

–Sorry, can't make it knee deep in tissue paper flowers and tulle for this party. S & G are pulling double duty for me XO–

S & G? Seems appropriate that the two who show up to 'help' share the same initials of Sodom and Gomorrah. Oh God, did I just do mental air quotes? Could this day suck anymore?

"I need water. I think I OD'd on scones and latte. Need anything?" I say to the girls. They both shake their heads so I head up to the counter.

"Hi, can I get an ice water please?" I say with a smile to the overly fake girl behind the counter.

"Umm, you have to buy something. We don't just give out water," the bimbette says to me with just a tad too much assholiness in her voice.

Now I am not one to judge someone from 14 seconds of contact with them; however, I feel that my initial impression of Tiffani with an 'i' is spot-on. Her hair is overly bleached, her boobs are overly fake, her lips are overly red, her clothes are overly tight, her nose and ears are overly pierced and her tone is overly bitchy. OK, large inhale and here goes.

"Well, let's see. Tiffani with an i, is it? I did just buy about $12 worth of drinks and goodies from this fine establishment. My friends over there," I turn and wave "Have ordered drinks and food as well. And, Tiffani with i, Icome in here so often I have a gold card with my name on it, because I drop a small fortune here, probably equal to your annual salary, a weekly basis."

I don't know what I am more impressed with, the fact that I managed to get that all out in one breath or the fact that I said it at all. I am not known to be confrontational but what do I have to lose after my embarrassing display at the gym? I'm just gonna let it all hang out!

"Is there a problem here?" the manager asks as he approaches. "No, not at all, Mark. Tiffani with an i was just getting me some water,"insert eyelash batting and smile here.

"Hi, Madi, how are you? How are things in the ER?" he asks.

"Great! You know I love my job, but coming in here to get my caffeine fix from you always makes it better," I reply to Mark the Starbucks manager. He is a nice guy and he makes a mean 7 pump light ice nonfat iced chai latte. I have been coming here since he was a brand new barista. I showed him how to make the perfect chai latte for me and have stuck by him as he worked his way up to manager. He's a good kid.

"Here you go, Madi. Good to see you," Mark says, handing me an ice water.

"Thanks, Mark. You too," I smile as I walk back to the table of unhelpful snatches I call my friends.

"What was that about?" Grace asks.

"Nothing. Make me nasty Barbie didn't want to get me a water. Apparently she thought I was some type of vagrant trying to get free stuff."

"Well, I told you that you need to get new gym clothes and maybe comb your hair before you work out. You do look a tad homelessy today," Savannah says sipping her drink.

"Thanks, bitch. I can totally feel the love. Let's not forget that I ran out of that gym so fast I'm surprised I didn't leave skid marks in the lobby. AND I DONT RUN!" I shout.

"She said skid marks," Grace says with a giggle. I swear to God, for a highly respected doctor, she acts more like a 12 year old boy.

"We need to take you shopping! You have been busting your ass at the gym to get your body back after Andy the Wonder Douche, and it's time we buy you some clothes that show it off. And maybe a new pair of FMPs for our girls night out. You wasted all that time on that dinkus you married—now it's your turn to live it up a little," Savannah will say anything for an excuse to go shopping.

"OK. Claire will be home later today so maybe we can take all the kids to the mall and pick up a few things and have lunch. Speaking of which, I need to get going. Andy should be there soon with Claire and I should shower before they get there."

"No need to shower. Andy is used to smelly, icky things. He married Sindee," Grace says with a smile. God, I love her sometimes.

I ARRIVE HOME in time to shower and change before Andy drops off Claire. I have missed my little Éclair so much the past few days. As much as I hate to say anything nice about Andy, and trust me it's hard to find anything nice to say, I do have to give him some credit. He does spend more time than I thought he would with Claire. When we decided to get divorced, Claire was only 2, and he was so busy in his own little world I really didn't think he would spend much time with her. Don't get me wrong, there are weeks that go by that he doesn't see her or call, but she always has a good time when they are together. And—oh, this is going to hurt—Sindee is good to her, and that's all I ask. Well, that and that all of Sindee's hair falls out. It can only be an improvement at this point. Catty Madi in the house, what what!

Being a single mom who works odd shifts at the hospital can be tough, but I am lucky enough that my parents are a huge help with Claire. Being an only child and my parents' only grandchild, she is pretty spoiled and overly loved by my parents.

Claire loves spending time at their house. She has her own room, computer, TV, a pool, trampoline, Wii, etc. I mean really, it's a kid's camp being run by two retirees. She has them wrapped around her little finger.

My parents have been so supportive of me and my decision to become a nurse. They spent countless nights taking care of Claire when she was a toddler so I could study for my Masters and work odd shifts at the hospital. Andy and Sindee decided to move to the opposite side of Phoenix so it was hard to find someone to watch her when she was little. My parents have always stepped up to help us.

I couldn't have done it without them.

When Claire was diagnosed with Tourette's syndrome about a year ago it was a devastating blow for me and the possible future she faced. My parents were by our side, and I can never repay them for being my rock when all I wanted to do was crumble. Being a kid is hard these days, harder than I remember it being. I hated the idea of Claire having to deal with anything other than the normal stuff kids deal with.

When the doctor told Andy and me that she had Tourette's, I actually felt all the oxygen leave my lungs. The room seemed to get very loud, but I couldn't help but notice no one was talking. I think it was the rush of blood flow in my ears that was deafening. It took a few days of crying to myself, tossing and turning in bed and a much needed junk food intervention by Grace with the world's best and most calorie filled hamburger I had ever had… but it was awesome.

Once I got done with my pity party (Madi, party of 1, your hissy fit is ready), I needed to realize that her diagnosis is a part of her life, but does not define it and certainly isn't the definition of her. I had a heart to heart with Claire and explained to her why she makes the little grunts and throat clearing noises. I explained that she isn't different or weird, she isn't sick, and she doesn't have cooties. She is just like any other kid, just a noisy one, which, let's face it—she is MY daughter so there was no chance she would be quiet anyway.

I have friends who have lost children in infancy, been diagnosed with cancer as toddlers or fallen at the hands of another's actions. As a nurse in the ER, I have seen my share of tragedy and I know it could be worse. If our lives are mildly inconvenienced by not being able to go to the movies without getting dirty looks from others or having people move away because they think she is sick, then so be it.

"MOMMY! I'm home! Where are you?" My Claire is home. I can hear her thunderous hooves running down the hall on the wood floors. Christ on a crutch, that kid is a bull in a china shop. BOOM! She plows into my side as I'm standing at the kitchen sink washing strawberries.

"Hi, my love bug, how are you? I missed you so much!"

"I'm good. I missed you too, bunches and bunches," she says as I lean down to kiss her sweet face.

"Did you have fun at Daddy's this past week?" *Did the icky monster Sindee touch you? Did it burn your skin? Oh, sorry, those are all internal thoughts.*

"I had fun, Mommy. We went to the water park and I got to watch a lot of cartoons and play on my DS." I hand her a strawberry. "I'm glad you had fun, sweets. Why don't you go put your bag in your room and let the dogs in? I know Zoe and Athena missed you too." Off she runs upstairs to her room.

Andy and I are left standing alone in the kitchen… awkward.

"Well, thanks for bringing her back, Andy. I appreciate it."

"No problem, Madi, and I was almost on time for once," he laughs.

Why is he laughing? It's not funny that he's always late, it's annoying as fuck! "Yep, mark the calendar! It might never happen again. Perhaps this would be the day for me to buy a lottery ticket," I say with a sarcastic grin.

"Well, I should go. Sindee is in the car and wants to run some errands before we head home." *Maybe she needs to have her fangs filed and her mustache waxed.*

"Bye, Madster," Andy says before walking away

Ugh, really? You had to use the nickname you gave me.

Inappropriate alert! Is it weird that my skin crawled when he said it?

"Saddle up, kiddo! We are headed to the mall with Savannah and Grace!" I yell upstairs.

"Are Landon and Drew coming too?" Claire asks.

"Yes, honey, the boys are coming with, and we thought we would stop and get lunch and maybe some cupcakes on the way home."

Landon is 10 and Drew is 8. They are Savannah and Luke's boys. They go to school with Claire, and if you didn't know any better you would think they are brothers and sister. The Brooks and Kennedy families spend a lot of time together. One would assume that Savannah and I, working together and seeing each other so much, would get tired of each other, but I am lucky enough to have formed a sisterly bond with her. She is like the sister I never wanted.

Luke has the patience of a saint. He tolerates Savannah's and my shenanigans all the time. We all spend so much time together it's like Luke has 2 wives, poor bastard.

"Aunt Grace is coming with us too, sweetheart."

"YAY! Are Sam and Soniia coming too?"

"No, honey, they aren't."

"Aww, why? I like when Soniia comes with us. She takes us to the playground while you guys spend F O R E V E R in the stores. It's SO boring, Mommy." (Insert huff and dramatic head drop here)

"I know, but she is in class today and Sam is at his dad's house."

Soniia and Sam are Grace's kids from her prior marriage to Clint the Wonder Tool, and that's not a compliment. Soniia babysits Claire for me on occasion, too. She is enrolled in

Cosmetology school and I have a feeling she is going to be the next "Stylist to the Stars" someday.

"Maybe one of these weekends soon we can go see Soniia and get your hair cut, how does that sound?"

"Oooh, OK, but can I cut it shorter or get bangs?"

Pick your battles, Madi, pick your battles. "No bangs, and yes, you can cut it shorter since it's summer."

"YES!"

Did my 8 year old just fist pump?

AS CLAIRE AND I climb into my overly small and frankly, silly looking car, we head towards the freeway when Claire waves and says, "Look, Mommy, that's where you work."

"Yes, it sure is." Internal thought: "Yep, that's where I get puked on, peed on, crapped on, yelled at and hit." Good times.

"Mom, why do they call it Bridgewater Hospital? There are no bridges or water anywhere around it."

"I'm not sure. That's a good question," I say with a laugh.

"They should call it dirt and train tracks hospital cuz that's all I can see."

Bahahaha, she has a point. Out of the mouths of babes. I love this kid!

Ninety minutes, countless wardrobe changes, borderline tears and several hissy fits later, Grace and Savannah are finally happy with the hooker inspired ensemble they have put together for me. For some reason they feel that a strapless, short, black and frankly SO not me dress is warranted for our upcoming night of debauchery.

"OK, and now for some FMPs! Time to get you some hooker shoes, hooker!" Savannah says with an evil smile. Who better to pick out slutty shoes than my former stripper friend Savannah?

"Oh come on, Madi! These are so cute and would look great behind your ears!" Vannah says with a snort, holding up a pair of heels and puts them behind her ears.

"Really? Ree-alllly? I'm sure my 8 year old appreciates that visual. I would rather not have to tell my daughter that I do yoga in heels. I don't want to scar her for life; she already has shrink visits in her future having to spend time with Andy and the troll. Let's not add to it, K, pumpkin?"

Grinning like the Cheshire cat, she hands me the extremely high, cheetah print shoes with a big, red, floofy bow thingy on them. To be honest, they are kind of cute, but not something I would EVER buy. I am more of a ballet flats, jeans and a t-shirt kind of gal.

"Well, Madi," I say to myself because I like to talk to myself in third person, "Time to make a change. Let's see if you can harness your inner slut for once."

I landed Andy the Douche being the wholesome, sweet, girl next door, and we all see where that got me. Maybe it's time to live it up a little, take a risk and do something completely anti-Madi! After staring at the shoes for what seemed like hours, I reach for them. "Give me those!"

The look of shock on Grace and Savannah's faces was almost worth the $175 price tag. ALMOST. This Amex bill is going to hurt! I may have to sell Claire to pay it off. She's adorable and a hard worker, she should fetch a shiny sheckle.

No buyer's remorse now, Madi. This is the new you. The

new you, who will wear an indecent dress, hooker shoes, go dancing with your friends, drink too much and dry hump a random hottie, perhaps get a tattoo or something pierced. Oh, God, I wanna throw up. YEAH! NEW MADI!

"Why do you look like you're going to throw up, Madi?" Grace asks with a concerned face.

"Because I just spent a small fortune a pair of shoes that should be on the feet of Cinnamon or Sapphire whilst bobbing for dollars. These shoes do not belong on the feet of a respected—SHUT UP, SAVANNAH—ER nurse and mother. What if Claire finds these in my closet and thinks her mother is working a local corner?"

"Let's go eat. You look pale, Madi," Grace says putting her arm around me.

"She's not pale, she's borderline albino. You need a tan, Madi. Your legs look like two glasses of milk in flip flops," Vannah says, laughing. Why do I voluntarily subject myself to this crap from these women?

"Food. Now," I say and walk with purpose from the store out into the vast open expanse of the mall.

After over indulging on chips, salsa and layers of cheese-covered Mexican food, it's time to make the drive back to the 'burbs. Claire and I climb into my mid-life crisis and hit the freeway.

"Mommy, can we listen to my favorite song?"

My head drops down in defeat. "Sure, sweetheart." I press a button on the stereo and prepare for the ear bleeding to begin as 'Call Me Maybe' starts to play and Claire sings along. I love this kid with every fiber in my body but if I have to hear that song again I may pull my hair out and stuff it in my ears.

Chapter 3

ARRIVING BACK HOME several hours later, I still feel like a bloated cow from all the food we ate at lunch. Claire and I stopped for some fancy cupcakes on the way home but those will have to wait until later. And not to toot my own horn, but… Toot Toot! Mine are way better, but this is a nice treat every now and then, plus my kitchen stays clean this way. Win Win.

Claire heads up to her room to read the new book I bought her today. I head upstairs to put away my day's purchases. I fear that when I put the clothes in the closet they may be rejected and spit out by my comfy jeans and t-shirts. Suddenly I begin to sing. "One of these things doesn't belong here, one of these things just isn't the same, one of these things is not like the others…"

Get a grip, Madi! It's a dress and shoes, it's not like you've grown a second head. Although, I think the second head would look more natural on me than that dress and those shoes.

As I hang up the dress and look at the shoes again, I feel a slight sense of pride. I own a slutty dress and awesome whore shoes—not to be confused with horse shoes, although I may sound like a horse clopping around in them. Tucked neatly between my standard sundresses, t-shirts, cardigans, capris, jeans and sandals is a killer outfit. I am going to rock this on girl's night out…? It sounds more like a question than a statement at this point.

After checking on Claire to find her on her bed "watching a movie" with her eyes closed, sound asleep, I decide to head down to the kitchen and indulge in one of the gourmet cupcakes we bought earlier. I should just shove the cupcake against my left thigh because that's where it's headed. "Look out below!" I say as I take a less than lady-like bite of red velvet deliciousness.

As I sit and scarf down the rest of the cupcake before Claire catches me, I hear my phone beep. Oooh, someone texted me. It's like a little electronic gift when my phone beeps. I love getting messages from people. Well, most people. I should clarify that when it's Andy, I equate that beep to a bag of flaming dog poop being left on my doorstep.

When I check my screen, I see it's Taylor.

–Put the cupcake down and step away–

How the hell did she know I was eating a cupcake? This is all very 'the call is coming from inside the house'. I look around and check outside the windows. I wouldn't put it past Taylor's realm of possibility to be watching me through my windows.

–How did you know I was eating a cupcake? Where R U?–

–Heard from G, said you bought shit cakes–

–What do you want??? Freak!–

–You didn't earn that cupcake; running from humiliation doesn't burn calories–

–I beg to differ–

–If it did you'd be a skeleton. Better see you tomorrow @ 9 no excuses–

–Can't show my face again, mortified–

–Then walk in backwards–

–Bitch!–

–Yep. C U 2morrow, or else–

Why did I just hear 'dun dun duuuun' after I read 'or else'? She doesn't scare me! OK, that's a lie. She does a little. Maybe I can show my face at the gym again if I wear huge sunglasses, a floppy hat that hides 3/4 of my face and bring reinforcements. I will make Savannah come with me. Maybe if she is there half naked it will distract from me. She has a membership and hardly ever goes anymore. Time for her to make use of it. I pull her up from my contacts list.

–V, tomorrow morning. You. Me. Gym. 9 am.–

–Nope. Don't wanna–

–Don't make me pull your hair. And I won't smack your ass like Luke does–

–Fine. See you at 9–

I decide to call it a night and head to bed. Maybe I will watch a little TV and pray for the gym to burn down overnight. I tuck Claire into bed and head to my room. After changing into jammies, I climb into bed and start flipping through the channels. I settle on reruns of my favorite sitcom from the 90's about a group of FRIENDS. I curl up and offer a silent prayer to the heavens above to please start a small fire in the gym—not enough to do any major damage, but just enough so Taylor will have to close if for a few months so I can regain my pride.

BEEP! BEEP! BEEP! 7:30am right on the dot! Ugh, I feel like I should have a fever or something. Maybe typhoid or scurvy; something that would prevent me from going to the gym today. Nope, picture of health. Damnit!

I change into my gym attire and search my closet for a wig or mask from a prior Halloween—something to hide my face—and shockingly, I come up empty. I guess I will have to go to the gym in my Humiliated Madi costume.

Why should today by any different?

I wake up Claire and decide that we will hit Starbucks before the gym. Don't judge me. I need copious amounts of caffeine in order to function. Today will just be hot tea; I don't need the extra calories after last night's cupcake-induced coma.

As Claire and I head into Starbucks I see that my new super favorite and happy barista Tiffani with an i is behind the counter. Yay. I get to start my day with hot tea and a side of snarky bitch. Maybe if I'm lucky, she will lick the rim of my cup before she makes it. I'm sure I am not her favorite person these days. I am fairly certain that Mark had words with her after our H_2O issue yesterday. As I approach the counter, I can physically see her attitude change as she huffs, pasting a plastic smile on her face that could give Barbie a run for her money.

"Good morning, welcome to Starbucks. What can I get you today?" (Insert eye roll)

"Grande black tea, please, with room for cream, and a kid's chocolate milk with one pump of chocolate, ice and whip. Thank you." (Bats eyelashes)

"I assume you would like a WATER with that too?" (Insert sarcastic tone)

"No thanks, Tiffani with an i, just the tea and milk. Thanks." (Insert removal of tip from jar)

As I walk over, retrieving our beverages, I turn around and almost run smack dab into someone with my hot tea. "Oh my gosh. Are you OK? I'm so sorr…"

Holy crap, it's him! It's Mr. HotTottie. The lone audience member that caught my Vanilla Ice tribute performance. Really, God? Really? I thought we had a deal!?!?!?!

"No no, it's my fault. Are ya'll okay?" he asks with a deep and sultry voice, and oh dear baby Jesus is that a southern accent I detect? I think I need to change my panties.

"Are ya okay?" Long pause. "Hello?" He waves his hand in front my face. Snap out of it, Madi!

"Oh, uh yes I'm thanks, asking for fine."

He looks at me, flashing a half smile. "Uh, I mean yes I'm fine, thanks for asking." Nice recovery, asshat.

"Alright then, you have yourself a great day," he smiles and gives me a wink before walking out the door. Really, he just winked at me? Are you freaking kidding me? I need to change my yoga pants.

I sit with Claire for a minute and we enjoy our drinks before we head off to the gym. Truth be told, I just need to regain my composure and get feeling back in my legs. He spoke to me. Holy crap on a cracker—he speaks, and it's beautiful.

As we walk into the gym we see Taylor behind the counter, Claire runs over to her and gives her a big hug and begins to tickle her. Taylor loves Claire and they play tickle monster all the time—little known fact, Taylor is SUPER ticklish. She takes Claire to the kid's center for me while I sign in. As I head over to the farthest possible treadmill—yes, the treadmills—I see Savannah is already here and walking.

"You're early. That never happens."

"I know, right? Luke got me up early so I figured I would get a jump start on the workout. It's been a few weeks since I've been here." I don't want to know how or why Luke got her up early, but I have no doubt that it involves dirty sweaty things and their own form of workout.

"OK. Well, I'm going to walk for about an hour then head

home." I put in my ear buds and keep the music down to a very dull roar so that I can still hear myself if I start to sing. No need to rehash the free show from yesterday. I'm not being paid to provide a floor show.

As I start to get into my groove and set a good steady walking pace, I happen to look around and find a set of eyes on me. NO FREAKING WAY! It's Hotness, party of one, from Starbucks! Don't panic.

I give a quick flustered smile and cut off eye contact uber quick. No need to prolong the embarrassment, just enough to acknowledge that I realize who he is.

Now, move on. He smiles back and nods his head towards me. No, he was supposed to move on, not smile. OK, we have established that we recognize each other from Starbucks. With any luck he will have no clue I was the one singing yesterday.

In an effort to look cool, I step up the pace on the treadmill. I don't want this guy thinking I just stroll along. I want him to be impressed with my mad workout skills. He is over in the free weight area with the cool kids. I work out on the side with the pasty kids and bookworms.

I get it going up to an almost run—OK, it's more of a light jog—but that's a HUGE deal for me. I keep it up for about 20 minutes until my lungs burn and I 'm gasping for air like a fish out of water. OK, Madi, cut the crap, slow it down, wrap it up and get out of here before you have a chance to do something stupid. Well, more stupid.

I crank the speed and incline down on the treadmill. As the belt comes to a stop, I take my towel and wipe down the surfaces. I turn around to take a step off the treadmill, and this is when I decide to do my most graceful face plant onto the floor. Apparently, there is a reason you are supposed to cool down after a workout. My legs were still in forward motion mode and my brain was not.

The only thing I remember after the sudden rush of concrete floor hurdling towards my face was the lovely "oooumphrtth" noise I made as I hit the floor and the edge of the treadmill.

"Madi! Jesus, are you OK?" I hear Savannah exclaim with a laugh. I open my eyes and look around quickly, hoping no one saw that but her. DENIED! I now have an audience, including Mr. HotTottie. You remember him, from Starbucks and my solo performance.

"I umm, yes, OK, I'm fine," I jump up in order to look cool, like I meant to do that, but my legs are still like Jell-O. Dusting off my legs and hands, I see Mr. HotTottie eying me up and down. Savannah has chosen this moment to head to the locker room to get our things.

"Are you OK?" he asks, with his dreamy southern drawl and a genuine look of concern on his face.

If I say no will you keep talking to me?

"Yes, I'm fine, thanks," I reply with a confident smile. Confident I look like an asshole.

The crowd has starting to disband and go back to feeling the burn.

"Looks like a pretty nasty scuf on your arm there," he points to my left forearm, gently touching it.

OH MY GOD, he touched me! It sent an electrical pulse up my arm. Is that the spark or tingle they speak of when you meet your soul mate?

Oh, right, that's probably just nerve damage from the header I just took.

"I'm good. I think it's my ego that's bruised more than anything," I mumble with a pathetic smile and shoulder shrug.

"Well, maybe I should get you some ice… Ice Ice Baby," he grins with a laugh and wink.

Moment of internal prayer: Dear Jesus, I thought we had an understanding. I wouldn't use your name in vain or scream it out during an orgasm if you stopped humiliating me on a regular basis. The deal's off!

"Wow, so you did see that. That's outstanding and not at all humiliating," I sigh and smile

"No, I didn't miss that. It was kind of epic. I've always enjoyed the classics."

Classics? DUDE. What the hell? "Yes, you can't go wrong with Bach or Vanilla Ice. They are both known for their timeless works of art."

Mr. HotTottie throws his head back and laughs. Wow, I think he even laughs with an accent.

"I'm Declan, Declan Hillier," he extends his hand to me.

"Nice to meet you. I'm Madi, Madi Kennedy. This is all very Bond, James Bond," I reply.

"Hahahaha, that's excellent."

I start to laugh. I fear that if I don't I will just burst out crying, so I might as well join him in laughing at me.

"So are you really OK, Madi? You're not just putting on a brave face?"

"No, I really am OK. Nothing a little alcohol can't fix, or maybe that memory eraser flashy thingy from Men in Black. Same diff!"

"Personally, I would go with the alcohol. The flashy thing probably causes cancer. Well that, and it being fictional and all," he chuckles.

"Riiight. That too," I smile. "Well it was nice to meet you, Declan. I really should go scrape together the last bit of my self-esteem and get going so I can go lick my wounds," Eww, that sounded gross. "I mean, put ice on them," I add as I start to limp backwards towards the main lobby. "Oh God, never mind. It was nice meeting you," I finish with an over the shoulder wave as I leave.

I swing by the kid's center to pick up Claire. When we come back through the lobby, Declan is gone. I'm sad that I didn't get to see that fine specimen again, but relieved that I can sneak out quietly with what remains of my dignity and not cause any more of a scene. Savannah walks up with my purse, and a shit eating grin on her face. "So, was that the hot guy that caught you singing?"

"Yes, how'd you guess?"

"Just a hunch," she says with a laugh.

Claire looks at my arm. "Ewww, what happened? That looks bad. Do you want me to fix it when we get home?"

"Do you have the ability to turn back time, sweetheart?"

Claire gives me a confused look and I laugh. "Just a kiss will make it all better." I bend over and Claire gives me a big smooch, and then kisses my arm and shin. "There, all better."

"Yes, thank you." I love this kid.

As Claire and I head home, Savannah calls to check on me and asks if Claire and I want to come over to go swimming and have lunch later. Of course, with my daughter being born part fish, she loves anything to do with water, with the minor exception of taking a bath. I don't quite understand that. It's the same as a pool, only smaller and you add a bar of soap. Whatever, she's weird. I think she gets that from Andy's side of the family. All of the weird crap I can't explain or the odd food things she mixes together like watermelon with ranch dressing (gag) I blame on Andy.

When we get back to the house, I head up to the shower and Claire starts to play on the Wii. “Claire, I’m going to take a shower, I’ll be down in a bit. Be good, OK?”

“OK, Mommy, I will. Pinkie promise.”

Chapter 4

STANDING IN THE shower, I let the warm water cascade over me and wash away the mortification that has created a crusty layer on my body from this morning. Jesus, Madi, first you almost scald what I imagine are very well defined and lickable abs of Mr. HotTottie at Starbucks, then you make a complete asshole out of yourself by swan diving off the treadmill at the gym. Could you be more of a spaz?

He's just a guy. Granted, a really hot, tall, southern, tattooed and muscly guy, but a guy none the less. Why am I making such a big deal about him and get all twittery when he is around? I work around some seriously hot and smart doctors all day long and I seem to manage my composure just fine. But this random gym guy, this Declan... makes me all gushy and nervous.

As I continue to let the warm water wash over me, I can't help but think about him. His dreamy electric blue eyes and those dimples—oh my God, I could lick cream out of them.

Mmmm, I bet he is a great kisser. Shit, I bet he is great at everything he does.

My hands move their way around my body, lathering up my skin. I bet he has great hands. They were firm yet gentle when touched me at the gym. As I work my hands around I begin to run them over my breasts, which are now sensitive and hard from thinking about him. Holy shit, I am turning myself on thinking about him in the shower. I close my eyes and begin to imagine what it would feel like to have his hands on my body. Would I feel that same electric pulse I felt earlier? Would he make me feel like that all over? What would his hands feel like if they were to gently caress and cup my breasts while standing in front of me, the water running over both of us? Mmmm.

As Declan bends down, he slowly takes my nipple in his mouth and sucks with the slightest pressure and the flick of his tongue. Oh God. My back arches and I let out a slight moan. He licks his way to my other nipple and gently sucks on it while cupping and massaging the first, gently biting down on the tip as I let out a playful yelp. He looks up at me with hooded eyes and a devilish grin. Sweet Jesus of all Jesuses—this man is amazing.

Standing up straight, the water beads on his chest. I run my hands up and down it, feeling how firm he is and lean forward to lick a trail up his torso. Declan looks down at me, grabs my hair and pulls my head back slightly to get better access, and begins to kiss and suck my neck. My hands work their way down his chest to his rock hard abs. I let them rest there for a moment, paying homage to the beauty that is his body. Declan kisses his way up to my ear and begins to suck on my earlobe. He murmurs a slight 'mmm' in my ear and I know it's my cue. Green light, Madi! You are cleared for takeoff.

I work my hands down his stomach, sucking and kissing as I go. Declan grabs me by the wrists and pulls me up swiftly. With both hands, he grabs my face, pulls me forcefully towards him, and kisses me with such passion my knees go weak. Our tongues are moving fiercely, tangling and clashing. He moans in my mouth and pulls me closer to him. I free my hands from his grip and begin to move them down towards his erect cock. As I slide my hand further down and wrap my hand around his hard length, he pulls away from our kiss and rests his forehead against mine. Looking deeply into my eyes, he begins to moan and growl through gritted teeth "Oh God, Madi. You feel soo…"

"MOM, CAN I HAVE AN APPLE???"

Sputtering, I am suddenly ripped from my erotic daydream back to reality. I look around in a panic. Is someone here? Did they see? Does anyone know that I was just rocking my own boat in the shower? Nope, you are in the shower, alone, and not being man handled by Declan. Damnit.

"Um, yeah, of course," I shout.

I finish my shower like a normal human being and feel worse than when I got in. Now, not only am I bruised and sore, I'm sexually frustrated. Nice combination.

After drying off and wrapping myself up in my favorite old ratty robe that I have had since college, I head downstairs to the kitchen. I find myself standing in front of the kitchen window, staring out into my backyard. I guess I must have been pretty lost in thought—I'm sure of the porn scene I just fantasized about in the shower has nothing to do with it—because I never heard Claire come in.

"Mommy, are you OK?" I startle. "Yes, sweetheart, I'm fine. Why?"

"Cuz when I went to ask you if I could have an apple, you were moaning and groaning in the shower like you might be sick," she replies with a concerned face.

This was not the most opportune time for me to take a drink of my iced tea because I promptly spewed it all over my kitchen counter and window. "Oh. Um, yes, ok. Sure, um, yeah honey, I'm fine. I think the hot water just felt good on my sore muscles after my fall at the gym?" I think that sounded more like a question then an answer.

"Hey, so why don't you go pack your bag to go swimming at Auntie Vannah's in a bit, OK?"

"OK, Can I bring Phelan?"

"Oh, I don't think it's a good idea to invite any other friends."

With an eye roll that could rival mine, she huffs. "Mother, Phelan is my doll,. Geez."

"Oh, right. Sorry." Mother? Really? My 8 year old just called me mother. And so it begins.

"Mommy must be too distracted by the aching and throbbing in her hoo-ha to remember all the names of your baby dolls," I murmur quietly to myself.

"What?" Claire asks with a questioning face.

"I love yooouu!" I reply with an overly eager smile. I guess I better go get myself ready to head to Savannah and Luke's for the afternoon. I shoot her a quick text.

–Hey, what can we bring?–

–Nothing, just your fine ass selves and your bikini.–

–Fine ass selves, CHECK. Swimsuit, CHECK–

–I didn't stutter bitch, I said bikini. You better bring it or I'll make you wear one of mine–

–Wearing of the bikini. CHECK–

Oh dear sweet Jesus. The thing you have to know about Savannah is she is built like a brick shithouse, which worked well for her as a stripper. She's 5'10", with long wavy brown hair, tan skin, curves and has tits for days. I, however, am 5'4", curvy in an 'aren't you adorable' kind of way, have long blonde hair, pasty white skin, and well, OK I do have a nice rack, but not nearly as nice as Savannah.

Savannah is the girl everyone turns their heads to see. I am the one they push aside to get a better view. I'm the girl next door; she is the girl in the poster on the walls of the men and boys in the house next door.

I bought a bikini on a shopping trip with Vannah one weekend because she strong-armed me into it but I have yet to wear it. Come to think of it, I have an entire section of my walk-in closet dedicated to poor choices made with Savannah. I should cordon it off with those cute little red velvet ropes and sell tickets to view the poor decisions and peer pressure purchases I have made.

Alright, I will bring the bikini only because I know if I don't she will literally drag me into her room, strip me down, and tie one of her barely there nipple covers on me if I don't.

Why am I friends with her? I subject myself to this voluntarily. Clearly, I am a sadist.

A while later, we head out to the Brooks' house, bikini in

tow. When we pull up in front of their house, I see their two matching phallic trucks with custom license plates and shake my head, just like I do every time I see them. Savannah's monstrosity is a red, quad cab, long bed diesel gas-guzzler of some sort with a "FOSHIZL" plate. Luke's is the same behemoth in blue with a "MYNIZL" plate.

For two cowpokes from Texas, they are surprisingly 'street'.

Being that Vannah and I are so close, we usually just walk into each other houses, which I should know better than to do. On more than one occasion I have come surprisingly close to a live porn show. With the boys being home today, I feel safe walking in.

I'm sure that they wouldn't full frontal their kids.

"Hey, we're here!"

"Come on in, I'm in the kitchen and the boys are out back."

As we walk into Savannah's kitchen, I see her standing at the sink in her barely there light blue polka dot bikini making lunch for everyone.

I put our stuff on the kitchen table and give Claire the nod that it's OK for her to head out back with Luke and the boys.

"What's cookin, stripper lookin?" I say with the most heartfelt love.

"Haha. Funny. Nothing, just making sandwiches. Ham for all of us and turkey for you, right?"

"Yes, please. No pig ass for me, thanks."

"You're not right. You know that, don't you? Everyone likes ham. Even the Jews. You won't eat ham but you love bacon."

"You don't have to understand it, Vannah. You just have

to accept it as part of the beauty that is me," I smile.

"So, how are your war wounds? What the hell happened with that? One minute I see you chugging along, at a pretty good clip I might add, and the next thing I see is a purple blur headed towards the floor."

"I really don't know what came over me. I just felt the urge to start jogging, and when I was done I guess my legs weren't."

"Yeah, I know. I caught the show. But here is my question—why were you jogging? You don't run and we all know this. Were you running to try and oh I don't know, impress someone?"

Shit shit shit shit. She figured me out.

"YOU WERE! Oh my God, you were trying to impress him!" Crap. I was silent too long.

"Yes, OK. There, I said it. I was jogging to try and look less moronic to the hot guy. And clearly, we all see how that worked out for me. First I get caught singing—scratch that, rapping—in front of him, then I almost scald him with my tea at Starbucks, and then finally I biff it in front of him. I was hoping to redeem myself, not make it worse. Obviously, that was a universal no. Five bucks says next time he sees me he hands me caution tape and a helmet."

"Baaaahahahahaha. Oh, can it, drama queen. He seemed like he was really concerned about you today. You should have seen him run over when you fell. You, of course, didn't see it because you were face down on the floor, but I have to say he made it over in about 5 strides. It was pretty quick."

'He did not. I bet he was coming over to see if there was carnage or something he could video and upload to YouTube under Gym Fail."

"Oh my God, Madi, he was not. What is his name, by the way? I saw you guys talking and shaking hands."

"His name is Declan. And why did you leave me? You disappeared when I was attempting to regain my cool and left me alone with him. You did that on purpose, didn't you?"

"Maybe," she replies with a shoulder shrug and a grin.

"Savannah Lynn Brooks, you answer me right now!"

"Jesus. OK, Mom, don't middle name me. Yes, I did leave you two alone on purpose. He was watching you and when you fell he started running towards you before you even hit the floor. I was watching him watch you; I think there was something happening there," she says waving her long well-manicured finger at me "I felt like it was my cue to vacate the premises and leave you guys alone for a minute. Hell knows you wouldn't make a move and talk to him, so I figured that this was an open door. Sue me."

"I'm not going to sue you but I am going to punch you in the ovary. I'm so embarrassed."

"Really, that is embarrassing to you? Not rapping like a white Republican sorority girl or eating cement? But him coming over to help you is embarrassing? OK, makes sense. For the record, all I did was let nature take its course."

"Nature? All of my encounters with this guys should have been narrated by Marlon Perkins and we all know how those scenes end, usually with some gimpy animal being devoured by another."

"OK, listen to me. I saw him watching you, and whether you want to believe it or not is your choice, but I saw him. He. Was. Watching. You. And I know this because I was watching him. He could devour me any time."

"Vannah, we know nothing about him except that he is

this amazingly hot gym guy. He was probably watching me to see what kind of show I was going to put on today, and as usual I didn't disappoint. For all we know, he could be some serial killer who wants to harvest my flesh and wear me as a hat for his drag show. He could be married with 7 kids or be a hoarder. Or worse, he could drive a VAN! Have you ever thought of that? He could drive a frickin' VAN."

"Alright. I want you to think about what you just said. You have a problem with him driving a van but are less concerned with the possibility of him being a flesh harvester or drag queen. You, my friend, are fucking crazy."

"HEY, you know how I feel about vans. No good, and I mean NO good, comes from a van. No slasher horror movie ever started with some creepy guy pulling up in a Prius. Think about it. That's all I'm sayin."

Vannah begins to laugh. "Well, you got me there. I guess the serial killer sect isn't known for being terribly ecofriendly. Although harvesting your flesh is kind of like recycling," she smiles

"See. Maybe his van is one of those that runs on old French fry grease. Could happen. I saw a show about people doing that."

"For the love of everything holy, you need to stop watching PBS," Savannah drops her head and shakes it slightly "Listen, I talked to Taylor and she knows a little about him. First off, he doesn't drive a van, gasoline or French fry powered, he drives a truck. He isn't in a drag show as far as we know, and she's never seen him wear anything to the gym that resembles human flesh."

My fears are legitimate. Watch Silence of the Lambs, you won't find a Prius, but you will find a van.

AFTER HELPING SAVANNAH finish making lunch, we head out to the backyard and set everything on the patio table. The kids are really more of a foraging bunch—they will come up and grab a bunch of grapes or a piece of sandwich and head back to the pool.

Savannah takes off her shoes, makes a running jump for the pool, and dives in. I'm shocked she didn't lose her top—or should I say, her triangular nipple covers.

"You better go get your suit on and come in, Madi. Don't make me send Luke after you. If he can rope a calf, he can certainly catch you."

"I don't know if I want to swim today. My arm is pretty sore from the treadmill road rash I got earlier."

"Suck it up, buttercup, and get in the pool!" Vannah shouts.

"Seriously. Not feeling it."

"LUKE! Get 'er!!"

Luke starts to make his way towards the edge of the pool.

"Ahhh! Fine!" I scream as I take off running for the house. I grab my bag off the table and head towards the bathroom to change into my bikini. As I get my things out of the bag, I see I have a text from Taylor.

–Saw your episode on the video system–

I take a second to text her back.

–That was recorded? WTF!!! I'm fine BTW–

–Good, don't want a lawsuit. Yes, popped popcorn and watched the play by play. Graceful–

–Please promise me you won't show anyone that video!–

–I can promise not to show anyone ELSE the video.–

–OMG, I have to move.–

–Reel it in Eunice, you're fine. Promise not to show anyone else.–

–Thank you–

–Oh wait, stipulation. You sign up for personal training.–

–Are you really blackmailing me??–

–Yep. :)–

–I expected more from you T. Never thought you'd resort to extortion–

–Don't big word your way out of this. 10 sessions and I erase the tape. No PT and I upload to YouTube.–

–YOU WOULDNT!!!!–

–Try me. :D–

–Fine. I. HATE. YOU.–

–No you don't, now go swim off some calories. Kisses–

I walk out into the backyard and find the kids sitting around the table eating. Looking toward the pool I see Savannah and Luke wrapped around each, they are probably having sex in the water. They don't see me coming so I cannonball right next to them.

"HA! Take that!" I say with confidence as I surface a few feet away from them. I managed to break up the love fest they were having. That makes me happy.

"I can see your tits," Luke says swimming past me.

"OH SHIT!" I yelp, sinking under the water line. Apparently my top wasn't tied as tightly as I thought and now it's more of a choker.

Savannah is dying of laughter and Luke just has a smug grin on his face. I guess it's fair. After all, I did see his 'fire hose' the night I passed out on their couch. It would do him good to remember to wear pants and close the bathroom door in the middle of the night. Thank God the kids were on the patio and I didn't just give their boys an anatomy lesson. Ooops!

Vannah swims over and helps me tie the top a little tighter this time.

"Thank you. Sorry I flashed Luke."

"Oh, please. Do you know how much T&A that guy sees a day at work? It's like an elbow to him."

"I know, it's no different than the hot guys we see come into the ER. We don't get turned on by them. But still, this was… MY elbow."

"He could care less. He's an ass man anyway," she says with a laugh.

WE SPEND THE better part of the afternoon and early evening playing in the pool with the kids and having a great time. For a while I actually managed to forget that I had made an asshole out of myself at the gym earlier today. That is, until Vannah asked me about my text chat with Taylor.

"So what did Taylor want?"

"Just checking on me. Apparently, she caught the highlight reel after I left."

"Hahahaha, you mean to tell me she has it on video? Oh, I have to see this."

"No, no, no you don't. You caught the live show. You're good. She strong-armed me into a few personal training sessions or she's going to upload it to YouTube."

"Wow, she will do anything to get people to use the PT at that place."

"Tell me about it. I agreed to 10 sessions. NO MORE than that."

"Well, I'm sure it won't be too bad. She hired those new trainers to get the program up and running."

"She hired new people for it?"

"Yeah. She's been doing it herself, and Bill was helping her, but they are getting quite a few clients now and needed help. I think she hired 2 girls and a guy to help out."

"That's cool. I'm sure the girls are popular with the women at the gym. Personally, I wouldn't want some beefcake guy watching me use that new machine she got. That thing looks like some type of medieval gynecological device."

"Well, I say you do those 10 sessions. I know Taylor she doesn't make idle threats."

"Oh trust me, I know. She is all business."

With much complaining, whining and several "5 more minutes" countdowns, I finally manage to tear Claire away from the pool and the boys. I know she is having fun but the poor thing looks like a bleached raisin. Although, thanks to her father's side of the family, that kid can tan and hold it. Sadly, I burn, peel and turn white again so it's not really beneficial for me to be in the sun. Well, that and I don't want to look like an alligator belt when I'm 60. Sunblock SPF 50+ it is for this Arizona native. I feel it's unfair that you can be born and raised in Arizona and still be pale. That's like someone born and raised in Colorado who can't ski. It's cruel.

I need to get Claire home and ready for bed. I have to work tomorrow night from 7pm to 7am, I need to get some sleep tonight. Thankfully, my parents are always there to help out when I need someone to come and spend 2 nights a week. I am home in time to get her to school and I sleep while she is there, then I pick her up, do homework and have dinner with her before it's time to head out again. I feel bad that my mom comes over here and sleeps away from my dad a few nights a week. She says it helps their relationship—you know, an 'absence makes the heart grow fonder' sort of thing.

HOME SWEET HOME again. Claire fell asleep in the back seat

of the car. I guess swimming and playing for 6 hours will wear anyone out. How a kid can be hunched over with their head almost in their lap and not wake up with a migraine is beyond me. If I got into that position, I might snap in half. It wouldn't be pretty.

As I pull into the garage, my cell phone goes off and it's Taylor. I let it go to voicemail since I am about to pull Claire out of the backseat of the car. Taking her upstairs, I don't even attempt to have her change into jammies. Poor thing, she is so exhausted, but seeing her like this—all floppy and ragdoll-ish—reminds me of just how little she still is. I must make a mental note of this sweet and endearing state, for I fear that tomorrow when she rolls her eyes at me and calls me mother, I will want to flick her between the eyes. She is still my sweet baby. I close her door and slip back downstairs to check my message from Taylor.

"Hey Madi, it's me. I set you up for the personal training. 10 sessions and they are an hour each. You and I both know you're going to do it and won't risk the possible humiliation of being posted on the internet. I am starting you off easy tomorrow. 8AM. I know you have to work tomorrow night so that will still give you time to go home and rest. Let me know when you get to the gym so I can get you started with your warm-up. Have a good night and tell my tickle buddy 'hi' for me."

I delete the message and decide to get my stuff ready for tomorrow night. It's too early for me to go to bed but I'm bored. I really do need a life. Maybe I will take up knitting or underwater basket weaving.

Oh well, back to the closet for scrub selections. I think I shall go with black scrubs and my pink polka dot socks tomorrow—not that anyone really sees them, but they are fun and make me smile. It's kind of like when you wear a matching bra and panties, you kind of feel like you have your shit together. I rarely have my shit together.

Well, that took 7 minutes, now what? I decide to call Elise and catch up. It's been weeks since I have gotten to actually talk to her and have a real conversation.

45 minutes into our chat about the girls, our lives (or my lack thereof), my humiliating escapades at the gym, work, people at work that we like, people at work that we don't like, the latest gossip, etc., etc., Elise tells me some shocking news. Eamon has been offered a job out of state in Washington and they are thinking of moving. They haven't made a decision just yet but are thinking about it. Elise is a California girl and doesn't care for the heat, and she misses the seasons. One thing you don't get in Arizona are the 4 seasons. We have 2—hot and a little less than hot. Elise also wants to raise Phaedra in a smaller town like she was raised.

Eamon was approached about the job out of the blue. He is happy with his current employer, but when the new company offered him twice the salary and a relocation package, it's hard to pass up. I am sad to hear that my best friend may be leaving me, but I understand that she has to do what is best for her and her family.

I always feel better after talking to Elise. Phaedra wanted to talk to Claire but she was sleeping, so we decided that on the days I have my personal training sessions I would drop Claire off at their house so she could play with Phaedra for a bit while I'm being tortured. I am feeling much better about my gym antics after talking to Elise and decide to suck it up and just pretend it never happened. That will be hard to do, given the scuff and the bruises I have, but when I walk into the gym tomorrow I will walk in confidently and will make the best of my PT sessions. I decide to head up to my room and read for a bit before I head to bed.

After a few hours of reading I decide it's time to turn down the lights and get some sleep. I set the alarm for 7. I only need 10 minutes to throw on my gym clothes, put my hair in a messy bun pony thingy, then a quick swipe of deodorant and I am out!

Chapter 5

BEEP BEEP BEEP BEEP. Fine, yes, it's 7:00AM, I know, I know. No need to shout about it. Stupid alarm. Maybe I can hit snooze—I don't need to swipe that deodorant, right? That's good for an extra 30 seconds of sleep. Can I go to the gym in my jammies? Ooh, better not. Boy shorts and a t-shirt are not appropriate gym wear. FINE, I will get up. Fricka Fracka Fruma Bumble Gobble. These are the words I mumble on my way to the bathroom to get ready.

25 minutes later, Claire and I are headed out the door to the McCaffery household. I run Claire in and give quick kisses. We are running late so I don't have time to chat but will surely catch up when I pick her up later. "Thanks, guys. I love you, Claire. Bye!"

I had better hurry. I don't want to feel the wrath of Taylor if I am late.

I quickly park and run inside, only to find Taylor standing at the desk, tapping her watch and glaring at me.

"I know, I know. Sorry, we had drama on what doll to

bring to Phaedra's this morning."

"Oh sure, blame the innocent kid who can't defend herself. And what did she settle on?"

"The one you got her. Feel better?"

"Surprisingly, yes," Taylor says with a chuckle. "OK, I can't believe I am about to say this, but I want you to start by warming up on the treadmill for 15 minutes and then we will get started."

"Okie Dokie."

I head over to the treadmill and pick my favorite one—the one that doesn't have a huge mirror in front of it. I really hate seeing myself when I work out. I feel it's cruel, and to be honest, what I can't stand even more are the guys that walk by to get a drink out of the water fountain and suck it in and check themselves out in the mirror. Gross. I don't want to know what I look like. I am always pleasantly surprised when I get home and find my eyeliner down to my knees, my face beet red, and my hair looking, as Savannah said, 'a bit homelessy'.

I get started on my warm-up and maintain a pretty good clip for about 10 minutes. The last few minutes are ticking down on the screen when I see something move to the left of me.

"Hey, Madi. How are ya?" I hear in a dreamy deep southern drawl.

"Huh?" I say, whipping my head around like a bobble head.

"Oh, umm, hi. I'm good, Declan, how are you?" Oh, yea me! I got it out and didn't stumble all over myself. Dear sweet baby Mabel—what is he doing here? Why isn't he bench pressing a Mack truck on the other side of the room?

"Good, thanks for askin'."

"So. What are you up to today?" I ask politely.

"Same thing you are," he smirks.

"Oh, you're here to humiliate yourself too? Glad to see I won't be alone. I always enjoy company," I say with a smile.

A deep booming laugh escapes his lips. Oh my God, it's seriously so hot when he laughs. "No, I'm here to work out with you," he states matter-of-factly as his lips turn up in a grin.

"Oh. Umm, well, I actually have a personal training session today. I'm sorry," I say with maybe just a hint too much sadness in my voice. But to be honest, I don't want this guy anywhere near me when I am working out. It's for his own safety, really.

"I know, Madi. I'm your trainer."

"THE FUCK?" Squeaks out of my mouth before I can stop it. Declan just laughs a little and raises his eyebrows at me.

"Seriously?"

"Yes ma'am, I am."

Jesus H. Christ! This man who, keep in mind I was fantasizing about in my shower—imagining him grabbing my tatas and me grabbing his 'thrill drill'—is now my trainer?!?!?!? Are you SERIOUS?

Oh, and for the record, the H stands for Harold. It's Jesus Harold Christ. Mystery solved. You're welcome.

"So, shall we get started?" Declan says with a smile and a head nod to the right.

"If you say so."

And now I take a moment of internal silent prayer. "Dear little baby Jesus, all snug in your bed. Please keep me from looking like a total asshole—errr, I mean idiot—in front of this guy. I know I have been coming to you a lot lately, and I will try and do better, but if you would just stop letting me act like a dumbass—errr, moron—I wouldn't have to bother you during your nap. Thank you. Amen."

As we make our way to the weight machines I see Taylor standing there with a smug look of satisfaction on her face. I stare her down and mouth 'I HATE YOU!' in shouty silent talk. She just smiles and blows me a kiss. God I hate her sometimes.

AFTER SEVERAL ATTEMPTS to use some of the weight machines to work different parts of my body I feel a full body muscle spasm coming on.

Declan finally ends our work out on the hip abductor machine. OK, so for those of you who don't know what this machine is, it's very un-ladylike to use. Imagine the stirrups at your OBGYN's office, only the pads are on the inside of your knees. You have to push your spread-eagled legs open and closed in a slow and repetitious pattern. Now it's not just open and close; it's open, hold for a few seconds, and then close. So here I sit, spread fucking eagle in a torture chair while this fine specimen of a man stares at me and counts down.

I wonder what he is counting down to. The moment I combust right before his eyes from how hot he is? Or from the mortification I feel having my beaver thrust to and fro in front of him? Oh, God. I hope I don't have a hole in the crotch of my pants.

"Alright. That was great, Madi. You're in pretty good shape and I'm impressed."

"Impressed? Why wouldn't you be? I mean, you HAVE seen my work on the treadmill."

Declan throws his head back slightly and laughs his deep throaty laugh. "This is true, and I know you're an excellent singer too."

"Oh, I didn't know you were tone deaf. My condolences."

"So why on earth are you taking personal training lessons? You seem to be doing pretty OK on your own," he says with a slight smirk.

"Umm, well, it's a long story, but I was extorted into it in order to prevent my swan dive off the treadmill from being broadcast on the internet."

"Oh, nice. Taylor?"

"Mmm hmmm. So how long have you been working here?" I ask between pelvic thrusts.

"Just a few months now. I was working out one day, and Taylor and I got to talkin' and she offered me a job."

"Why did you want to be a trainer? I mean, it's got to be exhausting listening to whiny sissy people like me all day."

"It's not so bad. Every now and then someone does liven it up by rapping or making a play for attention by falling off a treadmill," he says with a wink.

"Mr. Hillier, did you just wink at me? Doesn't that violate some type of trainer/trainee agreement?" Holy crap! Where did that come from?

"Well, MS. Kennedy, is it?" I nod. "Technically, there is no such agreement between trainers and trainees. We are free to talk about and openly mock our clients over a beer with our buddies at will. But rest easy, I have no intentions of mocking you."

"Oh please. I fully expect it, and might be disappointed in you if you didn't. After some of the things I have done in this building it's well warranted, I assure you."

He laughs that throaty laugh and flashes those perfect pearly whites. He has lovely teeth.

"So, Mr. Hillier, what is it that drew you to PT? The smell of the gym? Deep down you're a sadist who enjoys hurting people for money?"

"No, Ms. Kennedy." I can't help but notice that he emphasizes the MS every time he says my name. "I am actually in the process of trying to get hired on with the police department, and I enjoy working out, so until I am offered a job I figured this would be a good way to occupy my time and stay in shape."

"So sadist it is." I say, smiling.

He chuckles. "No, not really. I like staying fit and I don't live too far from here, so when Taylor approached me I figured why not. It would be a good way to make friends and stay busy while I wait and go through the hiring process for the department."

"Well, I know you say you aren't a sadist, Mr. Hillier, but I have done about a million and a half reps on this awkward and evil machine. Can I be done now?" I say with a bit of a pathetic look because quite frankly, my legs feel like Jell-O.

"Oh God, I am so sorry. Yes. Yes."

And with that, the weights clank down loudly as I free my thighs from the bonds of evil. "Oh sweet Jesus, I may not be able to walk tonight at work."

"So Madi, you seem to know a bit about me now. Can I ask you a question?"

"Well, considering I have been put in the most compromising positions by you today, I feel I am an open book." To go with my open legs.

"What is it that you do that has you working nights? Stripper? Nun?"

"Actually, I'm a stripping nun. They call me Sister Mary Tassels." I can barely get the words out before I start to giggle. Declan lets out the loudest laugh—I swear, it came from his toes, it was so loud.

"Oh my God, that was awesome."

Still laughing, I manage to tell him the truth. "I'm actually an ER nurse at Bridgewater."

"Well, I am sure that you are an excellent nurse, but I was kind of excited to think I could be training a stripping nun. When I mock you over beers with my buddies would it be OK if I tell them you are a stripping nun?"

"Oh, absolutely. Just speak of me in a kind manner. Or I may have to show you what I can do with a ruler." Holy hell, I just said that. Insert red blushing face here.

No words leave Declan's mouth but the expression on his face says it all.

"Well, I should go. I have some errands to run before I head home to get some rest before work tonight."

Oh God, too much, too much, take it back!

"Alright, Madi, well, you did awesome today. What are you doing Friday morning?"

"Oh gosh, ummmm…" I must have had a panicked look on my face because he quickly added, "second session Friday, then?"

"Yes. Second session. Friday. Same time. Yes. Training. Got it."

He smiles and winks.

AS I HEAD towards the locker room to get my things, Taylor corners me. "You two looked pretty chummy," she says with a smug look.

"What are you talking about? And don't talk to me. I am so mad at you right now."

"Really? Are you really mad at me, Madi? You didn't look too mad 15 minutes ago. You guys seemed to have hit it off pretty well. Speaking as a casual observer."

"He was being polite and making small talk while we worked out. Isn't that what you pay him to do?"

"Noooo, I pay him to make people want to cry and puke, not giggle and chit chat like you're sipping dirty martinis over brie and crackers."

"Whatever. He is just being nice. And why the FUCK did you pick him to be my trainer? Is it not enough that you extorted $500.00 in fees from me for these sessions that you now have to add insult to injury by making HIM my trainer?"

"For the record, I didn't extort it from you. You could have said no," she smirks. "But you chose to go with door number two. And I think he is into you." She turns to walk towards the door.

"Oh no, no you don't, you don't get to say something like that and leave. That's like farting and walking out of the room. What on earth makes you think he is into me? He is like, what, 30? He's not into me—he's into Xbox, Coors Light and 25 year old girls, for Christ's sake. He is just being nice to me because I am your friend and I am paying his salary. He knows that you forced me to sign up. He's a nice kid. Can we leave it at that?"

"Sure, we can leave it at that. But…"

"NO. NO buts!!"

"But… he asked me if he could be your trainer," she says as she waltzes out the door.

I stand in stunned silence in the locker room.

OK, what am I supposed to say or do with this information? Hmmmmm? Can you answer that for me because I could really use some help here.

My thoughts start to run a million miles a second. Well, it is me, so they are more than likely taking a leisurely stroll at about 2 miles a second but that's not the point. Why? Does it even matter? Oh God, I need a latte and scone. Should I place another "MAN DOWN" text to the girls or is it like crying wolf? Will they not show some day when I need a kidney and am sitting at Starbucks waiting for them?

I really need help, but I know if I call Savannah she's just going to tell me to 'jump on that pogo stick and ride it till dawn'—not exactly the nugget of advice I am looking for at this moment. I need a rational thinker who will take all the data given to her and then form an opinion and game plan.

As I leave the locker room I know I have to walk past the main floor and I am bound to see Declan. Yep, sure enough, he is standing by the front desk with Taylor chatting it up.

"Hey Madi, great job today. See you Friday?"

"Yep, Ok. Bye Bye then. See you Friday," I reply with no eye contact as I speed walk out to my car.

Plopping down in the driver seat I make the call. "LYNN! I need you!" I say when she answers her phone.

"Hey Madi, what's up? Are you OK?"

"I need your advice. Can you talk?"

"Sure, what's going on? Is Claire OK?"

"Yes, Claire is fine, thanks for asking, but I think I'm having a nervous breakdown. Remember that guy at the gym that I made an asshole out of myself in front of?"

"Yes. Which time?"

"Gah! Both times. Thanks for the reminder. And how did you find out?"

"Savannah told me," she says with a giggle.

"That bitch! Well, he's a personal trainer at the gym and I just had my first session with him."

"He's your trainer?" she asks, laughing louder.

"Again, yep. And thanks for laughing. So here is the thing. This kid is like 27 years old and built like… well, I don't even know because I didn't know they built anything like that. Apparently he asked Taylor if he could be my trainer and she agreed. She seems to think he is into me. What do I do?"

"What do you mean, what do you do? Why does this pose a problem for you? Does it matter that he asked to train you?"

"I… Well, no. I guess not."

"Why does it matter to you, Madi? Do you like him? Are you into him?" she asks a bit too smugly.

"No. Well, I mean… don't get me wrong, he is super-hot, and given the chance I would climb him like a tree," I mumble under my breath. "But he is just a piece of gym dandy eye candy."

"OK, then I don't see the problem here. He can be your trainer; that's nothing for you to get all in a tizzy over. So he asked to train you. Maybe he thought that Taylor would appreciate it, taking on the problem client and all. Or that it might be weird for Taylor to work with you," she says with a smile in her voice.

"Nice. Well, as usual, you put things into perspective. So there is nothing to do except keep my training appointments with him and try not to fall off the treadmill in front of him. Or anyone, for that matter. Thanks, Lynnie, I heart you."

"Right back at ya. Now that I talked you off the ledge, I have to get going. I need to take Bethany to the orthodontist."

"Thanks again. Tell the girls hi for us."

I hang up as I pull in front of Elise and Eamon's to pick up Claire. "Hey, baby girl. Did you have fun playing with Phaedra?"

"Yes, but I don't wanna go, Mommy," she says with a pouty face.

"Honey, we have to. I have to work tonight and Grandma will be over later to watch you. We need to get going. I have to get some sleep before work."

"Why don't you let her stay here tonight, Madi? It will be fine, the girls can play and you can get some sleep. You know we don't mind," Elise offers.

"I know, and I appreciate the offer, but you just worked a crap ton of shifts and must be exhausted. And I don't have any of Claire's clothes with me."

"Really, it's fine, Madi. They are about the same size—we have clothes here she can wear for the night. Besides, it's actually easier when there are two of them. They keep each other busy. It saves me from having to play Barbie's," she says with a laugh.

"Are you sure? I can pick her up tomorrow morning on

my way home around 8."

"No need, take your time. They can sleep in. I will feed them and then you can come get her."

At this point Claire and Phaedra are jumping around the room shouting "SLEEP OVER!! WOO HOO!"

With that, I kiss my little Éclair goodbye and head home to get some much needed rest before I head to Bridgewater to pull 12 hour shifts for the next 3 days.

Working 3 days a week is really nice, but having 4 days off is better. Having seniority at the hospital and being best buddies with the Chief Head Honcho Dr. Kelly helps too. I get to work mid-week and have weekends off. We all have to take turns working graveyards-that's not something we can get out of—but at least I work mine on Tuesday, Wednesday and Thursday. I miss the drama-filled, ass-on-fire weekend nights. The ER is not the place you want to be on a Friday or Saturday night. On occasion I will work an overtime shift if they are shorthanded but that's pretty rare. I covet my weekends off.

I get back home and decide to eat a little something before I head to shower and bed. As I am buttering my toast and applying copious amounts of apricot jam, my cell phone chirps that I have a new text.

–Don't forget 2 drink a lot of H2O. :) – From a number I do not recognize.

–Who is this? And why are you telling me to drink water?–

–LOL, its Declan. U left in a hurry, forgot 2 tell U–

–Why are you talking BINGO to me? – HA! Crack myself up

–LOL, Typing class drop out–

–How did U get my #? –

–Taylor, hope it's OK. –

–It's fine. 2 L8 now, but its fine. LOL ;) –

–LOL, Cool. What R U doing?–

–You don't want to know.–

–Try me. Now I am curious–

Is this really happening right now?

–I am ironing my habit and polishing my ruler– HAHAHA, I'm funny

–LMAO, That. Is. Awesome.–

–Actually I'm shoving my face with carbs then shower then bed.–

–Lucky.–

OK, what the hell does that mean? Lucky what? Lucky shower? Lucky bed? Is he being flirty with me? Is Mr. Hillier getting fresh?

–??? Lucky?–

–I <3 carbs–

Oh no, silly. He doesn't want you, he wants your toast. DUH!

–They are amazing.–

–Did U butter that toast?–

–Mmmm hmmmm.–

–Did U jelly that toast?–

OK, why do I feel like I am doing toast porn? If he asks me what kind of jelly my toast is wearing I'M OUT!

–I did, I jellied it good–

I can't help but laugh the entire time I am typing this and I can only imagine and hope he is doing the same. If he is doing dirty things to his own biscuit while we text, I will be slightly disturbed. Although, no… no, I would be disturbed.

–Wow, U made me really…–

"Made you really what?" I shout at my phone as I choke on my toast.

–Hungry–

–I'm not gonna lie, it was good. Oh so good, my toast was dripping–

Pause for effect…

–With butter and jelly–

Am I really toast porn texting Declan? You should be sleeping, Madi, not engaging in inappropriate toast talk here. Oh, maybe just one more.

–My sopping toast and I are hitting the showers, then I'm going to loaf around. –

–Toast Tease ;) – he sends back.

–I never tease when it comes to toast. Bye! –

As I head up to my room and start the shower I realize that I am feeling some pain. Not where you might think, considering I just worked out with a trainer, but my cheeks hurt. No, not those cheeks. My face hurts from smiling and laughing while we texted. I am still in shock at the things I said to him. I guess when they aren't standing in front of you it's easy to let your guard down. Oh well, no harm in a little friendly banter between gym acquaintances.

After a long hot shower and several inappropriate thoughts of Declan and buttered toast, I decide to hit the hay and get some sleep before work.

"Mmmm, hot buttered Declan," I mumble to myself.

Chapter 6

"MVA, 5 VICTIMS, ETA 4 minutes out. 2 critical!" I shout to the nurses and doctors standing around as I answer the call from the Fire Department.

"Well so much for a quiet night in the ER on a Tuesday," Savannah says.

"Fuck this. I am too tired to deal with this crap tonight," Dr. Kelly says. That's Grace, always the professional.

And within minutes, the ER is lit up with firefighters, paramedics, nurses, X-ray techs and doctors running all over the place as we try and assess the patients that have come in. "No rest for the weary!" I shout.

"One female, approximately 10 years of age, unrestrained in back seat of a van, breathing on her own but unresponsive," Hot Fireman #1 shouts as Savannah runs alongside him to Room 2.

"Male driver, drunk, minor injuries, unrestrained. Conscious," Hot Fireman #2 says as he comes in, I take this one and head into Room 3.

The other victims are brought in one by one via ambulance and taken to different rooms. The most critical of them all is the father of the family, who was driving. Luke brings him in and goes immediately into Trauma Room 1. It looks pretty touch and go at this point but Dr. Kelly is quickly accessing him and making a game plan.

Spending several minutes in the room with my patient, the drunk driver who crossed into oncoming traffic and hit a van filled with a family coming home after a night out for pizza. I can smell the alcohol on him and I am pretty sure he just pissed himself. Ahhh, the glamorous life of a nurse. Bandages are being applied, lacerations are being stitched and bed restraints are now attached. On more than one occasion, a suspect has tried to flee the ER after getting treatment.

About 45 minutes later, Dr. Kelly comes in to check on my patient. "So let me guess. The one with the least severe injuries is the drunk driver?" she says.

"Minor contusions to the face and head, a few lacerations to the right arm and a busted, fucked up left knee," I reply to Grace under my breath.

The drunkard is starting to get a bit out of hand. I think he is sobering up and starting to feel the pain.

"Give him 0.5cc's of morphine to calm him down, but no more. I think he should feel some of the pain he inflicted on the others," Dr. Kelly orders.

"You got it. 16 gauge in the top of the hand it is," I say with a smug smile to Grace

For those not in the medical profession, a 16 gauge IV needle is akin to a McDonald's drinking straw, only slightly sharpened on the end.

"OUCH, YOU STUPID CUNT!" he shouts as I pierce

the skin on his hand with the IV needle.

"Pipe down, hold still, and please remember your manners. I would hate to have to start a catheter on you too," I say with a plastic smile and saccharine tone. Right about then, Officer Nash comes in to check on the condition of his DUI suspect.

"I suggest you apologize to the nice lady before I turn my back and let her whoop your ass. She's little but she's feisty," Nash says with a wink.

Steve Nash—Officer Steven Nash, to be exact—is an officer with the local police department. The thing about Officer Nash is that he is SUPER hot, SUPER SUPER nice and SUPER SUPER SUPER good in the sack. How do I know this? Because I have tapped that… a few times.

Steve and I met when he came into the ER with an assault suspect one night. We got to talking, went out for drinks, then one thing led to another and his penis fell into my vagina. Repeatedly. Faster and harder. Again and again.

Steve was the first guy to clean out the cobwebs and knitting needles from my hoo-ha years after Andy and I split. At that point, it had been over three years since I had gotten any, and let's be honest—Andy wasn't all that great in bed, if you know what I mean. Let's just say it was a good thing he had a tongue.

Nash and I hooked up several times on and off over the next few months and even tried dating for a while, but I just didn't get a relationship vibe with him. So after several months, I called it quits.

I do get the awkward pleasure of seeing him now and then when he comes into the ER, and it's not at all uncomfortable that this man has seen me naked or heard me scream for more at the top of my lungs.

"Thanks, Nash."

"No problem. How have you been?"

"Good. You?" I ask.

"Pretty good, just living the dream," he says with his dimple laced grin and slightly stubbled face. HOT!

"I almost have him cleaned up and ready for transport. No need for observation on this one. I can already tell he's an asshole; don't need to observe anymore."

Nash laughs. "Alright, I'll take him off your hands as soon as you're done with the paperwork. How are the kids?" His facial expression changes to something more serious.

"Pretty beat up, from what I could see. Savannah was working the most critical one. I think they just took her to CT. She was unresponsive when they brought her in."

"Well, let me know when you're done so I can take him to his new home away from home," Nash says heading for the door.

"You got it," I reply with a smile as I apply the last of the bandages to the drunk's arm and go back to my duties of prepping and caring for this dick who almost wiped out an entire family.

"Hey, Madi?"

I pause and look up.

"You look good," Nash says quietly as he gets to the door, and looks back at me with a crooked smile.

I just smile. I really don't know what to say at this point. AWKWARD! I guess I could throw my head back and scream THANK YOU while I slap my hands on the bed and wad the sheets in my clutched fists. This is an action he is familiar with.

About 2 hours later, I get the all clear from Grace to

release Mr. Asshole into Nash's custody.

"Alright, Steve, he is all yours. Now make sure he is nice and safe. Wouldn't want him to hit his freshly bandaged face against the Plexiglas partition if you happen to take a rogue corner," I say with a wink.

Nash nods at me and puts the cuffs on the patient as I remove the bed straps from his wrists.

"So, ummmm, any chance I could talk you into a drink some time, Madi?"

"Oh gosh, ummm, I don't know, Steve. My schedule has been a bit..."

"Got it," he interrupts. "I understand. But if you ever change your mind... Call me." Nash takes the patient from me and escorts him out of the ER to his awaiting chariot of flashing lights.

Now if someone could please hand me my well-earned Bitch of the Universe sash and tiara, I will be on my way.

The rest of the night goes by with much less drama—just a few professional patients looking for their next fix or a refill of their oxycodone. Thank God it's almost shift change. I am exhausted.

Around 8am, Savannah and I walk out together to the parking lot.

"Hey, did I see Luke come in with one of the MVA victims earlier?"

"Yeah, he got called in. Marcus's wife went into labor so Luke said he would cover his shift."

"I was surprised to see him. Where are the boys?"

"He called my parents and they came over to watch them."

"I bet that was a nice surprise to see him at work," I say with a laugh.

"Yeah, it was. When he left, he told me to make sure I greet him at the door 'beaver first'," she laughs.

"Oh Jesus." I roll my eyes.

"So are you going to tell me what happened with Steve? I saw him talking to you earlier."

"Nothing much, just catching up."

"Please tell me you mounted him or at least made plans to in the VERY near future."

"No, I didn't mount him. What is wrong with you?"

"I don't know what your deal is with that guy. He is so hot and soooo nice and he is soooooooo into you. Why won't you give him a chance?"

"I don't know. I just don't feel that spark with him. He is a really nice guy but I don't want to lead him on."

"Well, he wants in your panties, Madi. You should give him another spin," Savannah says with a wink.

"I have given him a spin, remember? We tried dating, bu t I don't want to be someone's fuck buddy anymore," I reply, shrugging my shoulders.

"I know, but that boy has it bad for you. You should have seen him watching you tonight. He does it every time he comes in. And if you aren't here he always asks about you," she comments with a raised eyebrow.

"Please let it go. I already feel like a bitch."

"Sorry, not trying to make you feel like a bitch, just wanted to give you something to think about."

"Thanks. Now, go home and unleash the beaver for Luke," I say with a hand wave, dry heave and eye roll.

"I'M ON IT!" she shouts and she walks towards her truck. "See you tomorrow, B-Hitch."

"BYE!" I call back with a wave.

AS I HEAD towards the McCaffery house to pick up my little Claire Bear, I can't help but think about what Vannah said. Maybe I should give Nash a chance. He is a really nice guy—stable, responsible, fucking hot, caring, great in bed and gets along with my motley group of friends. My friends are my chosen family and mean the world to me. If my friends don't like you, it will never work with us.

Should I try and give him another chance? Maybe my head wasn't in the right place at that time for a relationship. Yes? No? Maybe?

Getting to Elise's house, I head up to the door and text her to tell her I am here. I don't want to knock if anyone is still asleep. They have 3 dogs and the commotion that ensues when the doorbell rings or someone knocks takes forever to calm down. I should know; the same shit happens at my house with Zoe and Athena.

"Hey, come on in, everyone is up," Elise says when she comes to the door. "How was work?"

"I'm exhausted. We had an MVA with 5 patients shortly after shift change and it was a nightmare."

"I saw it on the news. I was wondering if you ended up working it."

"Yep, sure did. I got the pleasure of treating the asshole that caused the entire thing."

"Nice," she says with a laugh.

"Is my kid still here or did you sell her to gypsies? Cuz I am OK with that as long as you got a decent price," I smile.

"She's in Phaedra's room picking up the mess they made making forts last night."

"How come she picks up at your house but not at ours? Doesn't seem fair."

"Eamon threatened them within an inch of their lives last night and said if they didn't, he would make them go out back and dig a hole," she laughs.

"Well, who am I to question your parenting techniques? Clearly, it worked!"

"So, I wanted to ask you. Phaedra has really been missing Claire and asked if she could come over again soon and stay a few days. You know, before school starts up and they hardly ever get to see each other again?"

"I guess, but I don't want to just pawn her off on you."

"Hey, I'm the one that asked. I know you get so little time with her when you're working. If you want to take her home today and spend some time with her, and then bring her back tonight on your way to work, you could just leave her here until you get off Friday. It's only a day and a half, really. We are going to hit the water park tomorrow and Phaedra would love Claire to come. Just pack a bag and send it with her tonight."

"Are you sure?"

"Absolutely. If Eamon decides to take this job in Washington they won't get to see each other for very long stretches."

"So he is thinking pretty seriously about it then?" I say with a sad pouty face.

"Yeah, we are. I miss the seasons and I want Phaedra to experience the small town feeling. You know I hate the heat."

"Don't we all? I only stay because my divorce papers

mandate it. I can't move Claire out of state without Andy's permission and I think he would say no out of spite," I reply, laughing.

"I bet he would, just to prove even more to all of us that he is an epic douche. What did you ever see in him?"

"I don't have any idea. I think I was a fresh faced, naive girl who wanted to be in love, and in waltzed Andy the Wonder Tool with his shiny suits and snake-tongue way of talking, and I fell for it. He's a salesman and a pretty good one. Look what he sold me!" I groan.

"Yes, but thank God you saw the light. A little later than the rest of us, but you saw it none the less."

"I guess we all have to see things in our own time."

"Well I, for one, am so glad YOU ARE HEALED!" Elise waves her arms dramatically, then pushes her hand against my forehead like a Southern preacher.

"Thank you, that was very evangelical of you. Dumbass."

"HI MOM!" BOOM. Power slam by Claire into my right side.

"Hi, Sweets, did you have fun? I heard you made forts."

"I did and they were so cool. Can I make a fort when we get home?"

"Yes, but we have to leave now. I am exhausted and need to feed us and get some sleep before work tonight."

"OK, but can I come back over? Elise said she would ask you and I hope you said yes." Insert Claire and the puppy dog eyes here.

"Yes, you are coming back tonight, BUT"—I have to insert that very quickly before the cheering starts, I need to inflict my blackmail—"Only if we leave now and I can get some sleep today. Deal?" I put my hand out to shake.

"Deal! Let's go!" Claire grabs my hand and pulls us toward the door.

"Thanks again, Elise. I will be back around 6, is that OK?"

"Sounds great. And don't worry about feeding her. Eamon is smoking a turkey today so she can eat with us."

"TURKEY! Awesome!" Claire exclaims.

"Well alrighty then. See you later!" I hug Elise goodbye.

Chapter 7

WHEN CLAIRE AND I arrive back home, we are greeted in our usual thunderous fashion by Zoe and Athena.

"Can you please feed the dogs for me?" I ask Claire.

"Sure Mommy, but then can I go up and pack my bag for Phaedra's house?" she asks with an excited smile and bouncing head.

"Of course. When you're done I am going to jump in the shower, OK?"

"Okie Dokie slow poky," Claire says with a giggle as she feeds the two hounds from hell.

I head up to my room to start the shower. As I am getting out my jammies and a towel, I hear a faint 'ping' coming from the other room. It's my cell phone alert to an incoming text message. I will have to check it after my shower.

As I climb in, I am suddenly flooded with flashbacks to my 'itching the fish' session the other day, dreaming of Declan and I all hot and wet in the very same shower. Maybe Savannah and Grace are right; maybe I do need to get laid.

Gah, I hate when they are right. Maybe I should just call Steve—he is amazing in bed, and apparently still wants to tap this even after a year.

I hurry and shower. I don't want to take my time for fear of a repeat performance and interruption by Claire. That was a close one.

As soon as I dry off and wrap my hair up in a towel, fancy turban style, I head off to fetch my phone to check the message. Maybe it will be Grace telling me the hospital decided to close for the day—you know, in honor of how hard we work. Mmmm, that would be delightful.

I see a message, it's from Declan. My tummy drops and I get all twittery inside.

What the hell is wrong with me? Why am I getting all nervous from an incoming text message? Dork.

As I swipe the screen, I see the words that make me smile from ear to ear.

–Good Morning, I hope U had a GR8 day at work.–

Oh my God, how sweet. What a nice kid.

–Thank U. It was, well… work ;) –

–I think it's cool what U do.–

–Thanks. I think what you do sucks–

–LOL. Hey now, B nice–

–I thought you were going to say B4, since U talk BINGO 2 me–

–HA HA. So why do I suck?–

–I didn't say U suck, I said what U DO sucks. I'm sore–

–I could make you even sorer.–

–I don't doubt that for a minute. You were very gentle with me, thank U–

–Friday I won't be so gentle. It's gonna get rough–

Holy hell! He just said that! I know he is referring to working out, but still in my filthy mind he is being dirty with me… and I like it. OK, here goes nothing.

–Sometimes I like it rough–

–I don't doubt that for a minute. ;) –

–Don't judge me. lol–

–Never. What are U doing?–

–Just showered now getting ready to make some hot buttered toast.–

–U sure do like toast. Is that all u eat? lol–

–No, but it's my favorite breakfast, with tea of course–

–Too bad Starbucks doesn't sell toast–

–????? Are you stalking me?–

–Lol, no. Just a good memory–

–Ohhh, so you are stalking me.–

–Why do U say that?–

–Most people wouldn't remember such mundane facts, except a stalker–

–I have an excellent memory–

–Damn, I was hoping you would forget about my rapping and swan diving. :(–

–Never. Taking it to the grave–

–Outstanding news.–

–And I don't like the term stalker, I prefer professional intense secret researcher–

–LOL. Call it what you will, you're a stalker–

–OK, fine. Lol ;) –

–Good thing I know you're joking.–

–Yep, good thing. Or am I? Nice towel. :D –

My head starts to whip around in a fury. Holy shit—he really is watching me!

–OMG! Where are you??–

–ROFLMAO–

–Declan you answer me right now or I'm gonna rap again, REALLY LOUD!!!!–

–Relax. I'm teasing U. U said just showered, I took a shot that U had on a towel of some sort–

–Well played asshole. Well played–

–I was right though huh? U have on a towel. ;)–

–No.–

–Hahaha, yes U do. Admit it–

–FINE, I did. But it was on my head so don't get any dirty thoughts–

Well, that was presumptuous of you to assume he would ever get a dirty thought about you in a towel.

–Too late.–

–Right, you forgot the LOL.–

–I wasn't lol-ing–

–Oh– Awkward.

–Well I better let U get some sleep, U work tonight right?–

–Yes I do. 7P to 7A.–

–Still coming to see me Friday?–

–Against my will. Yes–

–I will make it worth UR *while–*

–B7 I19 N41 G58 O73–

–?? What is that? Lol–

–Just BINGOing you back–

–LOL, G'night Madi. Sweet dreams–

–Thanks Declan. Stay muscley–

WTF? Stay muscley? Really? I shake my head.

–HAHAHAHAHA, I'll work on it.–

I tell Claire I am headed to nap for a bit. She decides to come into my room with me and watch a movie with her headphones on. Curling up next to me with her Hello Kitty headphones, she puts in her favorite movie and I drift off to sleep with a goofy doofy grin on my face. What is it about that kid that makes me laugh?

THE ALARM GOES off and it's time to get up and get ready for another day of working in paradise. I really do love my job, but some days it's very draining.

I get dressed in my standard issue black scrubs. All the ER nurses have to wear black. I like to liven mine up with fun socks. Yesterday it was pink polka dots; today I think I shall try purple stripes. I put on my makeup and pull my hair back in a loose, messy low bun and head out to get Claire. I find her in her room. She has made a fort out of her entire room with several blankets from the linen closet and guest room.

"What on earth happened in here? I thought you were watching a movie in my room while I slept? I see you were quite busy."

"I did, but then the movie was over and I was bored and you kept making noises so I came into my room to make a fort."

"Was I snoring again?"

"No, you kept smiling and saying something about a desk fan."

"A desk fan?"

"Yeah, do you have a desk fan at work?"

"No, not that I… Oooh," I answer nervously. Oh no, I was talking about Declan in my sleep. Desk fan… ha ha. Good cover, Madi. "Yes, I have a desk fan at work."

"Why were you smiling about it? Was it funny?"

"Mmm hmmm. OK, so get your things together. We need to leave in about 20 minutes," I say to Claire, changing the subject. Oh my God, I was talking about Declan in my sleep.

"I'm ready to go," she replies as she points to the 3 suitcase sized bags of toys and clothing she packed while I slept.

"Claire, you are staying 2 days, not 2 months!"

"I know, Mommy, but Phaedra wanted to see my new doll and then I had to bring her clothes and her bed and toys. She needs to have them for a sleep over too."

"You know what, why don't you narrow it down to one bag. I think that will work just fine. Phaedra is just as spoiled as you and she has plenty of dolly things for Phelan to use and play with, OK?"

"Fine," she says with a pout and a grumble. I think if she knew what a bitch was, she would have just called me one under her breath.

Twenty minutes later we head out the door, entire toy box in tow. I drop Claire off at Elise's and head off to work. Thankfully, this shift is much quieter than last night. Savannah and I even have time for wheelchair races and saline shooting contests.

Yep, we are always professional. And you people put your lives in our hands every single day. Suckers.

THE NEXT DAY and a half go by pretty quickly, to be honest. No real drama in trauma and I have managed to catch up on my sleep. With Claire being at Elise and Eamon's, I have been able to come home and do my signature swan dive, but this time into my bed.

Thursday night finally arrives and I know that I only have this one more shift until I am off for 4 days again.

Pulling into the ER, I see Savannah is already here. That's odd; she is usually screeching in at the last possible second before shift change. On more than one occasion I've have had to fill her in on her patients because she missed rotations.

As I walk into the unit, I see her already sitting at the desk and ready to work with charts in her hand.

I look around and then stare at Savannah. "Am I in the right place? This is Bridgewater, right? Why are you here? Is there an apocalypse?"

"Yes, you dumbass. Come and get your charts."

"Why are you here so early?"

"I'm not early, I'm right on time."

"I know, but for you that's early," I say with a laugh.

Savannah reaches out and slaps my ass as I walk by. "I had to drop the kids off at my parents' house. Luke got called in again to work tonight."

"Wow, that's twice in one week he has pulled another shift. Are they shorthanded?"

"No, he loves his job or something like that," she smiles.

"I can't relate." We both laugh.

"Hey there, chicas!" Grace calls out as she walks into the unit.

"Hey!" we say in unison.

"So, Madi, when were you going to tell me about your texting rendezvous with Declan?"

"What are you talking about, Grace?"

Savannah pipes up. "Excuse the fuck out of me. What did you say? She has been texting Declan and holding out on us?"

Both heads turn to look at me. "He texted me Wednesday morning. That was it."

"Are you kidding me with this crap?" Savannah says. "Why the hell didn't you tell me?"

"Umm, maybe because it wasn't a big deal and I didn't think it warranted the third degree from you guys. It was 5 minutes, tops."

"Taylor said he was walking around like a goofy schoolboy and it all started right after he asked her for your cell number," Grace deadpans.

"Knock it off. He was reminding me to drink water after my PT session with him. That's ALL!"

"Mmmm hmmmm, not what I heard. Tay said he was laughing out loud and smiling like a buffoon. She said she hasn't seen him like that since he's been coming to the gym."

"Whatever. Maybe someone else was texting him or he was looking up stupid videos on YouTube. Who knows?"

"Maybe funny videos of women falling off treadmills," Vannah adds.

I promptly give her the finger. She truly is number one in my book.

"Stop your shit. It was no big deal. He reminded me to drink water and that was about it. Nothing more." Secretly, I smile inside, thinking about our toast talk.

"Why are you smiling?" Grace asks.

Oh shit, I guess that smile wasn't as insidey as I thought.

"You LIKE HIM!!" Savannah squeals. "You do, you do, you like him!" She is so overjoyed with herself she just about falls off her stool.

"Karma, bitch! That's what you get for being a jerk," I growl to her.

"Karma nothing. You like him."

"HER HOO-HA LIVES!" Grace yells a tad too loudly.

"Fuck both of you. I don't like him; he's just a nice kid and is funny to talk to. He tolerates my stupidity and doesn't ridicule me for it. Well, not yet, anyway."

"Oh no… no no no no no. You don't get off the hook that easy. You like him," Grace says.

"Well who wouldn't? Have you seen him, Grace?" Savannah asks.

"No, but I heard he is hot," Grace replies with wide eyes.

"He is. He's like 6'7" and built like a brick shithouse. He's got these tattoos and these muscles and these tattoos on these muscles. He wears this 'Bama' hat backward and oh fuck me, it's hot."

"Aren't you married?" I ask Savannah.

"YES, but I'm not dead. That boy is fine."

"Operative word in that sentence being BOY."

"So, Kai is younger than I am. Is that a problem?" Grace gives me a strange look.

"No, but only a few years younger than you. This kid is like 10 or 12 years younger than me. When I was taking my SATs he was learning how to spell SAT, for fuck's sake."

"Oh Jesus Eunice, relax. No one said you had to marry the guy. What's a little harmless flirting? And if it leads to a balancing act on his penis… so be it," Savannah observes.

"A few harmless texts about hydration and now I have to fuck the guy. Nice."

"Yep, those are the rules. I don't make em, I just follow them," Grace says with a laugh.

"You guys suck," I reply as I walk out of the bay to go check on my patient who thankfully chose that moment to press the call light.

SEVERAL HOURS OF work and torture by Grace and Savannah and it's almost time to call it quits. I have exactly 2 hours left until shift change. It's 5am and I am kicked back at the nurses' station when a big old yawn escapes my mouth. Just as I have my mouth hanging wide open I turn to see none other than Declan walking into the ER.

"Working hard, I see," he says. I sit straight up in my chair and spin the rest of the way around, pulling my feet off the counter.

"Just taking a bit of a break," I reply, tucking a few stray strands of hair behind my ear.

"Nice socks," he says with a smirk.

"Nice hat," I observe, with a head nod towards the red Bama hat he's wearing.

"Thanks. So I take it you aren't terribly busy right now?"

"Not at this very moment. What's up? Are you OK?" I say as I stand up.

"I'm good. I went out for a morning run and thought I would swing by and say hi." He looks a bit awkward saying this. Is he embarrassed?

"You decided to take a run. To the ER?" I say with my head cocked.

"Well, kind of. I was running down Grand by the tracks and they come right by here. I thought I would take a breather and come in and say hi before I head back home."

"Well OK, then. That explains it."

"IS THAT DECLAN I SEE??" I hear Savannah exclaim from 4 rooms away. "IT IS! Well, what brings you to Bridgewater this time of the morning?" she says as she comes up and leans her arm on my shoulder, a self-satisfied smile on her face.

"Hey ladies, what's going on?" I hear Grace say as she saunters up.

"Nothing," I grind out with a smile.

"Who is this, Madi?" Grace asks. Is she batting her eyelashes?

"Grace… this is Declan. From the gym. My trainer," I mumble through gritted teeth.

"Declan, yes! I have heard SO SO much about you," Grace croons as she walks up in front of him, smiling and reaches to shake his hand. Declan stands there with a bit of an uncomfortable look on his face. Apparently he didn't know that my posse would be here with me.

"Hi, it's uhh, nice to meet ya'll."

"So, so nice to meet you too," she replies in a saccharine tone, still pumping his fist in an overly friendly and extended handshake.

"I know we haven't met personally, but I sure have seen you at the gym. I'm Savannah," Savannah pipes up, reaching for his hand.

"Yes, it's nice to finally meet ya."

"So, Declan… where on earth are you from? They don't grow em like you here in Arizona," Grace asks.

"I'm from Alabama, ma'am." Oh fuck, his accent is hot.

"I would assume so since you're wearing a Bama hat,"

Grace replies with a bit of an added accent herself.

"So what brings you here this time of day? Are you hurt? Don't feel well? Need some tending to?" Savannah asks, crossing her arms.

"Umm, no ma'am. I was just out for a run and thought I would come in and remind Madi about her training session later this morning."

"Wow, such personalized treatment from The Jungle Gym. I will have to commend Taylor on stepping up her customer service," Grace says with a smile.

"No need. I'll be sure to pass that on for you, ma'am," Declan replies with a smirk.

"OK, so yes, I will see you… in a few hours… at the gym. Thanks for stopping by and reminding me."

"No problem. See ya then." He nods his head and looks at Vannah and Grace, who are standing there looking so fucking pleased with themselves. "Ladies," he says with a head tilt as he walks out of the ER.

"Madigan Delaney Kennedy. THAT is the hot guy from the gym?" Grace asks. "THAT is the guy who caught you singing and your acrobatics performance?"

"Yep, that's him," I mutter as I sink down onto my butt against the wall, putting my head in my hands.

"I am only going to say this once, and if you ever every repeat it I will deny it was ever spoken. I would leave Kai for that man. So it is your duty as my friend to fuck him and report back to me. STAT," Grace informs me with a straight face.

"Grow up, Grace. No you wouldn't."

"Umm, is anyone else failing to see the big picture here? That man just ran here to see you, Madi. And don't think for a second that either of us believes that bullshit about 'being out for a morning jog thought he'd come and remind you about your training session later'."

"How should I know why he was here? Maybe he needed a drink of water and came into the waiting room to use the drinking fountain and then happened to see me sitting there so he thought he would remind me about our appointment later," I squeaked out in one breath.

"Ohhh, OK. Yep, I'm sure that's what happened," Savannah says with an over exaggerated wink.

THE NEXT 2 hours are nothing but pure torture for me thanks to Savannah and Grace, who, in mature fashion, continue to sing 'Madi and Declan sitting in a tree, f-u-c-k-i-n-g, first comes Madi and that's all that matters, then comes Declan and when he does it splatters.' They are my personal nightmare.

"KNOCK IT OFF! I hate you both!" I scream, and of course this is the moment the Hospital Administrator comes walking down the hallway.

"Ms. Kennedy, Ms. Brooks, Dr. Kelly," he states in his stern tone.

"Dr. Criswell," the three of us reply in unison. Oh shit, I have never seen Grace get so straight laced so quickly.

"How are things in the ER today?" he inquires.

"Good. Just off to do my last rounds before shift change," I answer as I quickly grab a chart—any chart—and take off. I round the corner so I can't be seen but I am still within earshot.

"Me too!" Vannah says, and with that we are both gone in a flash.

"So, Dr. Kelly, I would like to meet with you later today in regards to your staff and this department if you have the time. I would much appreciate it," Dr. Criswell says.

"Absolutely, sir. I will make the time," Grace replies, and with that he turns and leaves.

Minutes later, when the coast is clear, Savannah and I come out to find Grace. "What was that about?" I ask.

"I have no clue. He wants to meet with me later today. He said it was in regards to my department."

"Do you know why? Any clue?" Savannah questions.

"Nope, but he didn't look happy," Grace replies with a concerned face.

"He never looks happy. I bet he has that face even after he cums," Vannah says.

We start laughing. Gotta love Savannah.

Chapter 8

SOME OF THE other nurses start to filter in for shift change. We finish up what we are doing and Savannah and I head out together, as usual.

"I hope everything goes OK with Grace today," I say.

"I know, I haven't seen her look that scared in, well, ever."

"If you talk to her today will you let me know?"

Savannah nods as we walk to our vehicles. "Wanna catch a bite to eat before we head home?" she asks.

"No, sorry. I have my training session in like 45 minutes, remember?" I give her a sarcastic look.

"OH MY GOD, that's right! How could I forget? Well, far be it from me to keep you. You run along. Run along, little girl," she says, shooing me away.

"Asshat! I'm going."

"Yeah, you are! And I want a full report of how everything goes, you hear me?"

"Everything will be fine. We will work out, then I will go pick up Claire and go home to pass out."

Just then my phone bings that I have a new text. It's from Elise.

–Didn't go to Water Park yesterday, had a migraine. Taking the girls today. Will bring her home @ 6ish :) –

I send a quick reply back.

–OK, no problem, give her my love and thank you again! :x–

"OK, change of plans. Gym, then home. I don't have to pick up Claire. They are going to the water park right now."

"Alright. Well, you have fun 'training' with Declan and be sure to call me when you get home," Vannah says with a smile.

"Ma'am yes ma'am!" I reply with a salute as I head towards my car.

I AM JUST pulling up in front of the gym when I get another text. It's from Declan.

–Where R U?–

–Parked outside.–

–Can't work out from the car. U need to come inside–

–I beg to differ. Driving a stick is exercise–

–LOL–

I put my phone in my bag and head inside.

"Well it's about time, Madi. Nice of you to join us… 10 minutes late," Taylor drolls from the front desk as I walk in. I promptly flip her off and walk past the desk towards the locker room. I stare at myself in the mirror and give myself a little pep talk. "OK, Madi, you can do this. Suck it up and just get it over with." I take a moment to fix my hair and kiss my self-respect goodbye.

Heading into the main area of the gym I find Declan standing by the wall, waiting for me I assume.

"Hey there," he says.

"Hi. Sorry to keep you waiting."

"No problem. Everything OK?"

"Yeah, just last minute drama at work. I left late."

"Good, glad you're OK. Shall we?" Declan says with smile and motions me towards the weights.

Awww crap. This is gonna hurt. I hate the weight machine side of the gym.

"Are you sure we can't just walk on the treadmill for a bit?" I say with a sheepish grin.

"Nope, no more treadmill. I've seen your work on that piece of equipment," he responds with a wink.

We work out on a few of the pulley style pieces of equipment for a while. I am pretty impressed with my brute strength until I realize he only had 45 pounds on for me. We make our way toward a weight bench. He has me lay flat on my back and hands me a barbell loaded down with weights. I am apparently supposed to lift this bar up and down above my chest in a smooth and fluid motion. But we all know me—

I do nothing smooth and fluid. This is also the moment he decides to stand over me so his junk is just right above my head.

Here's the thing. I am not gonna lie; this guy is hot enough as it is, but with him standing above me like this wearing his black workout pants and that grey Crimson Tide t-shirt clinging nicely to his incredibly firm and muscley chest… How am I supposed to concentrate? Hmm? How?

"Come on Madi, give me 3 more," he says with his southern twang.

"I'm trying, but it's hard," I reply, whining like a bitch.

"That's what she said," he says with a smirk.

"Oh my God! Did you really just say that?" I ask, now laughing so hard I can't hold the weight up. It's getting dangerously close to coming down on my chest.

Leaning down, he takes the weight from me and sets it down. He laughs as he says, "I'm sorry. Are you OK?"

I sit up on the bench and nod, still laughing. Sitting next to me, he leans forward, locking his beautiful blue eyes with mine. "Are you really OK?" He looks worried. I wonder why—I am laughing, right? I didn't start to cry in the middle of my laughing outburst, did I? Because I have done that before…

"Yes, I'm fine," I answer, wiping the tears from my eyes.

"I had no idea it would make you laugh like that."

"Neither did I. I am going to blame it on sleep deprivation and lack of food."

"Well, you've done a great job today. Why don't we call it quits for now? Deal?"

"You don't have to ask me twice!"

This is where I should have stood up and started to walk

to the locker room to get my belongings, but I just couldn't tear myself away from his baby blue eyes. Instead I just sat there, admiring, gazing and just ogling him.

"Are you ready?" he asks

Oh look, you did have to ask me twice. I think to myself as I nod in reply.

"Looks like I did have to ask ya twice," he says with a smirk. Oh my God, he read my mind.

"Yes, I'm sorry. I am ready to be done," I reply as I start to stand up.

"Alright, I will see you on your way out," Declan smiles as he stands to leave.

I head into the locker room to get my bag. I don't look any worse for wear which is good. I straighten my hair back into a messy bun and put on a little lip gloss. Shut up, my lips are dry. I am not primping for Declan.

Oh God. Yes I am.

Walking out of the locker room toward the front desk, I see Taylor, Declan and Beth, the enrollment girl, standing there talking.

"OK, well, that was fun but I must away," I announce as I walk toward the door. "Bye!"

"Here, I'll walk ya out," Declan offers.

As we both reach for the door Declan says, "Please, allow me. If my momma saw you open that door knowing I was around, she would slap me upside the head." So I do what any self-respecting person would do. I let the momma's boy open the door for me.

"Well thank you," I curtsey and start to walk towards my car.

"Hey, so Madi, are you, ummmm, hungry?" he asks.

"Well, I was going to head home and grab something to eat. Why, are you going to prescribe an eating plan for me now?" I reply with a smile.

"Well, ummmm, no. I was going to see if you wanted to go get a bite to eat. With me. Right now," he looks down at the ground.

"The fuck?"

Declan looks at me and laughs. "Well, that wasn't exactly the answer I was looking for. Is that a good 'The Fuck' or a bad 'The Fuck'?"

"Ummm, it was more of a shocked 'The Fuck'."

"I mean, it's no big deal. I just thought you might be hungry, and ever since the other day I have been craving toast," he says with a wink and a raging dimple.

"OK!" I blurt out before I can even think or process my reply any further.

"Really?" His eyes light up.

"Sure, why not? I did just work up quite a sweat."

"Well I don't know if I'd call that a sweat," he smiles.

"Oh gosh, but I look a mess. I just pulled a 12 hour shift and then came straight here to our appointment. I don't have any other clothes, just these," I say, flicking my black pants and pink t-shirt.

"You look fine, Madi," he says with a sheepish grin.

"Well, OK. If you aren't embarrassed to be seen with me then I guess we are good."

"Want me to drive?"

"You aren't going to take me out into the desert, kill me and harvest my skin, are you?"

He starts to laugh. "Tempting, but no. Let's just start with breakfast and see how things go."

"Haha, funny man. OK, let me put my bag in my car." As we walk up to my car he laughs harder under his breath.

"Yes, I know. It's a ridiculous car and I am sorry I bought it," I say rather sternly.

"No, it's actually pretty cute and it fits you," he replies as I open up the trunk to put my bag in it.

"Did your license plate really say what I think it said?" He smiles as I close the back.

"Yes," I answer sadly with an eye roll. Apparently I had to name my mid-life crisis. Its name, you ask? Sofiat. Yep, I took a perfectly lovely girl's name and butchered it to fit my car.

"Nice. Come on, I'm this way," he grins and motions toward the side of the building. As we round the corner all I see is a motorcycle. "Where is your car?" I ask like a moron.

"Ummm, right there," he says, pointing to the aforementioned motorcycle.

"Ohhh, I didn't know you rode a hog," I say, harnessing my innermost bad ass.

"A hog, Madi?" He laughs. "It's not a hog, it's a custom bike. A buddy of mine back home built it."

"Oh, sorry. I don't know much about motorcycles."

"Clearly. Hop on," he says with a wink and pats the back of the seat where I get to sit.

Right about now is when I have visions of Clark Griswold standing on the edge of the pool swinging his arms back and forth saying 'this is crazy, this is crazy, this is crazy'. But, just like in the movie… I'm gonna go for it. What do I have to lose, right? It's just breakfast with my trainer. He's probably going to take me to some protein shack and make me eat something made with egg whites and twigs.

I scramble onto the back of the bike and Declan hands me

a helmet, then climbs on and starts it up. I swear to God that thing rumbled and vibrated like nothing I have ever felt. OK, well that's not entirely true, but it was infinitely more powerful than anything I own.

"Don't you have a helmet?" I yell in his ear.

"No, I just brought the one today. You wear it. I'll be OK. You may want to hang on."

"WHERE?" I yell, looking for handles as the engine roars.

"ME, you'll have to hold on to me. Wrap your arms around my waist," he yells back.

'This is crazy, this is crazy, this is crazy' replays again in my mind. I do as I am told and slowly wrap my arms around his waist. I am excellent at following directions.

"Any place in particular you'd like to go?"

"No, not really."

"I know a great place, but it's a bit of a drive. Are you OK with that?"

I quickly do the math in my mind. A bit of a drive equals more time on the bike which means more time holding on for dear life via his rock hard abs. "Absolutely!" I shout back.

"Just remember to lean. When I lean, you lean," he yells.

I nod. Hehehehe, it tickles.

ABOUT 45 MINUTES into our ride we pull into the dirt parking lot of a small dive restaurant. The sign reads 'Springs Cafe'. Declan parks the bike near some other motorcycles and helps me off. Oh God, help me. I have to take the helmet off,

which means my hair is going to look like a smashed down version of Medusa.

Declan reaches for the helmet and gently takes it off my head. I shake my head immediately in an attempt to rid myself of the epic hat head I am rocking.

"Are you OK?" Declan asks.

"Yes I'm great. Just trying to fix this," I say as I run my fingers through my hair.

"Here, let me." He takes his hand and gently strokes the side of my head, pulling a few loose tendrils back behind my ear. As his hand caresses my ear, he softly brings it around the side of my face and runs his hand along my jaw line. "Is that better?"

"Uhh huh," is all I could squeak out and I'm fairly certain my mouth is hanging open. My tummy feels funny.

"Come on, let's go inside. This place has amazing food." Declan grabs my hand to lead me towards the door. He must have realized what he had done, because as we got to the main entrance he dropped my hand and opened the door for me. "After you."

"Thank you," I say as we walk into the little hole in the wall place. We are promptly greeted by the hostess, who looks like a sweet little grandmother.

"Hey there, big boy! How are you? Two today?" she says with raised eyebrows.

"Yes ma'am. Mary, this is Madi. Madi, this is Mary, she runs this place," he says with a nod. He takes my hand to usher me ahead of him. I comply and follow Mary towards a table in the back near the kitchen.

"Here you go, hun," she smiles.

"Thanks, Miss Mary," he says as he kisses her cheek.

As we sit down, I can't help but look around. The place is small, pretty dimly lit and the tables are relatively close together. When I look at our table setting I notice that none of the silverware matches, our glasses for water are different colors and my plate has flowers on it while Declan's has shells.

"This place is adorable. How did you find it?"

"I went for a ride shortly after I moved out here and stopped in to eat. I fell in love with the place and come back as often as I can," he replies, and he puts his hands together on top of the table.

"I assumed you were a regular. Mary seems to be quite taken with you," I say with a smile.

"She is. She says I remind her of her grandson Jason. He was killed in Iraq about a year and a half ago."

"Oh my gosh, I am so sorry."

"Yeah, she gets pretty emotional when she talks about it. I like to come and check in on her every now and then. She runs this place with her husband and son, Jason's father. They are good people. Reminds me of some of my favorite places back home."

"That's really sweet. I bet you get homesick."

"Sometimes. Really, I just miss my momma."

"That must be hard."

"It can be. I try and go back home to visit her a few times a year."

Mary brings us some menus and a water pitcher to fill our glasses. "Thank you, ma'am," Declan says with a grin. Mary smiles right back at him and pats him on the shoulder. "Do you like pancakes?" he asks me.

"It's a carb covered in butter and syrup. I don't understand your question," I answer with a smile.

"Well, they have the best pancakes here, even better than my momma's."

"Then the pancakes I shall have," I say, folding up my menu. Mary comes back over and takes our order.

"A short stack for the lady and a regular for me please. Can we also get a hot tea and a coffee?"

"You got it, darling," Mary says, closing her tablet.

"Wait" I interject. "Why do I get the short stack and you get the regular? Are you monitoring my carb intake? Is this part of the personal training thing?"

Mary looks at me and smiles, then looks back at Declan. "Well it's just that…" he starts to say.

"Mary, can you please change that to 2 regulars?" I say to her confidently

"I can, sugar, and I did," she says with a grin and a wink to Declan as she walks away.

"Why did she look at you and wink?" I ask. "Is my hair all messed up? Do I have a boog?" I narrow my eyes at him.

"Jesus. No, Madi, you don't have a boog," he chuckles, "and your hair is fine, trust me. What'd you think of the ride up?"

"It was amazing. I never realized how pretty it is here. I guess when you are zooming by at 65 miles an hour in a car you miss a lot. But being on the back of your bike was so… so…"

"Peaceful?" he says.

"Yeah, peaceful."

We sit in silence for a few minutes as I look around and soak in all the quaintness of the cafe. It is really cute, with checkerboard and lace curtains, family pictures on all of the walls and, to be honest, a few creepy shriveled up looking doll things. Ugh, terrifying.

Declan sits back in his chair a bit and looks around too. "Those apple dolls freaking you out?"

"Oh my god, YES!" I say, looking back at him. He is watching me with a smile. "They're disturbing. Those are made of apples?"

"Yeah, I had to ask. They are pretty creepy."

"Yikes, I may never eat an apple again," I reply, laughing.

We sit in silence again for a few minutes when I suddenly blurt out, "wanna play 20 questions?" Oh geez, what am I, 12?

He smirks at me. "Sure, bring it on. Except how about 10 questions each? Back and forth like?"

"I can live with that. OK, so what brought you to Arizona?"

"I followed my brother out here. He works for the Sheriff's Office. There wasn't much keeping me back home anymore. It was time for a fresh start. Same question to you."

"My mother's womb. I was born and raised here." He smiles at me. "OK, ummm, how many siblings?"

"Just one, my older brother Clark. He is 6 years older than me. You?"

"None, I'm an only child."

"That must have been cool growin' up. Didn't have anyone taking your stuff or breaking things, blaming you for stuff you didn't do."

"It was OK as a kid. I was lonely, though. My parents built their house in a new development so there weren't many kids around for several years. You grow up fast as only child. Now, I guess my concern is that my parents are getting older and I am the only one to make decisions on their behalf.

And when they pass away, that's it, my family line is gone." Wow, way to crush a light hearted game of 20 questions, Madi.

"I guess I never really thought of it that way. It must be hard."

"It's OK, really. I don't know anything different so it is what it is." I smile and shrug my shoulders. "What's your favorite color?"

"Dark blue. You?"

"Green," I answer.

"Like your eyes," he says, playing with his napkin. Oh my God, I think I just started to blush. Did he really notice the color of my eyes? Well, he is sitting 2 feet across from me so it wasn't a stellar observation, but still… he noticed. Through my blushing, I manage to ask the biggest question I have had on my mind.

"Sooo. How old are you, Declan?"

"Well, I don't know my exact age as far as weeks, months as days goes, but I'm 29, almost 30."

I cough/choke on the sip of tea I just took. Great, I'm a dirty old spinster having breakfast with a toddler.

"I know it's in poor taste to ask a woman her age, but you asked first, so same question."

I can't tell him I'm 40! He's likely to leave my old ass here. "Well I am, ummmm… It's, ummm… OK, in February I turned…"

"Here you go, dolls, breakfast is served," Mary says as she places two of the biggest plates I have ever seen full of pancakes down in front of us. Thank you baby Jesus and the creepy apple dolls on the wall for bringing Mary to the table with our food. "Umm, are you serious?" I exclaim, looking at the plate in front of me. It is piled 5 high with pancakes the size of hubcaps.

Declan laughs. "I tried to order you the short stack but you didn't want me to monitor your carb intake, remember?"

I just want to slap that smug look off of his hot 29 year old face. "Yes, but had I known that these 5 pancakes could end world hunger I would have had Mary box and ship them to Darfur. What was the short stack? Enough to feed Denver?"

"No, honey, there are 2 in the short stack. You shoulda listened to him, he's a regular," Mary advises as she leaves with my tea cup to refill it.

"Is this why you're so tall? Eating pancakes the size of a Mack truck tire?"

"Yes ma'am," he smiles. "Maybe you should eat a few, might help you break 5 feet," he says as he cuts into the huge stack of pancakes. He is sooooo pleased with himself, he can't help but chuckle.

"Listen here, Jolly Green Giant. I will have you know that I am 5'4", thank you very much," I reply, cutting into my pancakes and shoving a very un-ladylike bite into my mouth.

"They're good, aren't they?" he says with a half grin.

"They're OK," I manage after I swallow the mouthful of deliciousness.

"Don't lie, I heard you moan," he laughs.

"I did not moan!" I reply with my best appalled look.

"You did. You moaned. It was pretty stellar," he says as I start to blush again.

"Alright, where were we? Oh yeah. How old are you, Madi?" he asks before taking a big bite of pancakes. I can't answer him when he has a mouthful of food. He could choke and drop dead right here. I can't be responsible for his demise. OH SHIT! Here goes… "I'm fff.."

"How is everything? Food taste alright?" Mary comes out of nowhere like a heaven sent ninja, setting my freshly filled tea cup down. Saved again by the blessed Mary! I think I love her. I may need to start praying to the Virgin Mary in her honor because clearly she has got my back. Mary for the block!

"Thank you, Mary," I say with a huge smile.

"Why do I feel like you are avoiding the question, Madi?" Declan asks with a puzzled expression that doesn't seem to slow down his pancake consumption.

"Why do you say that?" Insert innocent eyelash batting here.

"Oh come on, it can't be that bad. What are you, like 32?"

"Oooooh, so close," I reply, taking another bite of delicious, heavenly, melt in your mouth pancakes.

"Awww, come on. Higher or lower?" he deadpans.

I have a mouth full of food, so I use my thumb to point up. Way, way up.

"33?" he says, taking a drink of coffee. I shake my head and keep motioning up.

"34? 35?" My thumb is still pointed skyward.

"36? 37? 38?" I can't help but notice his facial expression is changing.

You remember that show The Price Is Right? As he is increasing the age higher and higher, I suddenly hear that little yodeling mountain climber as he struts his way up the Alps towards the highest price. Keep in mind you want him to get to the number without him falling off the cliff, or worse, leave you in this cafe.

"39?" he guesses, with a high influx in his voice. Still

chewing that same bite in an attempt to not have to speak, I shake my head one final time as he hits the magic number.

"40?" he says, puzzled, leaning back in his chair.

I simply nod my head and put my hand down.

"THE FUCK?" Declan says with a smile.

Pancake comes flying out of my mouth, landing on his face and chest. Immediately my hands fly to cover my mouth as my fork clanks loudly on my plate. I can only imagine the look on my face. My eyes must be the size of these pancakes. "OH MY GOD. I AM SOOO SORRY!" I squeal, scrambling with my napkin to wipe off my pancake and spit.

Declan doesn't say a word, sitting across from me as he laughs. What could he be laughing at? Maybe the fact that I am 40 and he has been dining with a soon to be AARP member? Maybe that I just spit masticated pancake all over him but managed to keep what he assumes are false teeth in?

"I'm so sorry, oh my God, I am SO sorry," I beg, standing over him as I keep wiping his chest. I feel my eyes fill with tears of horror. Sensing my unease, Declan smiles, takes my hand from his chest and gently cups it in his.

"It's OK, Madi," he says with a sincere tone and panty melting smile. Using his leverage with our hands he guides me back into my chair. Embarrassed, I put my elbows on the table, hiding my face in my hands. I can feel a tear getting ready to make its escape from my eye and come crashing down.

"Hey, what's wrong?" I hear him softly say as I feel his hands wrap gently around my wrists, pulling them away from my face. "Are you OK?"

I shake my head, looking away. I turn my chin to face him, just as the tears start to roll down my cheek. Gently running his thumb along my cheek, he wipes a tear away, looking into my watery eyes. "Madi, it's really OK," he says, nodding his head.

"I'm sorry, Declan. Do you want to go?" I ask as I start to scoot my chair back.

"Why would I want to go? I'm havin' a great time, pancake facial included," he says with a crooked smile and wink.

"I don't know, I just… I feel bad, and I spit all over you." I look away again.

"Why do you feel bad, Madi? Because you're 40?"

"Shhhhh, keep it down," I whisper, looking around.

He laughs. "Why do you think it would bother me that you're 40? Is there some Arizona law that doesn't allow people of different ages to enjoy a motorcycle ride and breakfast together? Because if that's the case, I have broken that law before," he says with a grin.

"No, there is no law, smartass. It's just that you thought I was 32, and I haven't been 32 for a long time."

"Eight years to be exact," he pipes up. "Is it a big deal that a 29, ALMOST 30, year old guy enjoys talking to and having breakfast with a 40 year old woman?" he whispers.

"No, you jackwagon!" I finally let out a slight laugh. "It was when your facial expression changed when you hit 38 and that STILL wasn't the right answer."

"My facial expression changed, Madi, because I would have never in a million years guessed you were 40. I knew you were older than me just by some of the comments Taylor has made, but I didn't know you were 40. Honest," he says, putting his hand up like a good little Boy Scout. Oh God, he could still be a Boy Scout!

"I will admit I was surprised when you said you were 40.

You really don't look it and you certainly don't act it."

"Hey!" I throw my napkin at him as he laughs.

"Everything OK here, dolls?" Mary asks, coming out of nowhere again.

"We're good, Mary, thanks," Declan says to her and she starts to walk away. "Oh hey, Miss Mary, can we get some more napkins?" he smiles.

"You're a jerk," I try and say with a serious face, but just can't quite swing it and end up smiling.

"So are you OK now? Or do you really want to go?" he questions as he takes another sip of his coffee.

"I'm OK. We don't have to leave unless you want to," I reply with a shoulder shrug.

He takes my hand from across the table. "I'd like to stay and finish breakfast if that's OK with you, Mrs. Robinson."

"OH MY GOD!" I exclaim, trying to tug my hands free.

He squeezes my hands tighter in his. "That's better. I like when you laugh," he says with a shy grin. Wow, this guy is good.

"Alright, so shall we continue with our version of 20 questions?" he asks.

"OK, but you ask first this time."

"What are your deepest, darkest fears? What keeps you up at night?" he questions, releasing my hands from his firm grip.

"Oh, you mean besides having to admit that I'm 40? That would be vans or clowns or clowns driving vans," I say with a full body shiver, cutting into my pancakes again.

"Hahahahaha. No, not what creeps you out and makes you scream like a little girl, but an actual fear."

After several moments of thought, the answer hits me. "Being alone. Growing old… or should I say OLDER, and being alone," I shrug. "I see a lot of patients come into the ER and they have no one. No one to stand beside their bed, hold their hand and calm their fears. No one to kiss them and tell them it will be OK."

"Madi, I don't think that will ever happen to you. I don't see loneliness in your future." I peek up to see him looking down at his pancakes, pushing them around with his fork. Swoon, how cute is he?

"What about you? What keeps you up at night?" I ask, looking back down at my tea cup.

"The fear of losing those I love," he answers quickly and matter of factly. I nod my head as I look up at Declan and note serious expression on his face.

"Are you OK?" I ask with a tilted head.

"I'm fine, it just reminds me of my Dad. He died when I was 13. It was hard watching my Momma go through that, ya know?"

"Oh Declan, I am so sorry." I had no idea he lost his father, and so young.

"Clark's my hero. He stepped up to the plate when my dad died and watched over my mom and me. I have always admired him for that. He was only 19 and ready to start his own life and make his own way in the world. Instead, he quit school at UCLA to come home and help us out. He transferred to the University of Alabama and went into Criminal Justice. He wanted to be close to home for us. It was all pretty hard on my momma."

Looking across the table into his blue eyes, I see they are so full of emotion and love when he talks about his family. "Can I ask what happened?" I softly question.

"Yeah, it's OK. He was killed in a car accident on his way

to work one morning. Driver ran a stop sign and hit him on his side of the car. He died at the hospital before we got there. We never got to say goodbye." I see tears welling up in his eyes. My heart breaks for him, and I reach across the table for his hand. He stops pushing the food around on his plate, putting his fork down. I take his hand in mine and squeeze.

"I'm so sorry, Declan. I can only imagine how hard that must have been on all of you."

"It was tough on my mom to suddenly be a single parent. We were a really close family, kind of like a Norman Rockwell painting," he says with a smirk. "I went through a pretty rebellious streak in my early teens. I think I was angry at the world for taking my dad from us. I gave my mom a lot of grief and gray hair," he laughs.

"Well, I think that was your job as an adolescent male, and you seem to have turned out OK so I think she did a pretty good job." I squeeze his hand again before letting go of my grip, but he doesn't; he keeps his grasp on mine.

"Thanks for listening. I don't really talk about it a lot so it was nice to have someone really listen. Thanks." He clasps my hand again before loosening his grip. "I think you were up with the next question," he adds.

"OK, in an effort to lighten the mood, what is your favorite food?"

"My momma's biscuits and gravy, they're the best. You?"

"Well, as of this very moment, these pancakes," I say, putting a forkful in my mouth.

Declan laughs. "Oh, that's right. Your favorite food is toast." He winks.

"What's your favorite song?" I ask as I keep eating.

"I have a lot of favorites, but right now I'd have to say 'I

Hold On' by Dierks Bentley," he replies. "Yours?"

"Ummm, like you should have to ask. 'Ice Ice Baby' for sure," I manage with a straight face. Choking on his most recent bite of pancake, he laughs.

"Cats or dogs?" I ask, taking another bite.

"Dogs. You?"

"Definitely dogs. Cats are too moody and want things on their terms. I already have me, why would I need a four legged version?"

Throwing his head back, he lets out a deep sultry laugh.

"Favorite sport?" I query, taking yet another bite.

"Football. I played for Bama on a scholarship. I was an offensive lineman for the Crimson Tide," he says proudly. "My dad went to U of A too, so I followed in his footsteps. Clark wanted to go to UCLA for whatever reason. We always said he was adopted," he chuckles.

I'm starting to get full from the 3 pounds of pancakes I have consumed, but you would never know it based on the amount of food left on the plate in front of me. I push the plate away, moving the tea cup in its place.

"How about you? Do you like sports?" he asks with some trepidation.

"Actually, I LOVE football. Growing up as an only child, I had to learn to adapt to both gender stereotypes. I can cook, I love to bake, I don't sew—I hot glue. I like to camp and fish. I don't hunt for anything other than a good bargain, and I enjoy and understand sports. I even played girls basketball for my elementary school in 6th grade," I beam proudly.

"Was that when you stopped growin'?" he laughs.

"No, you smug ass. I stopped growing in 9th grade, thank you very much!" I cross my arms in pretend indignation.

"Are you full?" he asks.

"I am. I bet if you just lay me on my side and give me a good push, I could roll my way back to my car."

He laughs. "Well, it's mostly hills, so you might get stuck. I would hate to have that on my conscience. You'll just have to ride back with me so I know you're safe," he grins.

Pressing the coffee cup to his beautiful lips, he pauses. "I think we are down to your final Jeopardy question, Madi. Shoot." He takes a drink.

"Why did you ask me to breakfast this morning?" I ask softly, looking down at my tea cup and biting the corner of my lip.

"I wanted to. I think you're funny, nice and… beautiful. I wanted to talk to you and get to know you a little better," he answers with a shoulder shrug.

Several moments pass, as does the silence between us. I peek up through my eyelashes to find him staring at me. I continue wringing my lip in my teeth.

"Is it bleeding yet?" He breaks the silence with a smile.

"Is what bleeding?"

"Your lip. You haven't stopped biting it since you asked your question."

I immediately stop. "Not yet, but it's close," I smile.

"So I have one more question for you, Madi."

"Technically I think 'Is it bleeding' was your final question," I note, running my fingertip around the edge of my tea cup.

"Well then, I am changing the rules of the game. I get another question. Can I see you again?" he asks softly, watching my finger circle the rim of the cup.

"Sure. I mean, I guess I could come back by on Monday

morning. Will you be there Monday?"

"No. I mean… yes, I'll be at the gym Monday but that wasn't what I was asking you." He grins, shaking his head "I don't mean at the gym. I want to see you again. Like this. No gym."

I can't help but stare into his baby blues as the Mothra sized butterflies start to swirl in my stomach. HOLY CRAP! HE JUST ASKED ME OUT ON A DATE! Moment of internal SQUEEL!

"I take it that's a yes?" he laughs.

"Why do you say that?" I ask innocently.

"Because your feet just started bouncing up and down under the table and you have a smile on your face that could rival the Joker," he says with a chuckle.

"Yes, Declan, I would love to see you again," I manage to squeak out with a giggle and apparently a larger than life smile.

"Good. I'd like that. Well, should we head out? I know you have got to be tired, you had a long night."

"Sure. Let me just use the ladies room. I'll be right back." I excuse myself from the table. On my way, I run into Mary and thank her for the amazing breakfast and apologize profusely for the mess I made spitting all over Declan.

"Oh, sugar, don't you worry your pretty little head about it. You let me worry about that. You just take care of that boy, you hear me?" she says, embracing me in a hug.

"Yes ma'am," I say with a smile and a head nod. I head into the restroom to wash up and well, you know.

As I head out into the dining room, I find Declan standing by the front door talking to Mary. I stop for a moment and watch them interact. It's really very sweet to see the two of them together. I can see why he likes it here. The cafe has such a homey feel and they really do care about each of their customers.

Declan leans over and embraces her in a sweet hug. She pats him on the back and kisses his cheek. When Declan stands up straight again, he notices me watching them and smiles.

I make my way over to them. "Mary, thank you again for the best pancakes I have ever had." She embraces me in another hug and says "It's my pleasure, hun. You remember to come back and see us, OK?"

"I will," I reply as I hug her back.

Walking towards the motorcycle, Declan looks down at me with a huge smile on his face.

"What? Why are you looking at me like that? Do I have a boog?" I ask sarcastically.

"No, you don't have a boog. OK, here's the deal. If I promise right here and now to tell you if you ever have a boog, no matter where we are, will you stop asking me that?" he asks with a smile.

"Deal." I put my hand out and we shake on it. "Thank you so much for breakfast, by the way. You didn't have to do that. I could have gotten it."

"I know you could have," he replies as we reach the motorcycle. Handing me the helmet, Declan smiles. "Do you want to hear some good news?" His face lights up.

"Absolutely!" I answer in an equally perky manner.

"When you excused yourself from the table, I checked my messages. I had a new voicemail. It was from my recruiter. He said I've been accepted into the Police Academy," he says proudly.

"Really? That's great. When do you start?"

"I report in 10 days. I am so excited, Madi. I have wanted to be a cop for as long as I can remember. I was telling Mary when you walked up. She called you my good luck charm." He smiles shyly. I softly smile back at him, putting the helmet on. Wrapping my arms tightly around his waist, he looks back over his shoulder and grins before cranking the engine. A tingling sensation rushes through me, but this time I don't know if it's from the motorcycle or Declan.

Chapter 9

AS WE ENJOY the last few miles of the ride back to the gym, I rest the side of my head against his back and increase my grip around his waist. Looking back, he smiles. I can't be sure, but it felt like he let out a huge sigh, as though he had been holding his breath.

Pulling back into the gym parking lot, he drives to my car. He turns off the engine and helps me climb down. Regaining my balance, I take off the helmet, handing it to him. "Thank you so much for a great morning, Declan. I really did have a wonderful time," I say, trying to fix my now unruly helmet head.

"Here, let me." He takes his hands and gently tucks the stray curls behind my ears again. Softly, the back of his hand caresses the side of my face. Our eyes lock on each other as he leans in closer, his face inches from mine. Slowly tilting my head upward, I lick my parted lips. As his lips are about to make contact with mine, he quietly whispers, "you have a boog."

"What?" I shriek in terror. Throwing his head, back he laughs. I reach up and smack him in the chest with my flat hands, pushing him back a few inches. I feverishly run my index finger back and forth across the bottom of my nose. I can't believe I thought he was going to kiss me. What a moron. As he continues to laugh, I stand patiently as he fishes my car key out of his pocket. I had forgotten he was holding it for me on the ride up.

Snatching it from his hand, I turn to unlock the door. Hearing the double beep indicating it's unlocked, I turn back around to say goodbye. Suddenly, he grabs the sides of my face with his large hands, pulling me towards him. His warm, soft lips gently touch mine as he kisses me with such tenderness it almost makes my knees buckle. The soft kiss continues for just a few seconds. Slowly, he pulls his lips away, then returns for just one more little kiss. My lips, immediately saddened by the loss of his, tremble.

"Thank you for an amazing morning, Madi," he says, kissing my cheek. "Can I call you later?"

"Mmmmm hmmmmmm," was all I could manage.

Reaching around, he opens the door to my car. Once I have settled inside he closes it and steps back. As I pull away, I look in the rear view mirror. He is still standing there, slowly running the pad of his thumb across his bottom lip with a smile.

Before I know it, I am home and pulling into my garage. I sit in my car for moment, thinking about everything that happened this morning, and smile.

Once inside I check my cell phone for any missed calls. As I swipe to open the screen I see that I have 4 new voicemail messages, 6 missed calls and 9 text messages. What the hell? I look through the text messages first.

1) **Taylor:** *I saw you get on his bike. Don't do anything I wouldn't do. lol*

2) **Savannah:** *Taylor said you left with Delcan. WTF!!! You better call me*

3) **Grace:** *You got on the back of a motorcycle with him!!!! DUDE! High 5! Call me*

4) **Savannah:** *I want details. You better call me ASAP!*

5) **Grace:** *Why haven't you called? What are you two doing?*

6) **Savannah**: *GET IT GIRL! You better be having sex if you aren't answering us*

7) **Taylor:** *He has a job to do you know. Unless you're the one doing the job!*

8) **Grace:** *Hey, Call me please. 911*

9) **Savannah:** *Madi, call Grace 911!!*

The last 2 messages came in about 15 minutes ago. I quickly check the missed call log.

Mom & Dad
Grace

Savannah

Grace

Savannah

Grace

I check my messages quickly. I'm sure they only want me to call them 911 so they can hear the gory details of me leaving on the back of a bike with Declan.

Message 1: **Mom**. *Hey Honey, it's me. Just checking in. Give me a call when you have a minute. I love you. Bye*

Message 2: Grace. *You had better be climbing that boy like a tree! Call me, I want to hear EVERYTHING.*

Message 3: **Savannah**. *Call me the second you get this message. I want details. Did you touch it? Is it big? GET'CHA GET'CHA SOME!!*

Message 4: **Grace**. *Hey, can you please call me, I need to talk to you.*

OK, that didn't sound like an "I want details" kind of message. I quickly hit recall on the last incoming call. Grace picks up quickly.

"Madi, hey. Are you OK?"

"Yes, I'm fine. What's going on?"

"Everything is fine; I just need to talk to you about something. Do you have a minute?"

"Yeah, what's up?"

"So, you know Dr. Criswell wanted to talk to me earlier

today, right? Well, he wants to make me ER Medical Director and he wants me to appoint a charge nurse. I told him I thought you would be perfect for the job, Madi, but I wanted to talk to you first."

"Wow, I really don't know what to say. I am extremely flattered and honored that you would even think of me for that. Can I take a few days to think about it?"

"Absolutely, that's why I wanted to talk to you right away. I didn't want anyone from the unit saying anything to you before I could."

"What about Savannah? Did you consider her?"

"I did. When I called and told her about what Criswell said and how he wanted me to appoint a charge nurse, she said you would be perfect. We both know you're up to the challenge, Madi."

"Well again, I am so flattered and honored. But I do need to take some time to think about it, if that's OK. That's a lot of responsibility to take on."

"It is. Just think about it, and honestly think about it. I think you'd be perfect."

"I will, I promise."

"OK. Now that the bullshit is out of the way, I want to know exactly what the hell happened today. I got a text from Taylor saying that you just climbed on the back of Declan's motorcycle and you guys took off together. SPILL IT!"

"Let me get Savannah on the other line. I don't want to have to explain more than once."

Within minutes, I have both Savannah and Grace on a 3 way call. Hello party line circa 1988. I give them the basic details of what happened—he asked me if I was hungry, we went to eat, talked and he brought me back. Period. They don't need the gory details… not yet, anyway. After hearing them giggle and laugh like school girls, we hang up.

I run a hot shower and clean up before laying down for a bit. I hadn't realized how tired I was until the hot water hit me. Several hours later, the incessant ping of my phone with incoming text messages wakes me. Claire will be home in a little while so I need to get up and around. I throw on a sundress and pull my hair up. Heading downstairs, I can still hear my phone. Jesus, someone had better be dead if they are blowing up my phone like this.

Picking it up, I see I have 10 new text messages. "HOLY SHIT!" I exclaim. I start at the beginning.

Savannah: *–YOU LYING BITCH–*

My stomach immediately drops. Why is she mad at me?

Grace: *Oh My God!*

Savannah: *OMG*

Grace: *OMG, I am so proud of you!!!!!!*

Savannah: *How could you not tell me??*

Tell her what?

Grace: *You're my hero!!*

Savannah: *I'm coming over!*

Grace: *I am on my way over*

What is going one with them? Then I get to the last message.

Taylor: *SMILE for the camera!*

Attached to the text is a picture of Declan kissing me in the parking lot of the gym.

"OH MY GOD! THAT BITCH!" I yell to no one in particular because I am home alone. Within seconds, the thunderous sound of feet running up my front porch echoes. The doorknob is now shaking and turning while they bang and ring the doorbell over and over again.

"Open up! We know you're home!" I hear Grace exclaim.

"Unless he is still in there. Then we'll wait for you to finish!" Savannah shouts and laughs. BANG BANG BANG!! They pound again. "We know you're in there, we can see you! Your door has a huge window in it, dumbass!" Grace says.

Oh, for fuck's sake. If I don't open the door soon they are either going to knock it down or embarrass the hell out of me with my neighbors. I slowly pull myself up off the couch and yell, "STOP IT! I'm coming!"

"That's what he said!" Savannah shouts, much to her own delight.

As I open the door, they both push their way in and embrace me in a group hug that I am not prepared for. "Ugh, get off me, you hags. What is your problem?"

"I cannot BELIEVE that you didn't tell us that he kissed you! How could you? I'm wounded," Grace pouts.

"Yeah, we asked you for details of your rendezvous and

you leave out the best part? Bitch!" Vannah exclaims with mock horror.

"OK, OK. Yes, we kissed. It was no big deal. I can't believe she sent you guys that picture!"

"THERE IS A PICTURE?" they shout in unison.

"Oh, Jesus." I hang my head. I should just learn to shut up. Bouncing on the chair, Savannah starts chanting, "Whip it out! Whip it out!"

"No. OK, NO! I am not showing you the picture."

"Fine. I'll just text Taylor right now and she'll forward it to me. So there, humph!" says the always dignified Dr. Kelly.

"You go right ahead." I just called their bluff. Yea me!

Savannah gets up and walks around the couch, I assume to get something to drink from the kitchen. They are no longer guests in my home. If you want it, you better get it yourself—I'm a nurse, not a waitress. As she rounds the sofa, she leans down and snatches the phone from my hands and holds it up over my head.

"HA HA! I got it! Grace, GO!" she shouts as they both take off for the downstairs bathroom. I attempt to run after them but I can't quite hurdle the sofa like Savannah. They managed to make it there and lock the door.

"I HATE YOU BOTH!" I shout at the locked door.

"We love you too!" Grace replies. Within seconds, I hear the delighted squeals of my FORMER friends. Heavy emphasis on the word former. They seem to be taking a bit too long just looking at a picture. What are they doing in there?

"What are you doing? Why are you quiet?" I hear them snickering.

"Oh my God, Madi, you toast porned the guy!" Savannah exclaims.

"GET OUT OF MY MESSAGES!" I scream as I bang on the door.

"Hydration talk, my ass! Madi got a little food dirty with gym hottie."

"I did not. We were being playful," I huff out in a pathetic manner.

"Mmmmmm hmmmmm, with your hot buttered toast and dripping jelly. That shit's gross. You need to see a doctor if your toast is dripping," Savannah says with a laugh.

Just then I hear a knock at the door. It's Elise with Claire.

"Get out here and give me my phone," I yell as I bang on the door one more time.

"Go get the door, Eunice. We'll handle the phone," Grace says.

As I open the front door, I see Elise standing there with a zonked out Claire. "Oh no," I say as she transfers her to my arms. "I take it they had fun at the water park today?"

"A better time could not have been had. They didn't get much sleep last night. They were camping in Phaedra's forts, which kept falling down on them so they were up all night giggling. Plus, the sun and fun at the water park? I think it was all a bit too much for her," Elise smiles.

"Thank you so much for bringing her home, I appreciate it."

"No problem. I'd put her straight to bed. Phaedra is passed out in the back seat and Eamon is sunburned," she replies.

"Thanks again, E. Coffee next week?" I ask before closing the door.

"Yep, call me!" She blows a kiss over her shoulder. Carrying Claire up the stairs to her room, I look down at her little, limp, exhausted body draped over me. As I place her on her bed I pull the comforter over her, kiss her cheek and whisper that I love her. She smiles and throws her arm around my neck.

God, I love this kid.

Running back downstairs I make a beeline for the bathroom. "Alright. You both listen here. Come out right now and give me my phone."

"Fine. Geeez, just trying to have a little fun," Grace says like a scolded child.

"Yeah, ya big meanie," Savannah adds to the comment.

As they leave the bathroom, they look at each other with a strange grin and quickly head towards the front door. "Yeah, we should go. We heard that Claire's home, so you should go spend time with her. We'll just get out of your way," Grace says, setting my phone down on the sofa table.

"Yep. Hasta la vista, baby," Savannah adds as she opens the door.

"Yeah, well, thanks for coming over… NOT!" Ok, that wasn't my most mature comment.

Why did they leave in such a hurry? Did they do something in my bathroom? I decide to check the room for damage. Savannah locked herself in there once when she was drunk and managed to pull my towel rod down. I wouldn't put it past them to have done some type of property damage. Hooligans.

As I walk out of the perfectly fine bathroom, I'm confused. Why did they suddenly bolt? I thought for sure they would prod me for more details.

I guess I should consider it a blessing.

Just then, I hear my cell phone beep. Picking it up, I see it's a message from Declan. Immediately,

I have a huge smile on my face just at the thought of what he may have to say.

–WOW, is that so? Lol–

Huh? Is what so?

–I never knew U climbed trees. LMAO–

What is he talking abou…

"NOOOOOOOOOOO!" I shriek.

Thumbing back through my text feed I see it, there it is in green and white.

Me to Declan

–The next time I see you I am going to climb you like a tree!! True story!!–

I immediately reply

–OMG! Declan, that was Savannah and Grace. I swear!–

–LOL, relax, I it's funny.–

–I am finding it less than humorous.–

As I hit send, the phone starts ringing in my hand. It's Declan, calling me.

Oh God, what do I do? What do I do? Do I answer it or send it to voicemail?

I can't talk to him. I am humiliated at the hands of my FORMER friend and boss.

I don't answer and let it go to voicemail. A few moments later he sends me another text.

–Really? U aren't going 2 answer? U said I could call u. :(–

*–No hablo English, senor.–*I'm cracking myself up when I hit send.

–OK, here's the deal. Calling again in 2 min U better answer. No hablo excuses.–

And right on cue, the phone starts to ring again. This time I take a deep breath and answer.

"Hello?"

"Madi?"

"No. I'm sorry, sir, she died of embarrassment a few minutes ago. In lieu of flowers, please donate to the National Arbor Day Foundation. She loved trees."

"Hahahahahahahahahahaha! Oh my God. Madi, 'I have no idea what your middle name is' Kennedy, you are too much."

"Declan, 'insert middle name here' Hillier, I am mortified. You have to know that I did not send you that text message. That was the work of the 2 morons you met in the ER this morning. You remember my former friends, Savannah and Grace?"

"No worries, Madi, I had a feeling it wasn't you. I mean, I could be wrong but it just didn't seem like something you would say. But it sure as shit was funny."

"I guess that depends on your perspective. First Twinkies are discontinued and now this?" I say, choking back mock tears.

"Yeah, that sucks. Twinkies were pretty good."

Walking over to the couch, I sit and curl into the pillows. "Pretty good, Declan? I don't understand what you just said to me. Pretty good? Twinkies are better than sex."

At the realization of what I just said, my hand flies up to cover my mouth. Apparently I feel this will take the words back. I hear a very loud laugh coming from the other end of the phone.

"Well, Madi, all I can say to that is… if Twinkies are better than sex, you're doing it all wrong," he says still laughing.

"So, how about that blue sky?" I say in a feeble attempt at changing the subject.

"Yep, still blue," he answers.

"Did they ever figure that shit out?"

"No, no, I think it's still a mystery."

"Great. Now I am craving a Twinkie." Deep sigh.

"That does sound pretty good. Too bad they are nowhere to be found."

"Can you hear that, Declan? Can you hear my heart breaking as you say those words to me?"

He continues to laugh. "So, Madi, ummm, are you busy Sunday night? I was wondering if you wanted to have dinner with me?"

The sound of silence fills the air.

Say something Madi! ANSWER HIM I scream inside my head.

"Madi?" he says softly.

"I'm here. Yes, Sunday would be nice."

"Are you OK? You got awfully quiet there. If you don't want to go, we don't have too. It's really OK," he says, sounding panicked.

"No. No, I do, I would love to go. I was just surprised, that's all."

"Why were you surprised? I told you earlier today I wanted to see you again. Sunday is again." I can hear his smile.

"This is true. I guess I just didn't think you would want to see me again so soon, that's all."

"I see. Well, I would love to take you to dinner Sunday, Madi Kennedy."

"It's Delaney."

"Your name is Delaney?" he asks, confused.

"Hahaha. No, my middle name. You didn't know it when you tried to middle name me earlier. My full name is Madigan Delaney Kennedy. Well, actually it's Madigan Delaney Banks Kennedy."

"Jesus, you sound like a law firm."

"How about you? Any hidden legal firms in your name?"

"Declan Henry Hillier, not too legal-ish sounding. Henry was my dad's name. Is Kennedy your married name then?"

"It is. Did Taylor tell you I was married before?"

"She did. I hope that's OK."

"It's fine. Too late now, but its fine," I say with a laugh. "It's not a secret and I'm not ashamed of it."

"Can I ask why you kept his name?"

"It was just easier. All of my nursing licenses are under Kennedy, so professionally everyone knows me as Kennedy. To go back to Banks would be like starting over. That, and it's a huge pain in the ass to change everything with the state and national nursing boards."

"I can understand that. How long were you married?"

"Four years total. Happily for two," I say, laughing.

"Can I ask what happened? It's none of my business. You don't have to tell me, I was just curious."

"No, it's fine. I don't mind. Andy had an affair with a transporter at the hospital. I turned the other cheek for a while, but one day I opened my eyes and kicked him out. I deserved better than that."

"You do."

"I do what?" I ask confused

"You DO deserve better than that, Madi."

"Thanks. I wouldn't change anything, though. I learned a lot from my relationship with Andy. I learned what I deserve and what I don't, and what I will and won't accept in a future relationship. And I learned a lot about myself, too."

"I bet you did. Well, for what it's worth, I think Andy is an idiot for doing that to you."

"Thanks," I say, smiling. "What about you? Any deep dark secrets you want to confess?"

"Just one."

His long pause is starting to concern me. Is he going to tell me he is a woman? Gay? What? Why the sudden moment of silence before he confesses something to me?

"I hate pudding," he says with the utmost seriousness.

"I feel as though our friendship may need to be reevaluated, Declan. How can you not like pudding? That's like saying you hate puppies. Or Santa."

"I don't know, I just never liked it. Even as a kid."

"Well, clearly you grew up in an unfit household run by people who didn't know how to make good pudding."

I can hear him smile through the phone. "Clearly, that is the case. Were you able to get some rest this afternoon? I know I kept you out a bit late this morning with the long ride to breakfast and all. Sorry about that."

"Why on earth are you apologizing? I had a great time."

"I did too. So what would you like to do Sunday night? Any place in particular you would like to go for dinner?" he asks.

"No. You picked a pretty good place this morning so I think I will leave it up to you again."

"Alright, then I know the perfect place."

"Care to fill me in?"

"Naaahhhh."

"Aww, come on. How will I know how to dress if you don't tell me?"

"Anything will be fine, just nothing too fancy."

"Well, I guess I'll cancel my plans to take my jewels and tiara out of the safe deposit box tomorrow then."

"Tiara is optional," he replies sarcastically.

"Did you want to meet someplace? Or I can pick you up and we can go in my car? Or you can pick me up on the motorcycle again? I'll just wear covered shoes. And I'm just rambling now, so if you could say something that would be great, or feel free to stop me at any time."

"Hahaha. How about I pick you up at your house, in my truck?"

"Oh, I didn't know you had a truck. I assumed you always rode the motorcycle."

"No, just every now and then."

"OK, well, that sounds great. What time?"

"How about 6:00?"

"I will be ready at 6:00 on Sunday night."

"Great. Let me grab a pen and I'll write down your address. OK, I'm ready."

"155 North Flower Ridge Lane."

"Alright. Well, I am going to let you go, because I heard that yawn you tried to mask a minute ago."

"Sorry. I tried to hide it, but apparently not well."

"No, not at all. But I have some things to take care of anyway." He pauses. "I'm glad we got to talk tonight." I can almost hear him blush.

"Me too." I smile even though I know he can't see me.

"You have a good night, Madi, and I will see you Sunday at 6."

"Goodnight, Declan."

I sit for a minute and reflect on my first phone conversation with Declan. He's so easy to talk to.

I like that about him. I run upstairs to check on Claire, and in true Claire style she is sprawled from one end of her bed to the other. That kid is a major bed hog. I turn off her nightlight and cover her back up, kiss her cheek and whisper "sweetet dreams, my Éclair," in her ear. I head off towards my room and quickly fire off a quick text to Grace and Savannah.

You. Are. Dead. To. Me.

I silence my phone and climb into bed. It's only 8:00 but I am exhausted from the last 3 days of work and my extended breakfast this morning with Declan. I had forgotten how tiring flirting is. Setting my phone on the night stand, I see the screen light up. Ordinarily I wouldn't look at it, but I was curious.

Goodnight, Madi

Goodnight, Declan ☺

Chapter 10

I AM AWAKENED in the morning by a messy haired little blonde with green eyes and morning breath.

"Good morning, Mommy," she says, putting the tip of her nose to mine and staring at me.

"Good morning, sweetheart," I reply as I kiss the tip of her nose. "Did you sleep good?"

"Yes. I. Did!" she says, so matter of fact.

"I would assume so. You were conked out when Elise brought you home last night. I had to put you straight to bed."

"I was tired, we had SO much fun at the water park," she squeals, taking off on a 20 minute dissertation on the joys of the lazy river and the kiddie wave pool. I love watching her animated face when she tells me stories.

"I am so glad you had such a good time with Phaedra the past few days, but I sure did miss you. What should we do today?" I ask her, rolling over onto my side to look at her as she lies on the pillow next to me.

"Ummm, I think we should go get something to eat from Starbuuuucks," she draws it out for effect, "and then maybe go to the mall and walk around, and maybe if we have time I could play in the playground."

"Wow, that would work out pretty well for you, wouldn't it? We just so happen to be at the mall, and if we have time for you to play, so be it? Is this what I am to understand?" I say with a smile.

"Well, or we could do something else," she grins

"No, that sounds fine, sweetheart, whatever you want to do. We are going to have a mommy—daughter day. Your choice."

"YEA!" she shouts as she starts to jump up and down on my bed.

"OK, kiddo. Go get dressed and make your bed, and we will stop by Starbucks on the way to the mall."

"Can I maybe get a doughnut at Starbucks?" she asks with an innocent face.

"Yes, you can get a doughnut. Now go get ready."

She hops off my bed and takes off for her room. I hear her distinct 'woo hoo' as she resumes jumping on her bed. Thirty minutes later, I come downstairs to find Claire sitting on the couch playing with her hand held game system. She is dressed and ready to go.

"Can we go, Mommy? I'm hungry."

"Yes, we can. Go let the dogs in and I will meet you by the back door."

WE MAKE A quick stop at our favorite Starbucks and run inside quickly. Thank God there is no sign of that snatch Tiffani with an i.

"Hi, kids. Chocolate milk with ice and only one pump of chocolate." I hear a very clear sigh come from Claire behind me. "And a grande nonfat light ice chai latte and an old fashioned doughnut," I say to the guy behind the counter. I don't recognize him, he must be new.

As I head over toward the pick-up counter, I see Tiffani with an i come out of the back room. She gives me a delightfully pleasant look and rolls her eyes. Just then, Claire comes behind me and asks me where her doughnut is. Handing her the bag and drink, she smiles up at me.

"Thank you, Mommy."

Lucky for me Tiffani with an i wasn't making the drinks today. She may have poisoned me out of spite.

After making our way in and out of several stores in an attempt to find something to wear on Sunday night, I come up empty handed. I guess when you don't have your girls with you it's hard to get an honest opinion on how things look.

The sales clerks are so eager for a sale they will tell you anything, including but not limited to insisting that you look SO GOOD in the gray cotton dress with the shoulder pads that made all 5'4" of me look like a linebacker for the Green Bay Packers.

I did find a cute pair of ballet flats, but I just wasn't sold on anything else this trip.

We stop at the playground for Claire to burn off some of her energy. Bless her heart, she was very patient with me today trying things on. While I am watching her play I get a text message from Andy.

Hey, do you think I can pick up Claire today? I miss her.

Sorry, we have plans today. How about next weekend?

Can I take her to lunch tomorrow?

Sure, what time?

Pick her up at 11, bring her back to you around 3?

That works, but don't be late, I have plans.

Andy is notorious for being late with both pick up and drop off. Actually, a more accurate statement would be he is usually late picking her up and early bringing her back.

OK, see you tomorrow @ 11.

"Claire!" I have to shout more than a few times to get her attention. "We should go, honey, we still need to swing by the store and get stuff for dinner." This is where she tries to solicit ten minutes every time I give her the 2 minute warning. It usually ends in an unhappy pouting child.

After our quick detour to the grocery store for a few girl's night essentials, we arrive back at home and whip up a little homemade pizza for dinner.

Claire and I snuggle up together on the couch, eat our pizza and watch a movie.

I realize I completely forgot to find a sitter for Claire tomorrow night. I send a text to Savannah, who I incidentally haven't heard from since my angry text to her yesterday.

–Hey, can you watch Claire tomorrow night for a few hours? You owe me!–

–OK, that's fine but you have to tell me why first.–

–Declan wants to go to dinner. Shut up.–

–OMG OMG OMG of course. What time?–

–He's picking me up at 6.–

–OMG I just peed myself a little. I'm so excited for you. Bring her by at 4–

–4 is a bit early–

–NO! You need time to get ready. OMG you are totally getting laid–

–Jesus, Vannah, it's dinner. He didn't invite me to an orgy.–

–You never know. Could happen.–

–I'm going to go get a mani pedi around noon, you in?–

–Like you have to ask. See you there.–

Claire and I fall asleep on the couch curled up together. We watched 2 movies and had popcorn and sundaes and almost made ourselves sick, but it was great. Looking down at my baby girl, I smile in amazement. We have had our ups and downs over the past few years, but Claire is the best thing that has ever happened to me.

I carry her up to my bedroom and lay her down on the other side of the bed. Climbing in next to her, she cuddles right back up to me. I am going to cherish these moments. I know that in a few years she is going to hate me and pretend I don't exist. Ah, the teen years, can't wait.

Claire and I snuggle all night long. Even though I don't sleep well when she sleeps in my bed, I still enjoy it every now and then.

WAKING UP THE next morning, I make our favorite breakfast of lemon waffles. Apparently I didn't OD on enough carbs yesterday so I should add a bit more to my diet today. Mmmmmm, they are delicious.

We spend the day lounging around the house, and by lounging I mean me schlepping 8 loads of laundry up and down 2 flights of stairs, vacuuming, dusting, and generalized housework, while Claire plays in her room. I did manage to carve out some time to obsessively rip through every article of clothing I own trying to find something to wear tonight for my dinner with Declan.

Dinner with Declan. Holy hell, I am having dinner with Declan. I still haven't decided if this is a date or him just being nice to me and wanting to make a new older friend.

Maybe he wants me to buy him and his buddies beer. Yeah, I bet that's it. He probably needs me to buy him a keg or rent him a car. I hear those can be tough to do when you're a young pup.

A little while later Andy arrives to pick up Claire. She's always excited to see her dad.

I cannot say the same.

"Hey, there's my big girl. Ready to go to lunch and maybe a movie?"

"YEAH!" she cries, jumping down from the last 2 steps. "Daddy, can we go to the mall and play in the playground? I never get to play there, Daddy," she asks him with so much sugar she could kill a diabetic at 20 paces.

"Christ on a crutch, Claire, you played there yesterday, remember?"

"Oh yeah, I forgot. Why do you always say that? Did Jesus trip over that desk fan you were moaning on about? I don't remember learning about that in Bible School. They never said anything about a desk fan or crutches," she says with a serious face.

"What is she talking about, Madi?" Andy asks, confused.

I, however, am trying to hold in the hysterical laughter that is now choking me from within.

"I have NO clue. Kids… sheeeesh. OK, you two have fun. Bye bye now," I say quickly, ushering them out the door.

Did my daughter turn my erotic moaning about Declan into a biblical passage?

God, I love that kid!

I grab my keys and head out the door to meet Savannah for our mani pedi date.

I hear the distinct ping of an incoming text, this better not be Savannah cancelling on me because she's too busy having sex.

Its Declan

–Looking forward 2 tonight. C U @ 6–

–BINGO! Me too :)–

–LOL, C U 2night.–

As I walk into our favorite nail salon I see that Savannah is already there getting her hooves buffed and polished.

"HEY! OK, come sit. Sit! Sit! Sit!" she says, patting the recliner next to her. "So where are you going? What are you wearing? How many orgasms are you going to have before you let him leave? Did you wax? Did you…"

"Relax, Vannah. Geeez! Come up for a breath, would ya? I haven't decided yet. I'm thinking jeans and a cute shirt with sandals. Or a sundress. Oh, God, I don't know. He won't tell me where we are going so I have no idea if I am going to be too casual or too dressy. What do you think?" I ask her, almost begging.

"Well, what were you thinking about? What were your choices?"

"First I thought about that long flowing grey skirt I have with a fitted white t-shirt and my sandals, or then maybe my skinny jeans rolled to capri with that white button up and my turquoise heels, or maybe my boot cut jeans with the coral top and my nude platform wedges with that cute gold bracelet. Vannah, I don't know!" I'm now panicking.

"I have the perfect outfit! Your boot cut jeans with those nude platform heels, that white button up dress shirt and that turquoise chunky necklace and bracelet set. And you should totally wear your hair in a side loose bun with the curls, like you did for that formal Christmas party last year. It looked sooo hot."

"Are you sure that's not too casual? What if we go someplace really nice? What if this isn't really a date and we are just hanging out?"

"That outfit is perfect, trust me. It will be fine. Plus, guys love a girl in a white button up dress shirt," she says with a laugh and an eyebrow wiggle "And it's TOTALLY a date."

MY FINGERS AND toes are perfectly polished and ready for a night of nervously picking all the polish off.

I'm glad she talked me into the gel manicure, I hear it may hold up to my nervous habit of polish picking.

When I get back home, I decide to rest for a bit before it's time to start getting ready. And by rest I mean lay there and stare at the ceiling, thinking about how tonight may or may not go. I am so anxious about tonight, I feel like I'm going to puke at any second. Why am I so nervous? I have been on dates before. I never got like this when Steve and I would go out.

Could I really like this guy? Is there even anything to be nervous about? I need to keep things in perspective. He is just a guy I know from the gym and we are going to be sharing a meal together. Yep, he is just a guy from the gym and he's going to come to my house and pick me up so we can talk and perhaps enjoy some more carbs together. OK, I got this. What's the big deal? He is just a guy that I know from the gym who is taking me out for an evening meal, alone, and who has pressed his warm soft lips against mine. OH GOD OH GOD OH GOD! And now I am panicking again.

Before I know it, Claire is home from spending a few hours with Andy.

We sit and share a snack while she tells me all about the movie they saw and what they had for lunch.

"Mommy, why am I going to Savannah's tonight?"

"I have plans to meet someone for dinner, honey."

"Well why can't I come? I eat dinner."

"Hahaha. I know, sweets, but this is a grown up dinner."

"Oh, like a date?"

Whipping my head, around I look at Claire. "What do you mean, like a date? Where did you learn what a date was?"

"Daddy told me. He was telling Sindee that you should go out on more dates because you never get any. Never get any what, mom?"

"Dinners, honey. I never get any dinners," I reply sweetly as my blood begins to boil.

"Umm, we have dinner every night," she says, confused.

"He just means dinner with other grown-ups, honey. Grown up dinners. And, God willing, desserts."

"OK, I guess. You guys are weird," she says with an eye roll.

Claire and I head out to go to Savannahs, who is standing in her driveway waiting for us. After many kisses and hugs Savannah helps Claire out of the car.

"Go ahead on in honey, the boys are watching a movie," she says ushering Claire toward the door.

Once Claire is inside I start to back out of the driveway as Savannah starts to blurt out "Did you shave? Did you wax? Did you pluck and tweeze? Oh, and don't forget to stretch,

Madi. It's been a while since your ankles have been behind your ears. You don't want to pull a hammy!"

Chapter 11

QUICKLY BUFFING, SCUFFING, scrubbing and rubbing, I jump out of the shower and dry off. I begin the herculean task of putting on makeup. I don't wear a lot of it and he has only seen me in the gym or that one morning at work. I manage to wrangle my hair back into a low left side chignon of loose curls and a side swept bang.

It's time to put it all together. I put on my fitted boot cut jeans, white tailored button up, the nude patent leather platform peep toe heels (they are hot, I'm not gonna lie) and then the finishing touches. I go with simple silver stackable bracelets and matching hoop earrings and a pendant. I don't want to overdo it.

A spritz of perfume here and there and I am ready to go.

Within minutes the doorbell rings. I slowly make my way down the stairs toward the door. As I reach the landing I can see his face through the window pane on the door. He's smiling. I take one last deep breath as I reach for the doorknob and turn it. As the door swings open, I get the full view of Declan standing before me.

He is wearing jeans and a black button up dress shirt. Oh, sweet Jesus. He has his shirt untucked and the sleeves are rolled up. I bite my lower lip as I take in the sight of him. WOW!

"Madi, you look… amazing," he says as he steps inside.

"Thank you. You look pretty amazing yourself," I reply with a flirty grin.

"Here, these are for you," he says with a shy and almost embarrassed smile. As I look down toward his hands, my eyes go wide and my mouth falls open from the pure shock at the beautiful sight I see before me. He laughs at my reaction.

"Oh, Declan, they're BEAUTIFUL! Thank you so much. Come on in, let's go put them away."

As I take them from his hands we walk together toward the kitchen. I lean down and inhale around the edges of the box, smiling up at him with pure pleasure. He laughs as I put them on my counter and take a moment to admire my brand new box of … Twinkies.

"I take it you found the house OK?"

"Yep, no problems. I umm… no. No problem finding it." I look at him with a slanted brow.

"I, ummm, got here about 20 minutes ago. I've been sitting out front in my truck," he says with an embarrassed grin.

"Oh my God, why?" I start laughing.

"Well, I was afraid I might not find it and I didn't want to be late, so I left early, but I didn't realize you lived so close. It only took me 10 minutes to get here. I didn't want to come to the door too early. So I waited in the truck," he smiles.

"Why didn't you want to come to the door early? I've been

upstairs overworking my hair and changing my shoes 147 times. You might have saved me about 52 of those shoe changes if you'd have knocked on the door." Oh God, he smells so good.

Can I get you something to drink?"

"Oh no, I'm fine. Thank you."

Oh yes you are, I say to myself.

"Are you OK?" he asks, standing on the other side of the kitchen island from me.

"I'm fine, why?"

"Because you're shaking," he says with a slight grin.

"I'm just really… ummmmm, cold."

"Cold? It's 102 outside," he laughs.

"I'm nervous," I mumble.

"I'm sorry, what?"

"I'm a little nervous," I say, a tiny bit louder.

"I'm sorry, I can't seem to hear you," he says again with a grin.

"I'm. Nervous," I reply, looking down at the counter.

"I heard you the first time. I'm just messin with ya," he says with a smile and a wink.

"REEEEALLY?!" I look up at him through my faux angry eyes.

"Why are you nervous?"

"I don't know. It's just been a really long time since I've been on a daaa… I've gone to dinner on a Sunday night." Oh my God! What if this isn't a date and you just totally assumed? It's true what they say—if you assume you make an ass out of you and me, but mostly me.

"You're nervous because you don't go on 'daaa-inners often on a Sunday night?" he says, laughing.

"OK, I am totally gonna Band-Aid this bitch, Declan." I inhale and take a deep breath. "Is this a date or are we just pals going to dinner? Because I am totally cool with either. I just wanted to know."

There. Got it out fast and painful, just like a Band-Aid.

Walking around the island, Declan stops in front of me. He looks down and takes my now sweaty, clammy and shaking hands in his.

"Well, Madi, I was hoping it was a date."

"OK. me, too." I look up with a smile. "So, to clarify my earlier answer. I'm nervous because it's been a long time since I've been on a date."

"Now that we have cleared that up, should we go?" he asks.

"Sure, let me just grab my purse."

As we walk out of the kitchen towards the front door, he comments, "This is a nice house, Madi."

"Thanks," I smile.

Heading down the front walkway of my house I can see Declan's truck come into view. It's a beautiful Black Ford F-150 Super Crew 4x4. I let out a long whistle. "Nice truck."

"Thanks," he says with pride as he opens the door and helps me in. Being that he is 6'7", his truck has to be lifted up a tad higher than a standard truck. But it's not obscenely high like Savannah's and Luke's trucks. I need a ladder to climb into those.

On the way to dinner we are both pretty quiet, enjoying the drive and the music he has playing on the radio. 'After Tonight' by Justin Nozuka begins to play. I love this song and I'm pleasantly surprised to hear it playing in Declan's truck. I never picked him for a Coffee House music type of guy, but rather more of a Giddy Up, Yee Haw, Ride 'em Cowboy kind of guy.

Yep, I just totally stereotyped the hot guy from Alabama.

I have no idea where we are going but I trust him, and I feel oddly safe with him.

Maybe because in a little over a week he will begin training to be a police officer, or maybe it's just a feeling I have with him.

A little while later we pull into the Old Town part of the city. It's filled with quaint little houses built in the1930's and 40's. Most of them have been turned into antique shops, little B&B's or restaurants. We park the behemoth truck down the block and walk into the courtyard portion of the square. Several of the shops are open.

As we walk towards the restaurant, we stop and look in a few windows. Standing in front of a toy store window, Declan slowly reaches for my hand, trying to gauge my reaction. I don't react, I just allow it to happen. Once our hands are together I give them a soft squeeze.

I can see out of the corner of my eye that he looks down and smiles at me.

Arriving at the restaurant, I am shocked at how cute and romantic it is. The old cobblestone house has a patio covered in ivy, with white twinkle lights strung over all the trees and gates. I can smell the fresh lavender growing all around. The tables are small, covered in white linens, and each lit by a flickering candle. We are seated in a far corner. I hear very faint music being played from a jazz bar a few shops down.

The waiter comes and takes our drink orders, white wine for me and a beer for Declan. Truth be told I'd love an ale with an orange slice, but I don't want to burp in the middle of our sweet dinner.

"This place is amazing, Declan. How did you find it?"

"I come down here every now and then, and I happened to walk past it and thought that it would be a neat place to take a da… someone for dinner," he says with a smile.

Tilting my head, I give him 'The Look'. "OK, I admit it wasn't the smoothest transition out of an awkward moment, but I did pull it off."

"Nooo, no you really didn't," he winks.

"Well, I beg to differ. I think it was a flawless move and I could have totally gotten away with it if you didn't have ears." Laughing, we start to look at our menus. Lavender encrusted ahi tuna for me and beef medallions for him.

"So, tell me more about you, Madi. I know your favorite color, your favorite song and that you have a newly discovered pancake addiction. What else is there to know about you?" he asks as he takes a swig of his beer.

"Well, let's see. I am terribly afraid of reptiles of any kind. I will scream and flail like a flamingo on acid if one comes in my house or touches me. I snore. I have a bad habit of picking off my nail polish. I was a virgin until I was 26. I will travel to Rome, Italy and Ireland before I die. I failed Biology in high school which is ironic, given my profession. I love the smell of coffee but can't stand the taste of anything related to coffee. I hate mushrooms and ham, annnnnnnnd my feet hurt. So that's me in a nutshell."

"OK, there is one obvious admission in there that I am just shocked to hear and cannot believe is true. Madi, how on earth could you possibly hate ham?"

"I really don't know, Declan. I have never liked it," I reply, laughing.

"What did you eat at Christmas growing up?"

'Chicken nuggets. Don't JUDGE me!" I smile, taking a sip of wine.

"Wow. Well, you might feel differently if you had my momma's ham. It's life changing."

"Doubtful. I can't stand pig ass."

"Pig ass?"

"Yep. Better get used to it, people are gonna start calling you that in a few weeks," I say, playfully running my finger up and down the stem of my wine glass.

"Madi, you are too much," he says, laughing. He takes another drink of his beer, his eyes watching my fingers. I watch his muscular arm flex as he brings his beer bottle to his lips. The rolled up sleeve on his shirt and his silver watch catching the light… I need a moment. As his lips make contact with the rim of the bottle, I find myself holding my breath. He has great lips. I watch as they move.

"Are you OK with that?"

"Ummm, sure. Absolutely. I am all for it," I answer even though I didn't hear a word of what he said. I was distracted by his lips.

"I thought so," he says, laughing. "You didn't hear a word I said, did you?" He's looking right at me.

Lowering my head, I bite the corner of my finger nail. "No, I didn't."

"I didn't think so. I asked you if you were OK with the gecko that's crawlin' on the wall next to you."

OK, Madi, it's time to put your big girl panties on. Or at the very least, the big girl thong you chose to wear tonight.

Don't panic; don't jump up and run screaming from this lovely establishment. It will not only embarrass your dinner guest, but you will probably fall and break a heel and that's not an option because you love these shoes.

"Yes. Yes, I do know about the gecko that is a mere inches from my head. I am fine. I am the master of my bladder and will not pee myself and run away."

Declan bursts out laughing and waves his hand, causing the vermin to run off. Several moments go by and he finally breaks the silence. "It's gone. Are you OK?"

"I'm good," I say as I down my entire glass of wine.

"Yep, that's the sure sign of a woman who is fine. You can exhale now," he replies with a grin. "What were you so distracted by?"

"Nothing," I answer quickly.

"Uh huh, nothing it is, then." He nods. Just then, the food arrives. It looks and smells amazing. We continue our conversation and enjoy the delicious food.

"So, I filled you in on a little bit more about me. What else is there to know about you?"

"Well, I have no aversion to reptiles and even had a lizard as a pet when I was a kid. I too failed Biology in high school. I am pro ham. But I do maintain a strict anti-mushroom policy. I also snore… or so I've been told. I would love to travel the world someday. My favorite place to visit is Hawaii. I think I may have a mild coffee addiction. I am terrified of needles, and my favorite movie is Willy Wonka and the Chocolate Factory; original version, of course."

"I have to be honest, it was touch and go there for a second. You lost me at lizard as a pet but redeemed yourself at anti-mushroom and pro Hawaii." We finish up our amazing dinner with witty banter and fun facts about ourselves.

"That place was amazing, Declan. Thank you so much for a wonderful dinner."

"It has been my pleasure, Madi. Would you like to walk around and check out more of the shops?"

"Absolutely. I love it down here. I use to come down here with my parents when I was growing up but I hadn't been back in years. I never knew this restaurant existed." Taking my hand in his again, we wander in and out of the antique shops.

We make our way back to the toy store we saw on our walk to the restaurant and head inside. The store is filled with nothing but toys dating as far back as the 40's. I happen to come across a Cabbage Patch doll that looks exactly like one I got when I was 10—you know, in 1983. "Oh my gosh! I had one that looked just like this when I was about 10. Her name was Raquel Carlotta and she wanted to be a jockey," I say, laughing.

"COOL!" I hear him exclaim as he holds up a blue Power Ranger in its original packaging. "I had one just like this when I was a kid, until Clark ripped his arms off and threw him in the lake by our house," he pouts.

"Awwww," I say, laughing. "You poor thing."

"What happened to Rocket Carmichael or whatever its name was?" he smiles.

"It was Raquel Carlotta, and she got burned in an unfortunate hair dryer incident," I add with mock tears. We leave the store a while later, feeling very nostalgic and laughing our asses off at the trip down memory lane.

"Are you OK? Are you limping?"

"I'm OK. My shoes are just getting a little uncomfortable. But I am fine." I try to fake a smile.

"Here, hop on." He motions for me to hop on his back.

"The hell you will. You are not going to carry me back to the truck. I'm a big girl, I can manage."

"Madi, I am not going to have you hobble back to the truck. It's 2 blocks away. Besides, you have a training session coming up and I will not accept 'my feet hurt' as an excuse to get out of it."

"Declan, I am not going to hop on your back. I can take off my shoes and walk. I will be fine."

"Can't you get worms from walking barefoot?" he asks with a smile.

"Umm, no, that's from uncooked pork, genius. You weren't kidding about failing Biology," I laugh.

"Well, this will have to do then." He leans down, scoops me up in his arms and carries me down the street.

"DECLAN HENRY HILLIER, YOU PUT ME DOWN RIGHT NOW!" I yell as I kick my legs.

"Simmer down or I will throw you over my shoulder and carry you like a sack of feed."

"THE FUCK!" I exclaim as I am toted down the street like a kid. I finally give in and wrap one arm around his neck as he carries me. Reaching the truck, he puts me down on the passenger side and disarms the alarm system. Leaning around me, he reaches to open the door. When he does, I lean in and kiss him.

Yep, I just did that. I made the first move. I couldn't help myself, his mouth was right there and I swear I heard it beckoning to me.

Declan is more than responsive and kisses me back. I part my lips slightly as he gently sucks on my bottom lip. His tongue slowly explores my mouth as mine explores his. He is an amazing kisser; his lips are soft and warm.

Reaching up, he grips the back of my neck, tilting my head and pulling me closer to him. Our bodies are pressed against each other so tightly I'm certain he can feel my heart pounding in my chest. A slight moan escapes his lips. He turns me in a fluid motion, pressing my back up against the truck, pinning me between the firmness of his body and the cold hard steel of the Ford. He attacks my mouth with his, slowly working his way around to my ear. Gently, he kisses and sucks on my earlobe as he lets out a slow breath near my ear, sending chills up and down my body. Kissing in a fevered frenzy, we are struck with the sudden realization that we aren't alone.

We are standing in a parking lot making out like two horny teenagers. AND IT WAS AWESOME! Yep, I just fist pumped myself. Breaking apart, we gain our composure and collect ourselves.

Declan clears his throat. "We, uh, we should get going," he says, wiping his bottom lip with his thumb.

"Yep," is all I can manage. My hoo-ha is starting to wake up from her long slumber. Opening the door, he helps me in like a true gentleman, but leans in for one more kiss before closing the door.

I can't help but notice that he is now limping when he walks around the front the truck to get to his side. Poor guy. I will pretend I didn't see him adjust himself. But inside I give myself a little high five.

'I did that,' I say to myself with a hint of pride.

The drive home is a bit of a quiet one. I think we are both in shock at what just happened. I am not normally one to initiate or make the first move unless I know for sure I won't be shot down. I have a problem with rejection. It's ugly. I don't really know what compelled me to kiss him first, but I don't regret it.

Pulling up in front of my house he is once again a gentleman, coming around to open the door for me. As we walk up the porch to my door, I am suddenly overcome with a feeling of sadness. I don't want tonight to end.

"Thank you so much for such an amazing night, Declan. I can't even being to tell you how much fun I had."

"Umm, you kind of already did," he smirks.

"I did?"

"Yeah, when you kissed me by the truck," he says with a sly grin.

"I don't really know what came over me," I begin to explain when I am suddenly cut off.

"I do," he says, slowly pushing me against the door. With my back firmly pressed against the door, he leans down and begins to kiss me again. Slower, but with the same heated need. Our tongues invade each other's mouths with such passion, I realize I am pushing myself against him in an effort to get closer. My hands wrap around his neck, pulling him to me. Holding him to me.

His large firm hands explore up and down the sides of my body. His lips break free from mine as he begins to make his way down my neck and up toward my ear, sucking and licking as he goes. Slowly running his tongue along the outside of my ear, he softly whispers "Oh, Madi." I am putty in this man's hands.

Releasing my grip on his neck, I wrap my arms around his waist and explore his firm muscular back with my hands. "We shouldn't be doing this," he says breathlessly.

Oh God, I just got shot down.

I pull away quickly. "I'm sorry. I don't really…"

"Neighbors. You have neighbors. Soooo…" he draws out with a smile on his face.

Turning quickly, I begin to unlock the door at a speed I can only compare to someone being chased by a zombie seeking shelter. Swinging the door open, we step inside. I throw my purse down on the sofa table as he closes the door behind us. I look up and see his face and suddenly feel like prey being pursued by a hot ass hunter.

Chapter 12

HE STANDS STARING at me. Stepping closer, I look into his eyes and smile. I take another step until I am inches from him. Declan reaches down and softly takes my face in his hands, pulling me to him. His lips reach mine as he caresses my face before running his hands through my hair.

One innocent kiss in a parking lot has sparked a fire storm between us. I want to explore every inch of his mouth with my tongue. Walking in a forward motion, he guides me backward into the living room, our lips never parting. He reaches down and grabs me below my ass, lifting me up swiftly. Wrapping my legs around his waist, my arms immediately find his neck.

When we reach the kitchen he sets me down on the island, face to face, our foreheads touching. Breaking the contact of our lips, he stares deeply into my eyes. "Madi, you are amazing," he says while gently running the tip of his nose against mine.

"Declan I… I… I," I stutter, staring into his beautiful blue eyes.

"I know," he smiles and nods.

"How can you know if I don't?" I close my eyes.

"Tonight has been the best date I have ever had. Just talking and laughing together, reliving my childhood in the toy store with you and now this. It's all been so…"

"I know," I say before gently kissing his lips again.

The feverish kisses from before are now replaced with softer, more passionate ones. Slowly our tongues explore each other's mouths. My lips break contact with his as I begin to work my way around to his ear, sucking and kissing as I go. His hands start to explore their way around my body. He grabs my ass and pulls me into him as I increase the hold on him with my legs, causing physical friction between us.

My hands wander to his chest and back, clawing and claiming him.

His hands find their way to the buttons on my blouse and I can feel our breathing become more rapid. He slowly begins to unbutton them, kissing his way down my neck as he does. Pulling my white collared shirt open, he exposes my breasts. They are being held prisoner in my white lace bra. Peeling the shirt from my body, we are one again caught in each other's stares. Unable to look away, I find myself getting lost in his eyes.

Kissing his way down my neck, past my collar bone and across my chest, he gets closer and closer to the tops of my breasts. I feel my heart rate quicken. I quickly unbutton his shirt as he kisses the exposed tops of my breasts. Swiftly, I pull his shirt back with such force I'm certain buttons have gone flying. It pools on the floor at his feet.

Oh, sweet mother of Troy, look at those tattoos and that chest.

I run my hands up and down his massive, firm chest. He smiles and kisses me before slowly working his way back down my nearly exposed breasts. Wrapping my arms around his torso, I run my fingers up and down his back in an almost clawing motion. I don't want him to stop.

Looking up at me as if to gauge my reaction, he slowly reaches around to undo the clasp of my bra. $45 Victoria's Secret bra be dammed! Rip that bitch! Here's a secret for you, Victoria. I'M GETTING LAID!

Peeling the bra from my heated flesh, it falls to the floor with the other articles of clothing. He wraps his arms around my back, pulling me to his chest. Our flesh is pressed together.

Tits to tattoos.

Arching, I throw my head back as Declan kisses his way down my exposed neck. As he works his way to my ear I hear a soft moan escape his lips once more, causing me to become incredibly wet. With both hands, he gently begins to caress my breasts, working my already firm nipples between his fingers, kissing his way down to them. In one fluid motion, he takes one in his mouth, softly stroking my nipple with his tongue. I am a bundle of raw nerves. They are so sensitive it's almost painful. Almost.

His hands move around to my back, supporting me, as he lays me flat against the cool marble of the island. Finding the other already nipple hard, he playfully bites at it, causing me to arch and let out a muffled yelp. I can see him smile as he continues to worship my breasts.

Writhing under him, I can feel myself become slick with

pleasure. He begins to lick his way down the center of my abdomen before sliding his hand down the front of my jeans. As he quickly unbuttons them I have a moment of panic. Oh God, he's gonna see a stretch mark. What if he thinks he's about to get it on with a zebra? Breathe, Madi.

As he kisses his way around my waist I sit up suddenly. Taking his face in my hands, I pull his lips to mine. I reach down and begin to make quick work of the buttons on his jeans as he works on freeing me from mine. Before I can undo his jeans, he picks me up and stands me before him, slowly pulling my jeans past my hips. Leaning on him for balance, he helps me free my legs from the confines of the denim. I am left standing before him in white lace boy shorts and my platform heels.

"Oh Jesus Christ, Madi. I don't stand a chance."

He picks me up and quickly sets me back down on the island. As I reach down to remove my shoes he quickly grabs my wrist. "Oh, please… leave those on." It almost sounds like he's begging.

A sly smile plays across his lips before kissing me again. My hands are free to explore his body. Running them down his chest to his lower abdomen, I can feel the massive erection pressed against his jeans. I attempt to unzip his pants to free him, but my hands are stopped quickly as he mumbles through our kisses.

"Oh, no. This is all for you."

He slowly lays me back against the cool marble of the island, and a shiver surges through me. His lips begin to kiss the edge of my now soaking panties. His teeth grab the edge and slowly tug downward, momentarily exposing me. As I writhe below him, he kisses his way down my inner thigh.

Deftly grabbing my legs, he lifts them, setting my feet on the counter on front of him. His lips are mere inches from my soaking wet core. I can feel his hot breath on me. My breath hitches as he uses the tip of his tongue to tease me through my panties. Arching beneath him as he torments me, I can't hold still against his skilled tongue.

Flattening his tongue, he presses it against my clit through the soaked lace, making a long, slow, licking motion. "Oh my God, Declan," I whimper, grabbing his shoulders, digging my nails into them.

"Mmmmmmmm," he moans. He reaches up and hooks his fingers into the waistband of the unnecessary barrier between us. Tugging them quickly, he frees me. He grabs my hips and pulls me forward swiftly, leaving me on the edge of the counter and of an impending orgasm. Leaning forward, he slowly runs his finger up and down my wet center. I can feel a rush surge through me as he looks up at me through hooded eyes.

"Oh, Madi, you are so wet and so sweet," he moans, using his tongue to lick his fingers. My head falls back to the counter as my hands grip the edges. Swiftly he slides them inside me, causing me to arch and whimper. "OH GOD, you're gonna make me cum."

As he works his fingers inside my aching pussy, he uses his tongue to tease my throbbing clit. Rotating his hand, he strokes his fingers in an upward motion, calling me to him, sending me over the edge.

"FUCK! I'm coming, Declan, I'm coming!" I scream out, thrashing below him.

He is relentless, my screams only intensifying his pursuits, causing me to climax again before I can recover from the first one. Gripping his massive arms I force him up, afraid if he makes me cum again I may never walk. As his eyes meet mine, I smile and kiss him fiercely, tasting myself on his lips.

Reaching for his zipper, I attempt to free him from his jeans once again. Again he grabs my hands to stop me. "No, Madi, please. I wanted this to be about you," he pants out between kisses.

"It was about me, now it can be about you," I answer, trying to find my way back to his zipper.

"I'm afraid if I don't stop myself now, I won't be able to stop myself at all," he replies breathlessly.

"Who said you needed to stop yourself?"

"Oh God, Madi, you have no idea how much I want you. Really, really want you," he says, resting his forehead against mine. I smile and gaze into his stunning blue eyes.

"You're shaking. Are you OK?" he asks, stroking my cheek with this back of his hand. I nod and smile slightly. Taking me in his arms, he carries me into the living room, gently setting me down on the couch.

He kneels in front of me and lightly grabs my foot, sliding off my shoe. As he does, he smiles. "These are fucking hot," he murmurs, softly kissing the inside of each ankle. Standing, he positions himself behind me on the couch, laying us both down and covering us in a blanket. He moves the hair from my neck and tenderly kisses below my ear before whispering, "you're amazing, Madi." He wraps his arms around me, pulling my naked body tightly to him. I can feel his rock hard cock pressed against my back.

"Declan?"

"Hmmm?"

"Why won't you let me touch you?" I ask, turning to face him.

"You really wanna know?" he chuckles. I nod.

"Because I was afraid that if you even looked at me, much less touched me… I would cum on the spot," he says sheepishly.

"Would that have been so bad?" I ask, slightly confused.

"No! Oh God no, Madi. I just didn't want it to take away from me enjoying every single fucking moment of that," motioning toward the kitchen, "because it was seriously… wow."

Looking down at his chest, I begin to trace his tattoos with my finger.

"Madi?"

"Hmmm?"

"Can I see you again?" he asks as his fingers trail up and down my back.

I roll on top of him, pushing him flat into the couch, straddling him. Looking down, I lean over and kiss him as I move closer to his ear. "You can see me any time you want," I whisper, softly biting his ear lobe.

Wrapping his arms around me, he flips us over, now hovering over me, my arms pinned next to my head.

"Tomorrow?" he asks.

Staring up into his gleaming blue eyes, the words escape my lips. "Stay."

"Madi, I… I can't," he says with sadness on his face. I try to hide the disappointment on mine.

"Oh, OK," I reply with a smile.

"Madi, it's just that…"

"Declan, it's OK, you don't have to explain," I say,

scooting out from under him. Grabbing the blanket, I quickly wrap it around myself. He sits up and rests his elbows on his knees before rubbing his hands over his face and head. I walk toward the kitchen to retrieve my clothing. He stands, looking at me with a horrified expression. "Madi, please let me explain," he begs as he follows me into the kitchen.

"You don't have to. It's fine, really," I reply, wrapping my white shirt around me. "But it is getting late and you have to work tomorrow," I add, biting my lower lip. I'm trying hard not to cry but I think I am losing the battle, quickly.

I don't know why I'm even upset. It was just a date with the hot gym guy. You got your parting gift and now he is headed out. You shouldn't be upset or surprised. Really, this is no different than what you did to Nash, so maybe this is that Karma bitch slapping you right here in your own home.

Stepping toward me, Declan slowly tilts my chin up with his hand, forcing me to look at him. "Please don't be upset, Madi. You have to understand…"

"I'm not upset, Declan," I say with a pathetic smile. "I really had a great time tonight, thank you so much." I hand him his shirt before I make my way toward the front door. Following behind me, he puts his shirt on, leaving the buttons undone.

"Can I see you again?" He pauses at the doorway.

"I don't know. I could probably come by the gym Wednesday morning after my shift," I reply, looking down at the ground.

"That's not what I meant, Madi," he says as he steps past the doorway. Looking back to me, he offers a sad smile before leaning in and kissing my cheek.

"Please drive carefully," I say softly into his ear.

Slowly closing the door, I let my head fall against it. As I turn the lock I look out the window one last time. I can see Declan's silhouette in his truck, his head resting against the steering wheel as he hits his fist against the dashboard.

The tears I was holding back make their way down my cheeks.

I walk into the kitchen to turn off the lights, grabbing the blanket we were entwined in. Wrapping myself in it I make my way upstairs to my bed. Eventually I drift off to sleep, my face stained with tears.

Chapter 13

WAKING IN THE morning, I find myself still half naked and wrapped in the blanket from last night. I hear my phone beep from the other room as I make my way downstairs. I fish my phone out of my purse, still sitting on the sofa table where I set it last night. I see I have two new text messages. The most recent one is from Savannah, sent about twenty minutes ago.

–Assume you had a blast, didn't pick up your kid. I'm holding her ransom for gory details. Kisses–

The second one I see is from Declan, sent at 1:30 in the morning.

–Madi, I need to talk to you. Please call.–

Oooh, he spelled out YOU, he must mean business! I also have a missed call from him at 1:02am.

No voicemail.

I reply to Savannah's message.

–Sorry, fell asleep. Be there soon! Bringing Starbucks XO–

Not knowing what to say to Declan, I don't reply for now. What am I supposed to say? Thanks for the Twinkies and the cunnilingus, see ya 'round? Maybe this is the hot young guy M.O. these days. I don't know, I've never been out with a guy 10 years younger than me before. Perhaps this is par for the course for those born in the 80's. I need to get my shit together before I see Vannah. She can read me like an open book and I am not really in the mood for a chapter by chapter recount of last night.

After a much needed shower, I throw on blue sweatpants and a white t-shirt. My hair is quickly pulled back into a ponytail before I head out. I swing into Starbucks on my way to Vannah's, hoping that maybe if I ply her with caffeine she won't pester me so much. Heading in, I see Mark behind the counter.

"Hey, Madi! How are you?"

"I'm OK, thanks. You?"

"Great! The usual?"

"Yes, please, and could you add 3 kid's chocolate milks and a venti unsweetened tea?"

"You got it!" he smiles.

Waiting patiently for my large order, lean against the high top counter and wait. I dig out my phone and see another missed call with no voicemail from Declan, along with a text.

–Madi, please let me know you're OK.–

They must have come I while I was in the shower. A quick swipe and I close out the messages.

And then, in walks a little salt to add to my wound. Silicone tits Tiffani with an i comes strolling in the front door, bright eyed and fake as fuck.

"Good morning, Mark, how's my favorite manager today?" she pukes out.

Christ, she is batting her eyelashes so much it's causing a breeze. I shudder at the chill.

"Hey," Mark replies with no emotion. I get the feeling he isn't a fan of hers, but I could be wrong.

"Excuse you," she says, pushing past me.

"The fuck!" I mumble not so silently to myself. Today is not the day.

Bring it on, Barbie!

"Hey Madi, here you go. Three kid's chocolate milks, a venti unsweetened tea and your usual, venti non-fat, light ice chai latte," he smiles, snapping me out of my homicidal rage toward Tiffani with an i.

Making my way toward Savannah and Luke's, I crank up the radio. Maybe some music will lighten my mood. What's done is done, no need to dwell. Flipping channels, I stop on 'Stay' by Rihanna. I've heard the song plenty of times, but never the morning after I've asked someone to and they didn't. Before I know what hits me, I am bawling like a baby. I park at the end of Vannah's driveway and take a few minutes to compose myself.

Luke is in the garage and tells me to just go on in. Walking past him, I enter their house. Savannah is in the kitchen cleaning up the breakfast dishes.

"OH MY GOD!" she screams, throwing the dish she was

rinsing back into the sink before charging me. Pushing me into a chair, she sits in front of me.

"OK. SPILL IT!" she squeals, her legs bouncing all over the place. I don't think she's blinked yet.

"We had a great time. He took me to a cute little place in Old Town and then we walked around the shops. Made out a little and then he went home. Not much more to tell, really," I smile.

"Bullshit. I call bullshit. Have you been crying? Why were you crying? LUKE!" she screams.

"Vannah, stop. I'm fine. I heard something on the radio that made me sad," I reply, trying to appease her.

"What?" Luke asks as he walks in the house.

"Madi's been crying," she says angrily.

"Who do I need to fuck up?" he asks flatly.

"No one! Everything is fine, you guys. I'm seeing him again Wednesday," I say, forcing a smile.

"You are?" her eyes light up as I nod. I can't bear to tell her it's for a workout session.

"You know if he hurts you, there are a line of people waiting to fuck his world up, right? And I will be front and center," Savannah says, patting my knee.

"I know, V, and I appreciate it." I smile to try and reassure her.

I know I bitch about my friends, but they really are the best, and I am lucky that they care so much about me.

After an hour or so of idle chitchat, I am on my way with Claire, headed back home. Another text comes in from Declan.

–Madi, can I come over tonight? I need to talk to you.–

This time I text him back.

–Can't, I have plans. But I'll C U Wednesday :)–

There, I added a smiley face. That makes it less bitch on wheels-ish, right?

I'm really not trying to be such a bitch, but I don't really know what to say to him. What is there to say?

I don't need some long drawn out explanation or excuse. I'm a Band-Aid kind of girl—rip it off, quick and painful. No use pulling it off one hair at a time.

The rest of the day is pretty much a blur of housework and sulking. Claire invited one of the neighbor girls over to play for the afternoon, so at least she is busy and doesn't have to see her grown ass mother pout.

Later that afternoon my mom calls, and we catch up about the events of the past week. Well, most of the events anyway. She informs me that they want to head up to the cabin for a week before Claire starts school and wanted to see if they could take her along. Claire loves going up to our family cabin. It's so pretty and peaceful, not to mention 30 degrees cooler than in town. They want to head out on Wednesday morning and stay for about a week. Since I'll be working three of those days she might as well spend time with my parents at the cabin.

Just before dinner time Brianna, Claire's friend, heads home. I decide to make Claire's favorite tonight. Spaghetti with meatballs, salad and garlic bread. I love talking to her about her day and listening to her tell stories about her dolls and what they did together. I remember being her age and the imagination that runs wild.

Later in the evening I grab my E-Reader and curl up on the couch for a bit. Waking several hours later, I find myself wrapped in the same blanket from last night—freshly laundered now, of course. I grab it and head upstairs to bed.

TUESDAY MORNING ROLLS around and it's a blur, filled with packing for Claire's trip to the cabin with my parents. She might as well pack a steamer trunk, she's bringing so much. She's going to the cabin but feels the need to pack her silver glitter ballet flats and a boa. That's my girl, I'm so proud! My parents are coming by tonight to pick her up before I head to work.

Once she is packed, it's time for me to focus on the next 3 days at work and what I am going to say to Declan at the gym tomorrow morning. I can't really worry about it; it doesn't matter what I think I'm going to say or how I'm going to act. By the time he is actually in front of me, all that will have been forgotten and I will mumble like in incoherent baboon. No need to stress, whatever's gonna happen will happen.

I finish getting ready for work a little early so I can visit with my parents and spend time with Claire before she leaves me for a week. As we say our goodbyes, we head off in different directions. I miss her already.

Walking into the unit, I still have a decision to make. Grace approached me the other day about a possible promotion to Charge Nurse. I was hesitant to accept it at first, but now I think it will keep me busy and give my hoo-ha a chance to hibernate again. Maybe this is the push I need—a sign telling me to focus on work instead of hot 30 year old guys.

When I see Grace, I tell her that I accept the promotion to Charge Nurse.

"This calls for a celebration! To our promotions!" Grace yells.

"Well, we are going out this Saturday for girl's night, right? Let's celebrate then," I say.

"Hells yeah!" Savannah pipes up

About 40 minutes into shift I am called to the main lobby.

I make the long journey toward the main lobby from the ER. Approaching the desk, I see Maggie, the receptionist.

She smiles and points to an obscenely large vase filled with pink and purple roses.

"Oh shit," I mumble.

"They were delivered a little while ago but I knew you were in the middle of shift briefing, so I didn't want to bother you," she smiles widely.

"No problem. Thanks for signing for them," I say, attempting to hoist the heavy arrangement.

"Oh, I didn't have to sign for them. But Lord all mighty, Madi, you should have seen the guy that brought them in. Holy crap, he was this really tall muscular guy with a dreamy accent. He didn't look anything like the delivery guys I usually see," she says with a laugh, fanning herself.

"I bet he was wearing a Bama baseball cap backwards too, wasn't he?"

"Yeah, how did you know?" she looks confused.

"Oh, I've seen him around before," I nod.

"Well, I didn't see a ring, and if he ever comes back, I'm jumping on that hillbilly," she wiggles her eyebrows.

"Ooooh, I heard he's gay, Maggie. Sorry," I say with a shoulder shrug as I walk away.

"THIS IS GOING to be so painful," I say to myself as I round the corner to the ER.

"WHAT THE?" I hear Vannah exclaim from her seat at the main nurse's station. Walking over, I put the arrangement down on the counter.

"He sent you flowers? Oh God, that is so cute. What did you do to deserve those? Huh? Huh?" Savannah asks, wiggling her eyebrows.

"Ewww, what is it with the eyebrows tonight? I expect that from a sleazy drug rep or used car salesman but not you guys. Gross." I roll my eyes. "Nothing. I told you what happened," I say as I reach for the card.

"What's the card say?" Grace asks. Opening the envelope, I read what Declan wrote.

Madi,

Please forgive me. I need to see you.

Please call… ANY time.

-D

P.S–I know they aren't Twinkies but they reminded me of you.

"Is that a tear? Are your eyes tearing up?" Vannah questions.

I hear Grace giggle. "I bet he wrote something about her

climbing his tree trunk and swinging from his branches," she says softly.

OK, that was funny. I laughed and put the card in my pocket. "He just wanted to tell me he had a nice time the other night." Yeah, so I lied. They don't need to know. I'm already embarrassed about being shot down. My fragile ego couldn't bear any more from the likes of those two bitches.

AN INTERNAL STRUGGLE begins. I do want to see him and I haven't stopped thinking about him. Not just the other night, but since I got caught serenading him, and the entire gym for that matter, with my rendition of 'Ice Ice Baby'. Should I call him?

Should I cut my losses and call Nash? Savannah could be right, maybe I need to give Nash another shot. He's never bolted after getting around the bases. I did, but HE didn't.

Ugh, too much! I can't think about all of this right now. Thank God for the minor injuries that just came in. Something else to focus on.

It's crazy in the ER for a Tuesday night. Typical stuff—sick kids, broken bones, elderly illness, MVAs with minor injuries, etc. Nothing out of the ordinary, just a lot of them. The area of Phoenix we live in is pretty much suburbia. We don't see a lot of gunshot wounds, stabbings or violent crimes, which is one of the reasons I live here, but it can make for long nights in the ER sometimes.

By the end of shift we have had our butts handed to us with puking people, broken bones and professional patients.

I'm ready to shower and go to bed. I am supposed to go to the gym this morning for a training session with Declan, but to be honest, I just don't have it in me today. I make a mental note to send him a quick text when I get to the car.

Grabbing my bag and huge vase of roses, I begin my trek to my car with Savannah.

"Why don't you leave those here to enjoy for the next few days? You're here more than you are at home," she comments.

"Because I swear to God above, if one more person makes a snide comment, sexual innuendo or sings a fucking childish nursery rhyme again, I'm going to give them a colonoscopy with the pointy end of these long stems," I growl. She knows that comment was directed entirely at her.

Approaching our cars, she begins to grin like the Cheshire cat.

"What?" I ask, peeking around the tall flowers.

"Nothing," she smiles. She is a horrible liar.

Looking toward my car, I see why she was smiling. There is Declan, leaning against the driver side door of my car, his arms crossed over his massive chest. I stop dead in my tracks.

I look at Vannah, who winks. "Bye," she murmurs before walking off to her truck.

"Hey," Declan says with a very small smile.

"Shouldn't you be wearing a trench coat and holding an oversized boom box over your head?" I reply with a slight grin.

He laughs. "I see you got the flowers," he says, stepping toward me.

I nod. "I did. They are beautiful. Completely unnecessary, but beautiful. Thank you," I smile.

"Madi, I'm sorry," he takes a few more steps toward me. "Why wouldn't you call me back?"

"Declan, you don't have to apologize. You have nothing to apologize for. You couldn't stay. I understand. I shouldn't have asked you to. I put you in an awkward position and that wasn't fair of me. I'm not mad at YOU, I'm mad at myself. I knew it was too much too soon when the words left my mouth, but I couldn't take them back. And now I'm dealing with the consequences of MY actions, not yours," I shrug.

Now standing in front of me, he takes the flowers from my hands and sets them on the ground.

"Then why wouldn't you call me back and tell me that?" he questions sincerely.

"Because… I'm embarrassed. I have humiliated myself a few too many times around you. I just had to cut my losses. We'll still see each other at the gym and at our training sessions, and I'm OK with that," I say, smiling and nodding.

"Well, I'm not OK with it, Madi. Do you want to know why I left that night?"

"No, not really," I reply, shaking my head and looking down at the flowers. "I already ripped the Band-Aid off, Declan, please don't rub salt in it."

"That's too bad because you're gonna to hear me out. I left because I didn't want to rush things with you or put too much pressure on you. I wanted to stay so badly, but I was afraid if I did it would scare you away," he says.

"But I asked YOU to stay. I don't understand," I answer, looking up at him.

"Madi, I haven't stopped thinking about you since you started belting out that horrible song at the gym. I've never met anyone like you, and I don't want to rush things. I didn't want you to think that I am only interested in a physical relationship. I really like you," he blushes.

"Then why not just tell me that?"

"I panicked. I wanted to stay. God, I wanted to stay," he says, arching his head back. "But when you asked me, I was surprised. I didn't want to leave you, but I was afraid if I did stay it would be too much too soon. I know you haven't really dated much since your divorce and I don't want to ruin things by moving too fast," he takes my hands in his. "Please forgive me," he begs, kissing my hands.

"There is nothing to forgive, Declan. You left because you really wanted to stay… I get it," I smile.

"See! You totally get me!" he winks. Taking our hands, he pulls them up, wrapping them around me.

"I do," I nod. "I need to tell you something, though, and I'm afraid you aren't going to like it," I add, biting my cheek.

"Okay..?" he questions.

"I'm not going to make it to the gym today for our session," I reply in complete seriousness.

"Oh, and why is that?" he smiles.

"Because I am taking you to breakfast. Unless you can't go to breakfast, because you really want to go to breakfast, which I would TOTALLY understand," I giggle.

"Come here," he says, pulling me firmly to his chest. Leaning down, he kisses me with his warm soft lips.

"It's a good thing you were my only appointment this morning. Where should we go?" he asks between kisses.

Looking up with wide eyes, I offer my suggestion. "How about the Springs Cafe?" I smile larger than life.

"That sounds like a great idea, but I have a client at noon. I don't know if we would be back in time," he replies.

"Well then, I don't care. Wherever is fine. I'm starving," I say, hugging him.

"How about my place?" he asks with a hesitant smile.

"Sure. Will it be OK that I'm in scrubs?" I question.

"No, MY place. As in where I live. I'd like to make us breakfast." He grins like a happy child.

"Sure, that sounds wonderful. Should I follow you?"

"I'll text you the address just in case we get separated," he squeezes me in a tight hug, picks up the flowers and helps me put them in the car.

Chapter 14

DRIVING TO DECLAN'S, I have butterflies in my stomach. I'm glad we talked about what happened the other night. I feel better knowing I didn't make a complete ass out of myself again. As much as I hate to admit, I am very insecure about myself.

I put on a brave face, but underneath it all I am still a bit damaged from the way my marriage to Andy ended. When I finally admitted to myself that he was cheating on me with Sindee it was a serious blow to my self-esteem. You see, the thing about Sindee is that although she might be a lovely person on the inside—doubtful—she is atrocious on the outside. Let's just say I look like Heidi Fucking Klum next to her. For Andy to choose Sindee over Claire and I was rough shot to my already fragile ego.

Over time the wound has healed, at least for the most part.

Arriving at Declan's condo, I pull in and park. He meets me at my car. Taking me by the hand, he leads me to his unit. Hehehehe, I said unit.

I take in a deep breath and prepare myself for the full-on bachelor pad experience. You know:

- Wooden cable spool for a coffee table
- Plastic milk crates with 2x4s and concrete blocks as an entertainment center
- Mattress on the floor in the bedroom covered with untucked sheets
- A pile of laundry in the corner that I could run and jump into like a pile of leaves
- The mandatory neon beer sign
- Some type of flag—I would assume University of Alabama, in this case—draped across the ceiling
- Some naked chick calendar thumbtacked to a wall
- Last night's beer pong table still set up, with bottles making a pyramid in the corner
- And the piece de resistance… it smells like a foot.

We have all been in a place like this, ladies. Admit it.

I'm certain my jaw hit the floor—the clean tile floor—when I walked in and saw the lovely sight before my eyes. There in the main room is a lovely brown leather sectional with coffee and side tables to match, and actual art on the wall that doesn't require an outlet, plug or thumbtack. There are no signs of a naked chick calendar and it appears to smell like fresh laundry rather than a foot.

"Come on in, make yourself at home," he says, closing the door behind me.

"This place is great. How long have you lived here?"

"About 4 years. Care for the tour?" he asks politely.

"Sure. Lead the way," I answer cautiously. Taking me by the hand, he leads me around the bottom floor.

"Obviously this is the main living room, and here is the kitchen." It's pretty big for a condo, I think to myself.

"Here is the downstairs bathroom." No signs of biohazard growing anywhere.

"This is my office," he says as he opens a door. "Ahhhhhh, there it is!" I laugh, pointing to the University of Alabama flag hanging on a wall.

"What?" he asks with a smile.

"I was wondering which of the stereotypical bachelor items I would find here. Where is the nudey girl calendar? Huh? Huh? Show me! Show me!" I say, bouncing eagerly.

"You're nuts," he says with a laugh. "Wanna see the rest of the place or is your scavenger hunt done?"

"I'm sorry, please continue." I curtsey.

Walking upstairs, he guides me to another bedroom, indicating this is a guest room. As we reach the wide double doors of the master bedroom I am flooded with butterflies again. We stand on the outside of the doors for a silent moment before he opens the doors.

Stunned is the only word I can use to describe what I see. Before me is the largest sleigh bed I have ever seen. Deep, dark woods make up the head and foot boards. Looking around I see a large matching dresser with bedside tables to match. It's gorgeous. The bed is covered in a dark chocolate brown and ivory comforter. It's all very masculine but not in a testosterone-riddled way.

"You can come in," he says, gently pulling me forward.

"It's beautiful. This bed is amazing," I remark, running my hand along the footboard.

“Thanks. My mom had it custom made when I was 16. Being 6’7”, you can’t just go to the local mattress store and buy something,” he shrugs with a grin.

“It’s gorgeous. It looks like… a giant brown marshmallow,” I say softly to myself.

“A giant brown marshmallow?” he repeats.

“Yeah, like you could take a flying leap into it,” I answer with a smile, looking up at him.

“Do it,” he says with an impossible grin.

“Do what?” I laugh.

“Do it,” he repeats as his smile widens.

“Seriously?” I question.

“I triple dog dare you,” he says before kissing me.

“Oh, it’s on!”

Slipping off my shoes, I make my way back toward the door. I gauge my trajectory, and before I know it I am off, like a really slow flash. “WEEEEEEEEEEEEE,” I squeal in delight as I fly through the air, landing on my back in the center of the big brown marshmallow.

As I sit up, slightly breathless, I see him doubled over, laughing hysterically. Throwing myself back onto the bed, I am also laughing beyond control, relishing the fact that I just took a flying leap into Declan’s bed.

Seconds later I am once again airborne. “AHHHH!” I screech as I feel myself being lifted 2 feet off the surface of the bed. I come crashing back down into the brown marshmallow, with Declan lying beside me, still laughing.

“Oh my God!” I clutch my stomach, now hurting from laughing so much. Declan’s deep laugh booms next to me.

“You made it look like so much fun, I had to try.” He turns, smiling at me.

"This is one amazing brown marshmallow," I say as I roll to face him.

"I'm glad you're here," he says before kissing the tip of my nose softly.

"Me too." I smile and gaze into his eyes. Pulling me closer to him, only our clothing separates us.

"Your heart is pounding. Are you OK?" He leans back to see my face.

"Mmmm hhmmmm," I slowly nod. I don't know if it's pounding from the flying leap I took several minutes ago or the fact that I'm lying in Declan's bed, wrapped in his arms. Inhaling deeply, I take in his scent. I feel so comfortable here.

Apparently so comfortable that I fall asleep wrapped in his arms.

STARTLED AWAKE BY the sound of a cell phone, I take in my surroundings. It takes me a moment to realize where I am. Climbing off the bed, I grab my shoes and head downstairs. Suddenly, I stop halfway down. I hear Declan on the phone and he sounds upset.

"No, I made it VERY clear where I stand. We're over. NO! It's over. It's been a year and a half, you need to move on. None of your business! Stop calling and texting me, got it?" Ending the call, he tosses his phone down on the counter before vigorously running his hands over his face and letting out an exasperated sigh.

Not wanting him to know I heard his call, I make a little noise as I come down the last few steps.

"Hey there," he says with a sincere smile.

"Hey. Sorry I feel asleep." I smile sheepishly as I make my way toward him.

"I'm not," he says, stepping closer. He opens his arms wide, scooping me into them. Embracing me in a tight hug, he sweetly declares, "I liked watching you sleep," then gently kisses the top of my head.

"That doesn't sound creepy at all," I reply, laughing.

Pulling me back from his chest, he smiles. "Are you hungry? I made breakfast while you slept."

"What time is it? Oh my God, Declan, it's almost noon. You have to go. Don't you have an appointment?" I say as I scramble to sit and put my shoes on.

"Madi, relax. I took care of it. I called Taylor and let her know I might be running a bit late and she told me not to worry, they called and cancelled," he replies, sitting next to me. "Take your sad little shoe off, breakfast is almost ready." He leans in, kissing me.

"Is there some place I can wash up?" I ask, taking my sad little shoe off.

"Sure, bathroom is over there." He motions with his head.

Grabbing my bag, I step into the bathroom. The sight of myself in the mirror is frightening. My once nicely pulled back ponytail is now magically on the side of my head like an 80's valley girl and my eye makeup is smeared, giving me a delightful Alice Cooper look. "Oh Jesus, nice!" I exclaim to myself in the mirror.

"Who are you talking to?" he yells from the kitchen with a laugh.

"My ponytail, like totally. Be out in a second," I mumble back through the door.

After my feeble attempt to fix myself, I exit the bathroom to find him standing next to the kitchen table, breakfast plated and ready. "Wow. That looks and smells amazing."

"Thanks. Come. Sit," he pulls a chair out for me.

Sitting down, I take the napkin and drape it in my lap as he sits next to me. Scrambled eggs, bacon, fruit and of course… toast.

"Aww, you made toast," I squeal with an excited hand clap.

"I know it's your favorite," he smirks.

"This is so good, thank you. I could have helped," I murmur, shoving bacon in my mouth.

"No need. You were tired and I enjoy cooking," he replies, taking a sip of his coffee.

"Yes, but I do believe the deal was that I was going to take you to breakfast. You somehow ended up making all of it, and alone."

"Most women wouldn't complain."

"Oh, make no mistake. I am NOT complaining. Next to toast, I think you might be my new favorite," I blurt out without thinking. My eyes go wide at my admission, but I choose to play it off and quickly change the subject. "Can I help clean up?" I ask, keeping my eyes averted.

Looking up at me, he smiles slowly. "Deal," he nods, choosing not to address my comment.

"Everything was so good," I say, pushing my plate away slightly.

"Good, I'm glad you enjoyed it. What are your plans for the rest of the day?" he asks, sitting back in his chair.

"A shower and another nap at some point. Other than that, nothing until I have to go back to work at 7:00. You?"

"Well, if you hadn't been receptive to me standing by your car this morning, I was going to spend my day figuring out ways to get you to talk to me. But since my original plan worked, I got nothing," he replies with a grin.

"I almost cried when I saw you today, standing there," I say, looking down at my plate.

"Why?" he asks, leaning toward me.

My voice lowers to a soft whisper. "I was happy to see you," I reply, looking at him through my lashes.

"I'm sorry I upset you, Madi. I don't want to blow this. I really like you," he says, reaching under the table for my hands. "I don't ever want to cause you tears, unless they are from happiness or laughter." He locks his eyes on mine. Leaning in, he kisses me slowly and with tender passion, making my knees weak.

After several minutes of post breakfast table kissing, he takes my hand and leads me to the couch. He sits down and pulls me beside him. Wrapping his arm around me, we snuggle in together. "Are you still tired?" he asks.

"A little, but I'm OK." I look back at him.

"Wanna watch a movie or do you have to go?"

"I can stay for a little bit."

"Good," he says while turning on the ginormous inch television that takes up an entire wall of his condo.

Flipping through the channels, he passes Dodgeball. "Wait! Wait, go back!" I exclaim.

Flicking back, he stops on the channel and I start to laugh. "I love this movie!"

"Are you kidding me? This day keeps getting better and better," he says with a huge smile.

"Why?" I smile up at him.

"Because most women don't like this kind of humor, they think it's juvenile and stupid."

"Well, Declan, being that I AM juvenile and stupid, these movies speak to me." He laughs and squeezes me tighter.

"It's gotta be the hair, Cotton. It's beautiful! Feathered and lethal. You just don't see it nowadays!" I quote from the movie, laughing hysterically at myself, of course.

Before I know it, it's almost 2:00pm. "As much as I hate to, I should get going. I still need to get some sleep and shower before work tonight." I sit up, reaching for my shoes. Pushing me back onto the couch, he straddles me. "Before you go, I am going to kiss the hell out of you," he says with a devilish smile.

Several minutes later, I am left winded and hornier than hell.

"When can I see you again, Madi?" he says, staring into my eyes, still pinning me to the couch.

"I don't know, Declan, when do you want to see me again?" I answer coyly.

"Saturday night?"

"Oh, I can't Saturday night. I have plans with the girls. We are going out to celebrate."

"What are you celebrating?"

"Oh my gosh, I didn't tell you." I slap his chest in excitement. "I accepted a promotion to Charge Nurse. And Grace was appointed ER Medical Director," I say with excited pride.

"That's amazing! Congratulations." He stares into my eyes before kissing me.

"Thanks! I'm excited. A little terrified at the responsibility, but excited. Grace, Vannah, Taylor, Lynn and I are going out

Saturday night to celebrate."

"Friday, then?" he asks, running the tip of his nose into the crook my neck before gently kissing my collarbone.

"Friday, then," I answer with a breathy nod.

AFTER A FEW hours of rest I start getting ready for work. I feel so much better after talking to Declan today. I know this sounds odd, but I really have missed him. It's been such a short time since we met, but I am so comfortable with him. I am normally really shy around men, but with Declan, it's different. He is easy to talk to, funny, cute as hell, sincere, sweet and cute as hell. Yes, I know I said it twice. Had to be done.

As I pull into the parking lot at the hospital I hear Vannah's monstrosity from 5 rows over. "Christ on a crutch, that thing is loud," I say to no one in particular. I wait for her to catch up to me.

"Hey," I shout as she comes walking towards me.

"Don't try and pacify me with pleasantries. I want details and I want them now. Why was Mr. Hottie here waiting by your car? Why did you get flowers? Why didn't you call me?"

"Pump your brakes, spaz. We actually had a bit of a rough patch the other night and the flowers were his way of opening the door. As for the waiting by my car, I think it's because I wouldn't return his calls or texts."

"I KNEW IT! I knew something happened. Sad song on the radio, my ass! What the hell did he do? Do I need to have Luke kick his ass? Screw that, do I need to kick his ass?"

"No, everything is fine. But thanks for the ass kicking offers. Good to know you've got my back," I say with a chuckle.

"What did Douche Knuckle do?"

"Douche Knuckle? Really? It was nothing major, just bruised my ego."

"Did he bruise your ego with his huge penis?" she asks, grinning.

I bust out laughing at her. "No, you idiot. We had a great time that night. When we got back to my house we were screwing around and I asked him to stay, but he said he couldn't."

"Couldn't or shouldn't? Big difference."

"Exactly. I didn't know either. But the look on his face freaked me out. It was a look of sheer panic and shock. I wouldn't let him explain because I didn't think I could handle whatever excuse he'd come up with. So I made it easy for him to leave by being a bit of a bitch. And then I didn't call him back or text him. You know how well I handle rejection," I reply with a pathetic laugh.

"So what did the card on the flowers really say?"

"Asked me to forgive him and call him," I shrug my shoulders.

"And that's why he was waiting by your car this morning. I gotta give that boy credit, he's pretty persistent."

"Yep. So we talked it out here in the parking lot and then went to his place and had breakfast."

"And by breakfast you mean you devoured his sausage link?" Savannah says, so proud of herself.

"What the fuck is wrong with you? No. I followed him there, actually ate food, fell asleep in his amazing bed and left.

Nothing happened except some making out."

"Jesus, Mary and Joseph. No wonder your vagina is dusty. Here's the deal. From now on, every time I hear you say you were with him and you didn't have sex, I'm going to buy you a cat."

"OK. For starters, I'm allergic to cats, and why a cat?" I ask, confused.

"So you can get your 'I'm forty and single' collection started."

"You're a bitch," I smack her arm as she laughs.

"Please tell me you're going to see him again soon?"

"Friday night."

"Did you invite him to come with us Saturday night?"

"No. It's GIRLS night, not girls and a guy night out. Besides, I don't want to scare the poor guy with all of you," I reply, making an exaggerated hand motion towards Savannah.

"Whatever. But I'm telling you right now, if you don't hump that boy Friday night I am going to pull your vagina card and bring you a calico."

Thank God we reach the doors to the unit.

Chapter 15

IT'S A SLOW Wednesday night in the ER. Just a few patients left over from the earlier shift that are going to be discharged soon, or admitted and taken up to their rooms. I'm pretty grateful for slow nights when I'm tired. I didn't get much sleep today—or the past few days, to be honest.

The next day and a half are pretty uneventful. Declan and I have talked every day on the phone for at least an hour or four. There are dozens of texts back and forth at all hours of the day and night. We've spent a lot of time talking about him starting the Police Academy next week. He is so excited and I'm so happy for him. I know what it's like to make your dreams come true. I felt that way when I found out I was pregnant with Claire. I have wanted to be a mother since I was a little girl. The day I graduated nursing school and of course, when I signed my divorce papers… dreams do come true!

Friday morning finally arrives and it's time to go home. I text Declan to let him know I am getting ready to leave work.

–Good Morning, Leaving work. Still on for 7 tonight? :)–

I wait a bit, but there's no reply. He must still be sleeping.

After finishing up with some charts, I call it a day and head out. Vannah isn't walking out with me this morning; she is briefing the next shift on the patient that has been a pain in her ass all night. Karma, is that you? Getting closer, I can see a tree-like being standing by my car again. Uh oh. Why is he here today?

"Hey there," I say with a smile as I approach.

"Hey there, yourself." Declan answers as he steps toward me.

"What are you doing here?" I ask as he leans in and kisses me.

"I just wanted to say good morning and bring you this." He magically produces a venti iced nonfat light ice chai latte out of thin air.

"Oh my gosh! How sweet are you? But how did you know my drink?"

"I remember seeing you at Starbucks that day. You seemed pretty chummy with the manager, so I asked him," he replies with a shoulder shrug.

"You mean you went out of your way to find out something I like just to surprise me?" I am shocked and I'm sure the look on my face is a dead giveaway.

"Well, yeah. I mean, I thought it may be information that could come in handy someday. And it did." He grins.

"Thank you, that was so sweet of you." I set the drink on the trunk of my car and wrap my arms around him. He looks down and kisses me.

"Well thank YOU for that awesome thank you." He laughs.

"So what are we doing tonight?" I look innocently at him while taking a sip of my drink.

"Nice try."

"Awww, come on. Not even a little hint?"

"I told you. Wear tennis shoes, long pants, and maybe bring a sweater. Something you won't mind getting dirty if it should happen."

"Fine," I pout.

"Oh, don't give me that pouty face. It won't work."

"I'm an only child. I can do this all day long." I shake my head.

"You're nuts." He laughs. "Go, drink your latte, have some toast and get some rest. You're going to need it tonight."

"Fine." I revisit the pout.

"I'll see you tonight." He leans in and kisses me again. This time, we are so wrapped up in our kiss I didn't notice Savannah until she decided to crank the engine on her beastly truck in an effort to scare the shit of us. It worked.

"Goddamnit, Vannah!"

"Hahahahaha! Get a room, whore! Hi, Declan!" she yells as she drives off.

After several more minutes of kissing those sweet soft lips of his, I get into my car. 10 seconds later, I hear my phone beep. It's a text from Declan.

–Yes 7 Tonight C U then. X–

He is still standing next to my car. What a nut.

Time flies when you're sleeping. I set the alarm for 5:00. I need plenty of time to get ready since I have no clue what to wear. I finally settle on my favorite comfy jeans, a fitted black t-shirt with a grey cardigan sweater and my black Converse. I curl my long hair into loose beachy waves, pull it back into a ponytail and add a little black headband. Cute but casual.

It's almost 7 when I hear the doorbell. I haven't had a chance to let the dogs out, so I guess Declan will have his first introduction to Zoe and Athena. As I open the door, the dogs run out and greet him.

"Oh, wow! Hi!" he says, trying to look at the beasts running around him.

"Hi. Sorry, hadn't had a chance to put them up when you rang."

"No problem. Wow, these are some big dogs, Madi. I knew you liked dogs, I just didn't know you liked big dogs," he laughs.

"Hahahaha. Yeah, I like 'em big."

My eyes go wide as I realize what I just said. "I didn't mean… I was talking about… oh, God. Forget it." I hide my face in my hands as I listen to Declan's hysterical laughter. "Zoe and Athena, go night night," I order, pointing upstairs. The dogs are kennel trained and head right for their beds.

"I'll be right back," I say, shaking my head as I walk upstairs, mumbling to myself. "I like 'em big, hahahaha. Stupid." But I can't help giggling.

As I come back downstairs I finally get a good look at him. He's wearing his Bama baseball hat, worn jeans, a black polo shirt and black Chuck Taylors. He looks so hot!

My eyes finally reach his and his expression is serious. "Madi," he says in his deep southern voice.

"Yes?"

"Are you wearing Converse?"

I look down at my feet. "Yes. Is that OK?" I look down at his feet to see the same shoes, only much, much, MUCH larger. You know, cuz I like 'em big.

"Abso fucking lutely!" he smirks. Stepping closer to me, he looks deep into my eyes. "You look awesome. I think the Chucks are hotter than the heels you had on the other night."

"Shut up," I say, smacking his chest.

"I'm not kidding, Madi, those are seriously hot on you. You look adorable. Perfect for tonight," he leans in for a kiss.

I wrap my arms around him and kiss him back. "You look pretty hot yourself."

"You think so, huh?"

"I know so."

"So, word is… you like 'em big," he's barely able to contain his laughter.

"You're an ass," I say, shoving his chest again and laughing. "So where are we going?"

"You'll see," he says taking me by the hand and leading me toward the door.

ABOUT 15 MINUTES into our 45 minute drive to wherever it is we are going, a song comes on the radio and he turns it up. "I love this song," he says as he cranks 'Cruise' by Florida Georgia Line. We both start to sing along as we coast down the freeway.

He steals little glances and smiles as he drives. Reaching

for my hand, he cradles it in his.

We talk and laugh, realizing we share the same eclectic taste in music.

We head west towards the White Bridge Mountains. They are a popular hiking destination, after it rains, there is actually a waterfall that cascades down the side.

I'm confused as to why we would be hiking at night; it seems dangerous. But I trust him.

As he pulls into the parking lot at the base of the mountains, I can see there are a few other cars parked here, but not many.

"What are we doing here? Are you taking me here to kill me and make yourself a Madi suit?" I laugh.

"Madi, I couldn't get much more than a pair of socks out of you. Maybe a new hat? Oooh, or some boots," he smirks.

"Ok. Enough serial killer skinning jokes. Now you're freaking me out. You have put way too much thought into this."

He laughs "Come on, let's get going so we don't miss it," he climbs out of the truck and comes around to open my door. He reaches into the back of the truck and pulls out a small cooler and a blanket.

Taking my hand, he asks, "Trust me?"

"I do." I place my hand in his.

He pauses and smiles.

"Let's go."

Chapter 16

WE BEGIN TO walk up a path that is dimly lit by solar lights. We reach a peak and I see a few people standing around and talking.

"What is this, Declan?"

He takes the blanket and spreads it out on the ground in a relatively flat spot.

"Come sit," he says, patting the spot next to him on the blanket.

"What are we doing here? Is this like a nighttime picnic club or something?" I ask, confused.

"No. There is a meteor shower tonight and they have telescopes set up so you can see them. I think there's even a planet within view tonight," he's almost embarrassed. "I thought we could look at the stars and have dinner."

I just keep staring at him as a smile forms on my face. "Declan, this is… I just… I love it," I lean in to kiss him softly.

He opens the cooler and takes out a few things. A few

bottles of water, fruit, cheese, crackers, pasta salad and a baguette of bread. We turn to facing each other on the blanket and enjoy our delicious meal.

"Where did you get all this stuff? That pasta is incredible."

"I made it," he says proudly.

"Oh my gosh. You can cook for me any time."

"I would like that," he says, smiling.

Enjoying the beautiful clear night sky, we don't really speak, it's so peaceful up here. I am just enjoying being with him. Sitting between his legs, I lean back against his chest, reaching around he wraps his arms around me, resting his chin on the top of my head.

"It's so beautiful up here, Declan," he kisses the top of my head.

"It is," he lets out a deep sigh.

"Ohh, I just saw one!" I exclaim.

"I did, too," he smiles down at me as I look back up at him.

"Would you like to look at them through the telescope?" I hear a man ask us. Looking at each other, we say "Sure!" in unison. Taking turns, we look into the telescope at the amazing view above us. It's breathtaking to see stars and planets so close up.

"Thank you so much," I say to the nice older man.

"My pleasure. You kids have a great night," he replies as he and Declan shake hands.

After stargazing for what seems like hours, we finally make our way back to the truck. "It's amazing how much beauty there is right before our eyes that we never take time to appreciate," I say, looking out the truck window at the night sky.

"You can say that again," he says, smiling at me.

The ride to the house goes pretty quickly, and before I know it we are pulling up in front of my house. In his usual gentlemanly style, he opens the door for me. "You know I can open my door on occasion," I remind him.

"Not with me around, you won't. Besides, if I don't open a door for you my momma will come out of nowhere and smack me upside my head." He laughs. Walking me to the front door, I am suddenly hesitant. I can't help but think about the other night and I don't know what to do. I want him to come in but I don't want to put pressure on him again.

"It's OK, Madi," he knows what I am thinking.

"Umm, do you want to come in?" I ask with trepidation.

"I would love to," he smiles.

As we walk into the house, I turn on a few lights and set my bag down on the table. "Can I get you something to drink?"

"No thanks, I'm fine."

We walk into the kitchen. I stop on one side of the island and he stops on the other. We stand staring at each other for a few seconds but it feels like an eternity.

"Madi, can I ask you a question?"

"Of course," he looks nervous.

"I was wondering if you would, well, if maybe you wanted to start seeing each other," I can barely hear him but I get the gist of what he just asked me. Oh hell yeah, let's have some fun with this.

"I'm sorry, I didn't hear you," I reply, looking very serious. He says it again, but a bit louder.

"Declan, you're going to have to speak up. I can't hear you." Haha, this is fun for me.

He repeats it one more time, but this time I am laughing halfway through it. It's at this point he realizes that I've heard him all along. "Oh, you're in for it now," he says as I take off running into the family room and around the sofa. I am in hysterics and so proud of myself.

Declan is standing on the other side of the couch, ready to pounce. I take off running towards the front door. Shit! I didn't think this through—my only option is up the stairs. I bolt up the steps and he is hot on my heels. He grabs my foot a few steps from the top. I manage to break free, but with his long legs he quickly catches me on the upstairs landing. He throws me up over his shoulder like a sack of potatoes and smacks my ass really hard.

"Owwwwww," I cry, laughing.

He walks us towards the double doors which lead to my room. He steps inside and throws me down on my bed. I scream as I go flying from his height. I'm laughing so hard I can't catch my breath. Pinning my arms down by the sides of my head, he straddles me.

"Oh, you think this is sooo funny, don't you?" He glares at me.

"Yes sir, I sure do." I smile at him, still giggling.

"I'll show you funny." He lifts up my t-shirt and blows a giant zerbit on my stomach!

"Ahhhhahahhhhhhaaaaaaaah!" I laugh.

"Still funny? Huh? Huh?" He starts to tickle me.

"Uncle! Uncle!" I yell. As he looms over me with a smile, his expression changes.

"Are you OK?" I ask.

"I've never been better." He slowly leans in, kissing me. My arms are still pinned by my head. I try and wiggle them free, but he has a tight hold on me. Breaking the contact of our lips, he releases my hands.

He smiles as he leans in for another kiss. My hands are free to wrap around his neck.

The intensity of our kisses grow and before I know it, my arms and legs are wrapped around him. He works his way down my neck toward my ear. Arching, I give him better access. A soft moan escapes his lips as he lightly rims my ear with his tongue.

I am so turned on I can't hold still. I run my fingers down his back, pulling his shirt up and attempting to pull it over his head. He stops his feverish kissing and yanks the shirt off, throwing it down on the floor.

I make a beeline for his chest, running my tongue over the tattoos on his massive pectorals. I work my way up his neck, sucking as I go.

As my lips reach his jaw, he begins to peel off my cardigan and pulls the bottom of my shirt up and off in one fluid motion. "Madi," he moans, making his descent down into the cleavage of my aching breasts. He pulls them from the cups of my bra and begins to suck on my nipples. "Oh God," I whimper.

Reaching under Declan, I make quick work of his zipper and button. I slide my hands down the back of his jeans and firmly grab his tight ass, pulling him into me. I can feel his massive erection against my leg.

I work his jeans down behind him, using my feet as leverage to push them past his thighs.

Declan stops sucking my nipples and begins his southern descent towards the waist of my jeans. As he is undoing the zipper and button I lift up, allowing him room to slide them down my legs. He kisses my hip bones and stares up into my eyes as he peels my hot pink panties from my soaking wet pussy.

He stands, looming large over me. I lay flat on my bed, staring up at the beautiful man before me. I take a second to memorize his body. His tattoos, his muscles, his smile and his eyes. He is amazing. I want to remember this moment. I am suddenly filled with a sense of calm as he looks deep into my eyes; not just at me, but into me.

I smile and sit up in front of him. I slide my hands into the waist band of his black boxer briefs, freeing his very large erection. Gently, I take my fingers and wrap them around the base of his hard cock. I lean forward and begin to lightly run the tip of my tongue up and down his shaft. He uses his hands to carefully caress the sides of my face and removes the band from my hair, causing it to cascade down around my face.

Looking up at Declan, I can see his eyes firmly fixed on me. Not breaking eye contact, I part my lips and begin to take him into my mouth. I take his length to the hilt of my throat. “Oh God, Madi!” he growls as he pulls my hair away from my face. I stare into his eyes while my mouth is full of his hardened cock. “FUCK, this feels so good,” he grunts.

Sliding my tongue back and forth against the seam of his erection while plunging him in and out of my mouth, I am getting more and more turned on. Declan gently grabs my shoulders and pulls me up to stand in front of him. Without care or thought, he leans in and kisses me, knowing he was just in my mouth. Son of a bitch, that’s hot!

He lifts me up and lays me on the bed before him. He leans down and pulls a condom out of the jeans, now discarded on the floor. Grabbing his hard cock by the base, he begins to slowly rub against my wet center. He slides his tip up and down, teasing my clit. I am writhing below him. Leaning forward, he slowly eases himself into me.

With a sudden and deep inhale of breath, Declan stops, a look of concern taking over his face."Madi, are you OK?"

With an exhale just a sudden, I look into his passionate blue eyes. "Yes," I smile.

Declan continues to ease himself into me, being careful not to hurt me by going too quickly. Before I know it, he has filled me to my core and begins a slow and steady rhythm. He leans forward, resting his forearms on the bed beside me, and kisses me with intense passion while continuing his deep, even thrusts. He is being so gentle. I know he can sense that he is almost too large for me. I wrap my legs around him and pull him deeper into me, causing me to gasp and my eyes to go wide, but I pull him toward me again. He feels so good inside of me, filling me completely.

"Oh God, please don't stop," I manage between gasps of breath.

"Madi, you feel so good," he moans, his face buried in my neck.

I can feel myself getting close. I use my legs to continue his slow and passionate tempo. Before too long, I can't hold back any longer and I start to shudder in his arms. "YES! YES! YES! Oh God, Declan!" I scream as I begin to spasm around his cock. I throw my head forward over his shoulder, completely wrapping myself around him. Digging my nails into his back, I pull them upward as the intense orgasm rips through me.

I can hear him hiss through his teeth as he starts to

increase his force and rhythm. "Fuck, Madi, I'm gonna cum," he grunts. Pulling me closer, we are almost one. I can feel him pulsating inside of me as I continue to spasm around him.

Several minutes go by. The only sound heard is our panting as we try to catch our breath. Lifting his head, he gently moves the wet strands of hair from my face. He stares deeply into my eyes as he kisses me softly. Still inside me, Declan rolls over onto his back, pulling me with him. I rest my head on his chest and listen to his heart beating, pounding like a drum.

"Are you OK?" I ask him, still slightly out of breath.

"Madi, I…" there is a pause. "Yes. You?" he asks, pulling me up a little so he can see my face. I smile and nod.

"God, you look so beautiful," he whispers as he gazes into my eyes, softly tucking the hair behind my ear.

I suddenly feel shy, I can't explain it. Resting my head back on his chest, I use my finger to trace the tattoo on his chest, following the pattern as it wraps around his shoulder and down his arm.

"What are you thinking about?" he murmurs, slowly stroking my hair.

"Do they have meanings behind them?" I ask, still tracing his tattoos.

"Yes, they all do," he replies, looking at me. I lift my head and rest my chin on his chest. We lay on my bed for a while as Declan explains the meanings behind his tattoos. I am fascinated by his explanation of each of them. They all truly mean something or represent a pivotal moment in his life. They aren't just art; they are his story.

Declan stands and reaches for my hand, pulling me to stand by him. He pulls back the covers on the bed, motioning for me to climb under them. Then he grabs his boxers and pulls them on. I am suddenly filled with panic. Is he leaving again? Is this what he does? Sweet talks a girl, fucks around with her and then leaves? I can't do this. I start to sit up to say something when I notice he is walking out of the room in just his boxers. As he walks away, I can't help but notice the long scratch marks I left on his back.

A few minutes later he comes back into the room with a glass of water, handing it to me. He leans down, removes his boxers and gets under the covers with me. I snuggle up along his side and take in a deep breath of Declan.

As we lay together, he runs his hands up and down my back and arm. "Declan, I ummm, I am so sorry," I say, looking up at him.

"For what, Madi?"

"I, ummm, I scratched your back… pretty bad," I answer with a scared look.

"I know," he says with a grin.

"You do?"

He nods.

"You're not mad?"

"Mad? Are you kidding? That was hot. That's what did me in. You were so hot and into it," he says with a slight smirk.

"Wow, you really are a sadist," I laugh.

"Seriously, do you have any idea what a turn on that is? I have never been with anyone so responsive and free. You just let go."

"Free? Let go?"

"Nothing. I didn't mean anything by it."

"Well, now you have to tell me," I say, turning to face him.

"It's just that… well, normally the girls I have been with in the past are so concerned about messing up their hair or makeup that it's like they just go through the motions. Putting on a show of what they think I want to see or hear. But you… you are something else. I knew exactly what to do to you. I've never been with anyone like you. You're so in tune with your body. You know what you like, and you aren't afraid to make noise, get sweaty or claw the shit out of my back," he explains with a sheepish grin. I can tell he is worried about my reaction.

"So are you saying that because I'm a little older my body is different?" I ask with a raised brow.

"Well, I mean…" he pauses.

"BOOO YAAAH, bitches! About time I have something on those 22 year old skanks!" I yell with a laugh.

"Oh my God, I thought you were going to be pissed at me."

"No, I asked you. I had to be prepared for your answer, even if it wasn't the one I wanted."

"So you're OK?"

"HELL YEAH! If I have to have a few wrinkles in order to have mind blowing sex, so be it! It will be my burden to bear," I reply with a giggle.

"You are something else," he says, kissing me.

"Declan?"

"Yeah?"

"Stay," I say quietly.

"On one condition," he replies, looking me straight in the eyes.

"OK." I nod.

"Answer my question from earlier, in the kitchen," he

softly kisses me again.

"Yes."

Round Two! Ding Ding!

Chapter 17

AS SUNLIGHT BREAKS through my bedroom window, I am awakened by the sounds of snoring, and it's not me this time. I open my eyes to see Declan's face on the pillow next to mine, and I smile. What a great way to start my Saturday.

I watch him sleep. Nope, not at all creepy.

I can't believe that I slept with this guy last night and he is waking up in my bed the next morning. OK, well, let's be honest; there wasn't a whole lot of sleeping going on, but you get my drift. Declan was so passionate and caring, it was… amazing. Usually when you have sex with someone for the first time, it can be awkward, nerve wracking, uncomfortable, etc., but last night was just different.

I must have been deep in thought about last night because I didn't notice Declan's eyes on me.

"Good morning, beautiful." His deep voice is scratchy from sleep.

"Good morning, handsome. How did you sleep?"

"Better than I have in I can't even tell you how long."

"You snore." I giggle.

"Hi Pot, I'm Kettle, you're black." He laughs.

"Hey, I told you I snore. I own it."

"Well, Madi, I have a confession to make. I snore too," he says with a smile.

"Noooooooo!" I say with a fake look of shock.

"That's not what you were saying last night." He smirks.

I throw myself on my back, fist the sheets up in my hands and start thrashing my head from side to side. "YES! YES! YEEESSSSSS!"

I stop suddenly and look at Declan, who is wide eyed with a very large grin on his face. "Better?" I smile.

"Hell yeah, that's better! Let's see if I can make you do that again," he says with a raised eyebrow as he rolls over on top of me and kisses me. Morning breath be damned, this man is hot.

After yet another vigorous round of mattress pounding, I finally limp out of the bed to the shower. I leave Declan lying in my bed, clicker in hand. I'm sure ESPN can distract him long enough for me to shower.

Holy hell, my hoo-ha hurts! I had no idea my poor girl could handle so much. I am impressed with her, though—she must have cleared out all the dust, knitting needles and cats to make room for Declan's huge cock. I think I'm going to rename my hoo-ha Timex. She took a licking and kept on ticking.

A few minutes into my shower, I feel that I am not alone. I lean out of the water spray and open my eyes to find him standing behind me. "You look like you needed help washing your back." He grins.

"By all means," I say, handing him my shower puff. He

gently runs the scrubber up and down my back, slowly moving my long hair to one side and kissing the back of my neck. All I can manage is a long moan. The hot water mixed with Declan's hands and lips are amazing. I am standing in a mosaic tile heaven with a 6'7" god.

Although this was very close to my shower porn episode that Claire almost caught me in the middle of, we manage to keep it pretty PG. Stepping out, he grabs a towel and wraps me in it before grabbing one for himself.

"Are you OK?" I ask him.

"Never been better, why?"

"Well, we were both naked with our hands on each other in the shower but nothing happened."

"Madi, sometimes I just want to be with you. We don't have to be having sex. Besides, I think I saw you limping to the shower. Maybe you need a break," he says, laughing.

"Oh my God, I was not limping!" OK, maybe I was.

"Your center of gravity looked off," he replies, still laughing.

"You're an ass!" I grumble, shoving him back on my bed. I climb up next to him and curl up in the crook of his arm and chest. Laughing, we lay together on my bed wrapped in our towels. Snuggled up to each other, we both enjoy the silence as he rubs my back in a soft soothing rhythm.

I hear something very faintly whispered but I can't be sure if I heard what I think I did. Did Declan just whisper, "Can I keep you?" Did he just quote my favorite part of Casper to me?

I don't know what I should do. Should I answer or pretend like I didn't hear him? I don't want to embarrass him or myself—that might not have been what he said. I decide to pretend like I didn't hear it. I don't want to embarrass myself. What if he said "Can I have a tissue?" I would feel like an asshole.

"Are you hungry?" I say instead.

"I could use some coffee. What about you?"

"I could run to Starbucks and grab some. There is one pretty close to here."

"Are you sure? I could go get it, you don't have to," he offers.

"I don't mind. I can be there and back in about 15 minutes. Why don't you stay here and watch something man-ish and I'll run up there." Kissing me, he agrees and tells me what he would like.

I throw on some sweats and a tank top and toss my hair up in a damp ponytail. Running downstairs, I hop in my car and zip to my favorite Starbucks. Walking in, I am overjoyed to find Tiffani with an i working this morning. Well you know what, Tiffani with an i? Not even your bitch personified look can dampen my mood today.

"Hi, can I get a venti iced nonfat light ice chai latte?"

"$4.3…"

"AND…" I say, cutting her off. Clearly she didn't think I was ordering two. Bitch. "And a venti soy Americano with 1 espresso shot and 2 pumps of vanilla." Tiffani with an i rolls her eyes and gives me my total.

"Thanks!" I chirp, dropping a dollar bill in the tip jar. I should probably put it in her G-string, I bet she's more accustomed to getting her tips that way. I retrieve our drinks and head out the door.

As I get back to the house, I am suddenly filled with butterflies. The thought of seeing him again always does this to me. Walking in the house, I shout "Lucy! I'm home!" in my best Ricky Ricardo impression.

I climb the stairs and find him still lying up against the headboard on my bed, still in his towel. It's a lovely sight. I flick off my flip flops and put the drinks on the nightstand as I curl up next to him.

"That was fast."

"Told ya!" I say, smiling.

"So are you excited for your girl's night out tonight?"

"I am, I guess."

"You guess?"

"Well, yeah, I mean… We made these plans a few weeks ago. Savannah was convinced that I needed to go out and—oh God, please don't judge me—'dry hump some hot guy and get drunk'," I say with a mortified look.

"Hahahaha. So is that what you're going to do tonight? Get drunk and dry hump some hot guy?" He smirks.

"Well, we made these plans before you and I had ever…"

"Ever?? Ever what, Madi?" He is still smirking.

"You're enjoying this, aren't you?"

"Immensely." He grins as he takes a slow drink of his coffee.

"OK, so before I met you officially and before we… Yes. I was going to go out tonight and get drunk. But I really never had any intentions of dry humping anyone."

"No?" He takes another slow sip.

"No. I mean, I can cross dry humping off the list. And can we stop saying dry hump?"

"Oh no, Madi. I wouldn't dream of you changing your plans. You go out tonight and dry hump away."

"Oh stop. Declan, these plans were made before I met

you. And, for the record, you are the only one I want to dry hump," I say, reaching up to kiss him. "What about you? Any plans to go to a strip club with your 'bros' and toss a few back, maybe pay some girl's tuition via her panties?"

"Haha. No. I may go hang with some buddies, get a beer. Nothing exciting. Speaking of which, I'm supposed to be meeting some of the guys to play basketball later. I should get going. I need to head home to change and get my gear."

"OK," I say with a pout.

"Can I see you tomorrow?"

"Sure, I would like that. Lunch?"

"Sure, lunch works. Will you text or call me when you get home tonight just so I know you made it home safely?"

"I will," I reply, kissing him.

After several minutes of making out on my bed, we both make our way downstairs. I walk him to his truck and kiss him goodbye.

"Have fun with your bros tonight."

"Thanks. Have fun with your ho's," he says, laughing.

I lean in and kiss him through the window. "I will let you know when I get home."

THE AFTERNOON FLIES by and before I know it it's time to start getting ready. I have managed to dodge several texts from the girls about last night. I told them I would talk to them tonight when we were all together as I didn't want to have to explain it 97 different times.

Taylor, Lynn and Grace have ridden together and

Savannah had Luke drop her off so she wouldn't have to drive. We are all going to go in Taylor's Mercedes SUV. She can fit us all, and since she isn't much of a drinker, we have a DD for the night. Yay Taylor!

I feel so out of place in this short black strapless dress and these ridiculous animal print shoes. But since everyone else is dressed like a whore, I might as well be too. I am pretty proud of myself for wearing it and as much as I hate to toot my own horn (TOOT TOOT), I'm pulling it off.

We all pile into Taylor's SUV we head to GalleryScape, an outdoor complex filled with bars, clubs and stores. On Friday and Saturday nights, the clubs are packed and everyone is dressed to impress. It has everything from a wine bar to a rodeo bar with a mechanical bull, and everything in between.

As we walk into SIXX, one of the upscale dance clubs, I see it's largely filled with 20something year olds.

We approach the bar and the bartender asks what he can get us. I am feeling pretty adventurous, so I tell him to surprise me, just leave it roofie free. He makes us all a vanilla vodka and Coke. Not gonna lie, it tasted exactly like a vanilla Coke, only with an ass kick at the end. It was amazing.

The girls and I find a table in one of the corners and sit for a bit. I am not quite ready to dance just yet. I have a very firm 3/10 rule when it comes to dancing. Three drinks and ten people on the dance floor. The dance floor is pretty busy but I haven't had my third drink yet.

The waitress comes back with a tray full of shots for us.

"Here you go, ladies. Compliments of an admirer."

"Umm, we can't accept these," Grace objects.

"The fuck we can't!" Savannah shouts as she starts to grab them off the tray.

"Vannah, someone could have put something in them. How many times do people come into the ER drugged? Dumbass."

"Don't worry, ladies, I watched the bartender pour them and no one else touched them. The guy just paid for them." the waitress assures us.

"See? It's safe!" Savannah says, taking the rest of them off the tray.

"Who was it?" I ask.

"He told me not to say, just said to tell you ladies to hit the dance floor and have a great night," she shouts as she walks away with a smile.

Taking a glass, we all hold them up in the air together. "To us being hot bitches!" Savannah yells. As a group, we yell "HOT BITCHES!" and down the shot. The music is pumping loudly and I'm feeling that shot already. As JLo's 'Dance and Love' comes on, I decide it's time to dance. Yep, I'm pretty buzzed.

I grab Savannah and Lynn and we head out together to the dance floor. Waving my arms over my head and dancing to the beat of the song, I feel someone come up behind me a little too close. It's pretty crowded, so I don't use my signature accidental elbow to the gut move just yet. I am getting lost in the music when I open my eyes and realize the girls are walking off the dance floor without me. We have a 'no man left behind' policy when we go out and those bitches just left a man behind. Feeling slightly pissed, I take a few steps to follow them when I feel an arm wrap around my waist and pull me back.

OK, time for the elbow to the gut move. Pulling forward as far as possible, I thrust my arm back as hard as I can, making contact with the soft part of the abdomen. I hear a loud "ummphhh." and the arm around me loosens. As I whip around to give this asshole a piece of my mind I see Declan looking down at me, holding his side and smiling.

"Simmer down there, Bruce Lee. What's with the Kung Fu on the dance floor?"

"OH MY GOD!" I yell as I reach out to touch the spot I just nailed him in. "Are you OK? I am SO sorry!"

He laughs. "It's OK, you didn't know it was me. But good to know that you can hold your own," he says with a wink.

"What are you doing here?" I ask with a huge smile.

"My buddies wanted to get a few beers and we ended up here," he yells in my ear.

"I am so happy to see you," I slur in my borderline drunk ass state.

"Madi, are you drunk?" he asks, laughing.

"So close. I think it was that shot I just did," I answer.

"You did a shot? One shot? And you're trashed?" He laughs harder.

"Hey, I had 2 vanilla vodka and Cokes and some dude just bought us all a shot. So there!"

"Wow, you're pretty hard core, Madi." Still laughing. Jerk.

"That shot was strong. It was soooo good, though. Lemony." I smile.

"What was it?"

"I don't know. The drink girlie brought it to us. She said some guy bought them for us and told us to dance and have fun. So we are. I'm very good at following directions." I get the very distinct feeling that Declan is enjoying this drunken sight before him. Damn, he is sexy.

"It was a lemon drop," he says into my ear.

"Let me drop what?" I shout back.

"Hahahaha. No, the shot was a lemon drop. And I'm glad to see you can follow orders." He winks.

"Mr. Hillier, are you winking at me? Are you trying to be sexy? Because I should tell you, it's working. You're very hot. Did you know that? Did you know that you are very hot? And tall? You're very hot and tall." Yep, that shot is definitely hitting me.

"Well you, Ms. Kennedy, are very short and beautiful and clearly a tad buzzed." He laughs. "Hey, I don't want to keep you from girl's night. You go dance and have fun. If ya'll need a ride please call me, OK?"

"Declan, dance with me," I shout in his ear.

"Seriously?"

"Please?" I beg, smiling up at him.

"Alright, but then you'll go back to your girls?"

"OK."

As the song changes to 'Clarity' by Zedd, Declan comes up behind, pressing into me. He wraps his arms around my front and we move to the bass thumping of the song, swaying and grinding together.

He leans down and says in my ear, "you look so fucking hot, Madi, seriously," as he kisses my ear.

"I want to take you home with me," I say.

"Gladly," he answers as he grinds into me.

I turn around and press myself into him. Wrapping my arms around, I pull him down for a kiss. Yep, gross PDA right here on the dance floor of SIXX. Our lips are interlocked and our bodies move as one on the dance floor when Declan suddenly jolts upright and I hear what sounds like a dolphin caught in a net, squealing.

"ARE YOU FUCKING KIDDING ME? ARE YOU SERIOUS? Are you fucking this… this… old lady?"

Chapter 18

WELL, SON OF a bitch, if it isn't Tiffani with an i… right before my drunken eyes.

"Ummm, no one ordered any coffee, but thanks. Run along! OH, and yes, he is," I reply with a shitty smile.

Yep, I'm drunk. I'm surprised my balls fit in this dress.

"What do you want, Tiffani?" he asks as he steps around me, positioning himself between us.

"I can't believe this!" she's screeching again. I throw my hands over my ears and wince. For Christ's sake, it's like when Daryl Hannah tries to talk as a mermaid in Splash. It could peel paint off the walls.

"What business is it of yours, Tiffani with an i? Why the fuck do you care?" I yell, leaning around him.

"It's none of her business. And she's my ex-girlfriend, Madi," he says over his shoulder.

"THE FUCK?" I shout.

Declan approaches her in an effort to avoid a larger scene than the one she's already started to make.

I can see my girls coming up behind Tiffani with an i. Apparently they saw some of commotion.

"None of your business, Tiff," Declan growls to her and turns back around to face me.

"You ARE fucking her! Oh my God! This is why you won't talk to me? THIS?" she says, flicking her hand towards me. "I knew you liked some kinky shit but I never knew you had a grandma complex, Dec!" she yells, crossing her arms with a head swerve.

"What the hell is going on here?" Savannah shouts as her and the girls walk up behind them.

"Fuck off, Tiff," Declan says, turning back to face her. "Move on, go find your next sucker."

I am stunned and don't really know what to say.

That snatch just called me a grandma.

I have half a mind to knit an afghan and choke her the fuck out with it. I'll show you grandma!

"Bitch, I gave you a dollar today!" I say in my slightly overly intoxicated state.

I hear Vannah and the girls bust up behind her.

"I knew that was your coffee order! I knew it! But never in a million years did I think you'd be hooking up with HER. She has a kid, for fuck's sake! Did you know that? She has a KID, Declan!"

Wow, I never knew one could sober up quite so quickly.

"What are you talking about, Tiff? Go the fuck home."

"It's true, Declan, ask her. Go ahead," she puts her hands on her hips and waits with a smug look on her face.

Yep, I'm gonna puke.

"Madi, what is she talking about?" Declan turns and looks at me. I think the look on my face just answered his question.

"It's true? You have a kid?" He looks so confused, and I don't know what to say.

"Listen here, you little fuck tart, you better pump your weave and back off," Savannah says, stepping between Declan and Tiffani with an i.

"You're pathetic!" she shouts as she walks off the dance floor back towards her Pussy Posse.

Ugh. She needed to shave to wear that skirt, and I don't mean her legs.

"Madi, answer me," he says with a hurt look on his face. I don't know what to say, but my blank look and the slight head nod tell him all he needs to know.

Declan turns and walks to his group of friends, downs his beer and heads towards the exit.

I finally regain cognitive thought process and I quickly walk towards the exit to cut him off.

"Declan, wait!" I yell.

He keeps walking, I follow him outside as the girls file out behind me.

"Declan, please!"

He stops abruptly. "Madi? Is it true? Do you have a kid?"

I nod.

"For fuck's sake, you didn't think I should know about that? It's a fucking kid, Madi! It's kind of a big deal."

"She," I say quietly.

"She what?" he shouts angrily.

"She. My daughter. Her name is Claire. She's not a FUCKING KID. She's my daughter," I reply coldly.

"FUUUUUCK!" he shouts and runs his hands over his face. "Anything else you need to tell me?" I can see the intense hurt in his eyes.

I shake my head and look down at the ground as tears begin to fill my eyes.

"Were you trying to hide it?" his tone is filled with pain.

"HER, not IT! And no, I wasn't hiding anything, Declan," I say pleadingly.

"Then why the hell wouldn't you tell me about her, Madi? Jesus Christ!" he asks loudly.

"Declan, I have only known you for 2 weeks. I don't make a habit of introducing her to guys I fuck," Oh shit, I didn't mean to say that.

"Oh, so now I'm just a guy you're fucking. Good to know." He nods, lets out a hurt laugh and walks quickly away.

"Declan, please wait. I didn't mean it like that. Let me explain, please!" I try running after him but can't keep up. Before I know it he is out of my eyesight.

I slump down on a bench outside of a store and start to sob.

The girls are by my side in a heartbeat. I didn't realize they were still there. They must have kept their distance during our fight.

"Oh Madi, I'm so sorry," Lynn says, sitting down next to me and wrapping her arm around me.

"Fuck him!" Vannah spits, rubbing my back.

"Come on, let's get her home," Grace says with a look from Taylor.

They girls help me get up and we make the long walk to the car.

The drive to my place is a quiet one. Sitting in the backseat between Savannah and Grace, I rest my head on Grace's shoulder. Savannah strokes my back. "Are you OK?" Lynn asks as she turns around in the front seat to watch me. I nod between sniffles and sobs.

As we pull up in front of my house the girls walk me inside. All I can manage to do is lay myself down on the couch. Vannah grabs the blanket and covers me with it. "You guys can go. I'll stay here with her tonight and have Luke pick up me up in the morning," Savannah tells everyone.

"Are you sure? I can take you home now," Taylor replies.

"No, it's fine. I don't think she should be alone," Vannah says.

I can only make out the gist of their conversation. I can't get the vision of Declan's face screaming at me out of my head. I never meant to deceive him, but my job as a mother is to protect my daughter. I have never introduced Claire to anyone I have dated, partly because I haven't had a serious relationship since her dad and I split and I certainly wasn't going to introduce her to Nash.

Vannah walks the girls out and locks up the door behind them. "Do you want me to help you up to your room?"

I shake my head no and stare blankly at the wall.

She goes into the kitchen and gets me a glass of water and something for the headache I am sure to have later. After I take the pills and drink some of the water I lay my head down on the couch. My sobbing has stopped but the tears continue to roll freely from my eyes.

"Are you OK, Mads?"

"I can't get his face out of my head, Vannah. He was so mad."

"Well, I mean, it had to be kind of a shock for him. You never told him about Claire?"

I shake my head.

"Why?"

"I have only known him a few weeks. I don't tell just anyone that I have a daughter. If I thought this was going to go someplace I would have told him. But I didn't know…" I start sobbing again.

"You didn't know what?" Savannah asks softly.

"I didn't know that I was going to fall for him. Now he's gone," I say as the sobs rack my body.

"You really like him, don't you?" Vannah asks with a guarded face.

I nod "And I just ruined it," I moan as my sobbing slows.

"I don't think you ruined it, Madi. You just need to give him some time."

"I saw his face, Savannah. It's over," I shake my head and wipe the constant stream of tears from my face.

"Well, would you want to be with someone who didn't love Claire? Or want to be a part of her life?" she asks.

"Absolutely not. We are a package deal."

"Just give him some time. Just keep in mind, though, he thought it was just you, and in a span of about 45 seconds he found out it's you plus one. That had to be surprising."

"I fucked it up, Vannah. I fucked it up. What am I going to do?"

"There's nothing you can do, honey."

"What if he doesn't want to see me again? What if that was it?" I wail.

"Well, sweetie, then it wasn't meant to be," she replies, rubbing my back as I begin to sob again.

"Oh God. I just want to tell him I'm sorry."

"I know, hun," Savannah says with a sad face.

Chapter 19

I TOSS AND turn through a restless night of sleep.

All I could picture was Declan's face, he looked so hurt, so deceived.

I wake up in the morning curled up in a ball on the couch, still in my dress. My head is pounding and my eyes are swollen and still wet from crying.

I leave Vannah sleeping on the other end of the couch and make my way upstairs to shower.

I run the water as hot as I can stand it and climb in. I start to sob all over again as I think about yesterday morning; Declan and I in the shower together. What a difference a day makes. Yesterday I was falling head over heels for this guy, and today he's gone.

Sitting down on the bottom of the tub, I let the water run over me. Maybe I can wash away the look on Declan's face last night. Maybe if the water is hot enough I can rid myself of the sick feeling I have in my stomach. I stay in the shower so long the water begins to run cool.

Getting out, I throw on a pair of red cotton shorts and a white t-shirt.

As I make my way downstairs I can hear Vannah talking, I'm sure she's called Luke to have him come and get her and fill him in on what happened last night. I walk toward the kitchen, as I round the corner, I stop mid-step.

Declan is sitting at the kitchen table with Savannah.

He is wearing the same clothes from last night and looks awful.

As he looks up our eyes meet, I can see the anguish in his eyes.

My eyes begin to fill with tears. I did this to him. What do I say? What do I do? I just stand there and stare at him as the tears run down my cheeks. I'm frozen.

"Well, you two clearly have things to discuss, so I am going to go wait out front for Luke," Savannah says as she gets up from the table. As she heads towards the door, she stops and hugs me. Quietly, she murmurs in my ear. "Just hear him out. Call me later. I love you," kissing my cheek, she walks away and out the front door.

Hearing the door latch, panic sets in.

"Madi, we need to talk," Declan says in a quiet but very serious tone.

I nod.

"Can you please come sit down?" he pushes out the chair next to him.

I walk across my kitchen and suddenly the term 'dead man walking' comes to mind.

"You look like hell," he says as I approach.

All I can do is let out a slight laugh. "So do you,"

I can barely look at him as I bite my upper lip. "Why did

you come?" I ask as I sit down.

"Because, I… I needed to see you and talk to you. The way things went down last night was…"

"A nightmare?" I respond quietly.

"To put it mildly, yes," he says, nodding his head. "So," he lets out a deep sigh "You have a daughter?" he asks in a very matter of fact tone with his arms crossed over his chest.

I nod.

"How old is she?"

"Eight."

"Does she live here with you?"

"Yes." I nod

"How is it that this never came up in conversation, Madi? How do you hide a human being?"

"I never hid her from you Declan, not intentionally."

"So when we were playing 20 questions and sharing interesting facts about ourselves, you never thought to add in 'by the way, I have an 8 year old daughter, please pass the syrup'?"

"It's not that easy, Declan. I didn't tell you because it's my job to protect her."

"What do you mean protect her, Madi? Do you think I would hurt her?" he looks offended.

"No! But you have to understand, as her mother, I have to set an example for her.

I don't have the right not to be selective when it comes to who I expose Claire to.

I have only known you for 2 weeks. I didn't know if this relationship was going anywhere.

I don't want to bring someone around that might not be here in a week or two. I don't want her to get attached to someone and get hurt if it doesn't work out.

My house isn't a revolving door of men," I say as the tears start to fall from my eyes.

"Is that to protect her? Or you?"

I lower my head again and softly say, "both."

He shakes his head and takes a deep breath. "OK, I understand your point. But then, why not mention you have a child? You didn't have to elaborate beyond that, we could have worked up to it. But a heads up would have been nice, and not from my ex-girlfriend in a club," he replies.

"I know, Declan. I am so sorry. I wish I could change what happened, but I can't. I wanted to be the one to tell you, and I was going to, soon. I know you're hurt and I wouldn't blame you if you didn't want to see me again. But Claire is the most important thing in this world to me and I would die to keep her safe," I say solemnly.

"Why do you keep saying that? Keep her safe? Protect her?" he asks "Did something happen to her?" He looks concerned.

"No," I say, shaking my head.

"You? Did something happen to you?" he asks.

"Declan, please," I protest, shaking my head.

"Madi, If you can't be honest with me…"

I cut him off mid-sentence. "I was molested as a child, Declan," I reply, looking up at him. "The moment Claire was born, I vowed I would never let anyone hurt her. Ever. And I mean it when I say I would die protecting her," I blurt.

"Madi, I… I…" he stutters over his words "Oh my God. I had no idea," he says as his eyes well up with tears.

"Declan, don't. Please don't. I didn't tell you to upset you or for your pity. I want you to understand why I am so cautious with Claire and who I bring around her."

"God, Madi..." he says as he kneels in front of me. He takes my hands in his and kisses the tops of them.

"I should have told you about Claire, and I was going to tell you. All of it," I cry, shaking my head.

"Madi, don't. I understand. You did what you felt was right as her mother."

"Then, after Andy betrayed me... I just never wanted anyone to come into our lives and get too close. I keep everyone at arm's length; then I don't have to worry about getting hurt. But then I met you, and... I never meant to deceive you," I say as my tears drop onto our interlocked hands.

Neither of us says anything for several minutes. Then Declan stands up and brings me with him. "Come on."

"You don't have to stay, Declan. It's OK. I understand and wouldn't blame you if you want to go." I wipe my damp eyes.

"Madi, I'm not going anywhere. I just want to talk. Let's go in the other room." He takes me by the hand, walks us into the living room and sits us on the couch facing each other.

"Madi, I am so sorry that you had to go through that." His eyes well up with tears again.

"Declan, please don't cry. I can't handle you crying too." I say with a slight chuckle.

"Who was it?" he asks as anger outlines his face.

"A babysitter's husband. The second my parents found out, it was handled."

"God, I can't imagine what you went through, Madi," he replies, squeezing my hands.

"And I never want you to. Ever. It's in the past, it's over.

Nothing can change what happened." My tears are finally subsiding.

"I wish I could, Madi. God, I wish I could fix it," he says kissing the top of my head.

"But you can't. I handled this all wrong, but I am new to all of this," I admit, waving my hand between us.

"What do you mean?" he asks.

"Dating, Declan. Having feelings for someone. I have only gone out with one other guy since Andy and I split 6 years ago, but Steve and I were very casual, no real relationship. I never had any real feelings for him, so I didn't have to worry about Claire being involved."

"Wow, yeah, wait. I don't really want to hear about your exes," he smiles.

"Oh right, but having Tiffani with an i, the bitchy barista from hell, come up as your ex was delightfully pleasant for me?" I note through a sniffle.

He lets out a slight laugh. "OK, fair enough."

"She hates me, by the way."

"Well yeah, ya think?" he says with a grin. "But there's a reason she is my ex and I have no intention of going back," he adds matter of factly.

We sit in silence for several minutes. I wonder what he is thinking. Is he angry? Is he thinking of a way to leave without looking like an asshole? Is he making his grocery list in his head? I look up at his face and it just breaks me. I have to look away as the tears start to form again.

"I don't want to lose you," I say softly.

"Hey. Madi, look at me."

"I'm sorry, Declan. I fucked this up," I mumble, looking down at my fingers wringing together in my lap.

He places the palm of his hand on the side of my face, using his thumb to wipe away my tears. I lean into his hand. "We're ok, Madi," he murmurs, looking into my eyes.

"I hurt you."

"You didn't hurt me, Madi, I just needed time to process everything that was screamed at me in 60 seconds time," he replies, shaking his head.

"The look on your face, Declan. It was pain. I saw it and I caused it."

"I wasn't hurt about you having a child, it was hearing it the way I did and from the person I did. I was blindsided. I needed some time to think."

"And?" I ask quietly.

"And. I'm here," he says with a sad smile.

"Where did you go?" I ask. He is in the same clothes he was wearing at the club so I assume he didn't go home.

"I went to my brother's, and then I went for a very long drive."

"And that helped?"

"Well, that drive eventually brought me to your doorstep, so, yes," he says with a smirk. "Clark gave me some things to think about. I needed to see you and talk it through. I needed to find out… more," he looks at me and smiles. "And if I heard you correctly, you said that you have feelings for me?" he grins.

"No. No. I didn't," I deny, shaking my head. FUCK! I so did! It slipped out. Panic is setting in.

"Yeah, you kind of did," he says, nodding. "You said that you are new to dating and having feelings for someone. No takesies backsies," he winks.

“Uhh, we aren’t talking about me right now, we are talking about you. Focus,” I reply with a serious face. “What did Clark say?”

“Just… stuff.” he is starting to get shy.

“What’s wrong, Declan? Why won’t you tell me?” I ask, tilting my head toward him. “I mean, I dropped 2 pretty big nuggets on you in the last 12 hours, so I feel like maybe you could even the playing field.”

“He just put things into perspective for me, that’s all. Reminded me that sometimes you have to look at the big picture.”

“Oh.”

We sit on the couch in silence for what seems like an eternity.

“Oh, God. As you would say, just Band-Aid it!” he mumbles to himself. “I’m falling in love with you,” he blurts out.

“You fell and love Band-Aids? What?” I ask, confused.

“Jesus, no,” he says with a laugh. “Madi, I’m falling in love with you. More and more every day.”

“Huh?” My face must be precious at this moment. I’m certain my eyebrows have joined my hairline.

“I. AM. FALLING. IN. LOVE. WITH. YOU,” he uses his hands to imitate sign language.

“Huh?”

“Huh? That’s all you can say?” he laughs.

“Uh, huh?” I say with a smile.

He rolls his eyes at me and smiles from ear to ear. I lean forward, so close our foreheads are touching and we are looking directly into each other’s eyes. “I’m falling in love with you too, Declan. And I’m terrified,” I smile as my eyes fill with happy tears this time.

"I know," he says, lightly kissing me. "Me too."

Chapter 20

WE HOLD EACH other in a tight embrace on the couch, taking quick glances and long stares at each other. I'm relishing this moment with him. An hour and a half ago I thought I would never see him again, and now we just admitted that we are falling for each other.

Maybe that fucktart Tiffani with an i did us a favor. I should send her a note of gratitude, perhaps in a gift basket filled with body glitter, vanilla lotion, antibiotics, herpes cream, and FDS.

"Can I ask you a question?" I ask hesitantly.

"Of course."

"How long were you with Tiffani with an i? Why did you break up? I mean, as much as it physically pains me to say, she is a pretty girl and she's closer to your age."

"We just admitted to each other that we are falling in love and you want to know about my ex? That's odd," he says with a laugh.

"Well, I mean… yeah, it is. I guess I'm just curious.

Why it didn't work out. So I don't make the same mistakes, maybe?" I answer with wide eyes and a shoulder shrug.

"Well, we dated for 2 years on and off, and one day I realized she just wasn't a very nice person and was a gold digger who was only with me because I could buy her things."

"Oh. And that's a problem for you? Cuz I should tell you, I'm only with you for your money."

"Haha, Madi," he says with a smirk. "How did she know you have a daughter?"

"She works at my favorite Starbucks. Claire and I go in a lot. Actually, you were there too."

"I was?" He looks shocked.

"Yep. The morning that I almost scalded you with my tea when I ran into you, Claire was sitting at the table behind you."

"She was?"

"That's her." I point with pride to the pictures on the entertainment center.

"Oh my God, I saw her. I remember she was sitting at the table playing with her doll. She was talking to it and laughing." He smiles at the memory.

"Mmm hmmm, that was my Claire," I say, nodding with pride and a shy smile.

"Madi, she is beautiful. I should have known. She looks exactly like you."

"Thank you. But I do need to tell you something about her." My tone is serious again.

"OK."

"Claire has Tourette's syndrome. Do you know what that is?"

"Like when you yell out cuss words and bark and stuff?" he questions.

"Well, it's very clear to me you have seen Deuce Bigelow," I laugh. "Yes, that is a very extreme and rare form of Tourette's. Claire has a vocal and physical tic form. She clears her throat and coughs repeatedly. After a lot of testing last year, the pediatric neurologist made the diagnosis."

"Is she OK? I mean, does it cause her any pain or problems?"

"No, it's not physically painful for her, but she has been teased at school, and sometimes people move away from us in public. They assume she is sick or get aggravated by the noises. It is what it is." I shrug my shoulders.

"So how do you handle it?" he seems genuinely interested.

"There's nothing to handle. It's just the way it is. Claire knows that she is no different than any other child, she's just a noisy one. And if people make comments or ask why she does it, I tell them the truth. Most people are very understanding once you explain it."

"Jesus, Madi, you are so strong," he says with compassion on his face.

"Not really. I'm a hot mess, or haven't you noticed?" I reply with a smirk. "I have my moments and break down just like anyone else."

"But you do all of this on your own. Do you get any help from her dad?"

"In some ways. He sees her when he can, and when they are together it's always a great time for both of them. He isn't here for the day to day stuff. He's your typical weekend dad—around for the fun but not for real life. I take care of all that."

"But who takes care of you, Madi?" he asks sadly.

"I take care of myself, Declan. I have for years. But I am lucky enough to have an amazing support system with my parents and the girls. They would, and have, done so much for me, I could never ever repay them. I'm very blessed."

Leaning forward, Declan kisses me and says, "I want to take care of you, Madi."

"Declan, you don't have to take care of me. I am a fort… well, we know how old I am, no need to rehash that," I smile.

"I know I don't have to, Madi. I want to," he leans in for another kiss. This one lasts a bit longer.

"Your friends really do love you, ya know," he says, running his fingers through my hair.

"I know this. But why do you say that?"

"Because Savannah told me if I hurt you she was going to cut my balls off," I can't help but burst out laughing.

"Hey, that's not funny. I think she was serious," he pulls back to look at me.

"Oh she absolutely was," I reply, nodding my head and laughing. I lean into his side and run my hand up and down the seam of his jeans while he plays with my hair. "Declan?"

"Yeah?"

"Are you really scared?" I don't have to elaborate, he knows.

"Yeah. You?"

"Yes."

"What are you scared of?" he asks, kissing the top of my head.

"Falling for you… so fast… getting hurt," I can feel the tears approach my eyes again.

"Me too, Madi. I have never felt this way for someone, especially someone I have only known a few weeks."

"So what do we do?"

"What do you mean?" he says with a slight laugh.

"I don't know, Declan. I'm so… I don't know what I am doing. We are so different. Our lives are on totally different planes. I have a child. I go to PTA meetings and drive carpool to cheer and soccer. I have a mortgage and a car payment for a fucking clown car I hate. You're about to start the police academy and live out your dreams. You're 29! You should be out with your bros, tossing back brewskies and checking out girls with tight asses and mile high fake tits, not helping me fold laundry and do math homework because you know what, it's hard!"

"OK. First of all, I need you to take a breath. I don't think you inhaled once during that little rant," he says, rubbing my back. I sit up and face him.

"It's true, Declan. I don't want to hold you back."

"Now you're just pissing me off."

"I'm sorry. I just…"

"You just what? You just want to push me away, right?"

"No," I say quietly.

"Good, because I'm not letting you. Everything in life that's worth having requires work, Madi. Is it going to be easy? No, probably not. But I'm willing to try if you are."

"What about your friends? And Clark? Do they know that I am 10 years older than you? That I have a daughter?"

"As a matter of fact, they do. Next?" he says with a smug look on his face.

"And they didn't give you shit for it?"

"OK, here is the thing, Madi. My friends knew I was interested in someone but they didn't know anything about you. All they knew was that we had been out a couple of times and that I really liked you and wanted to see where things were headed. Last night, when we were at SIXX, we saw ya'll sitting at the table. Two of my buddies told me I should go talk to you and Savannah because you were hot, but then they noticed Savannah's wedding ring. Dave said if I didn't go talk to you then he was going to, and he would have you screaming his name by sunrise," he laughs at the look of shock on my face.

"I ordered the shots and sent them to your table. When you went out to dance, they told me I should make my move, so I did. They had no idea that you were the girl I've been seeing. They just thought you were some hot chick in a club."

"Did you tell them who I was later?"

"Well, not right away, we kind of got interrupted by Tiffani… with an i? Is that what you call her?" he asks, laughing.

"Yes, only because it's socially unacceptable to call her Snatch Von BitchAss."

"Hahahahaha. After everything went down, I told them I was leaving. They assumed it was just because of Tiffani giving me shit for dancing with someone. They didn't know who you were. But I told 'em later. I'm pretty sure if they could have high fived me over the phone they would have," he smiles.

"What about your brother? Does Clark know?"

"Clark has known about you since I told him about your stellar Vanilla Ice remix, that first day I saw you."

I can feel myself turning red from embarrassment. "Why does he know about that? Oh my God," I say, shaking my reddened face.

"Because we were talking and he asked me how things

were going. We talk every few days," he starts to turn a little red himself.

"OK, and…?" I ask with raised eyebrows.

"I told him I saw the cutest girl at the gym and that you had me cracking up. That you were singing 'Ice Ice Baby' at the top of your lungs on the treadmill. I told him that I was going to find a way to meet you."

"Oh," I smile and turn a brighter shade of red.

"He told me it was about time someone made me smile," he says with a shy grin.

"I make you smile?" I ask coyly.

"A lot," he laughs.

"So I take it that Snatch Von BitchAss didn't make you smile?" I say, shaking my head.

"No, not really."

"Then why were you with her?"

"I don't know. We met when I first moved out here, through some mutual friends. Do you really want to hear this?" he questions.

"No. But yes," I laugh.

"Well, Tiffani—excuse me, Snatch Von BitchAss—and I met through some friends. We all hung out here and there. One night she asked me out and I said yes. She was cute, so why not," he says with a shoulder shrug.

"Ugh, I just threw up in my mouth a little," I imitate dry heaves.

"Do you want to hear this or not?"

"Please continue," I say dryly.

"Anyway, she asked me out and I said yes. We had an OK time, but I could see she was going to be a handful. I went out with her a few more times, and somehow it evolved into us dating exclusively. To be honest, I didn't really like her all that much, and I don't know why I stayed with her. She was bossy, rude to my friends, disrespectful to my family, and possessive of me and my time. And she spent my money like she'd hit the lottery. After about 2 years of this on and off, I found out she cheated on me and I caught her trying to steal one of my credit cards."

"The fuck?" I exclaim. "Why did you stay with her for so long if you weren't happy?"

"I think it was you who said 'one day I opened my eyes, and I knew it was over'. She didn't make me happy and I would rather have been alone than be miserable. So I told her to stop calling me and stay away from me or I would press charges for the credit card thing. She pretty much did until a few weeks ago when I ran into her at Starbucks."

"Ran into her? Ooh, you didn't know she worked there?" I ask, surprised.

"No. I didn't know she was capable of work. I didn't realize she was there until after I ordered my drink. It was actually the day I ran into you. Literally," he smiles.

"Wow."

"Yep, and she started blowing up my phone, saying she made a mistake and wanted me back."

"I'm sorry."

"For what? I knew what she was like. I knew I shouldn't have gone out with her. I knew better when Clark warned me and told me he didn't like her or trust her. But we all learn our lessons in our own time."

"That still sucks, though. I don't understand why people have to be like that."

"Well, I once heard from a very wise person that

sometimes we learn from our past relationships. We learn what we deserve and what we don't, and what we will and won't accept in a relationship with someone. And I learned a lot about myself from dating Snatch Von BitchAss," he says with a wink.

"I should copyright that shit!" I say, laughing. "I have to confess something to you, Declan."

"Umm, OK. Are you hiding another kid?"

"Haha. Funny man. No, but that day I fell asleep and you made us breakfast…"

"Yeah?"

"When I woke up in your bed—frickin amazing, by the way—well, when I was coming downstairs I heard you on the phone with someone, and I didn't want to disturb you so I waited at the top of the stairs until I heard you hang up." I look at him wide eyed and innocent.

"Yes. It was her."

"I know," I look down at the couch. "I didn't mean to eavesdrop, but it sounded like a serious conversation and I didn't want to interrupt."

"It's OK. I have nothing to hide from you, Madi."

"Of course I had NO CLUE that SHE was your ex," I say with a full body shiver.

He laughs and pulls me to him. "Come here. I don't want to talk about her anymore. She is the past and this," he kisses me, "this is now, and the future, I hope."

I look up into his heavenly blue eyes and smile. My heart just skipped a beat.

"So you know I am starting the academy Monday, right?"

"I do. Are you excited?" I reply with a smile and a nod.

"I am. It's going to be a lot of work, but I'm looking

forward to it. But I want to talk to you about something. It's gonna be 5 months of training, and it's mostly all during the day when you're home. I'll be home at night when you're at work. We aren't going to get to see each other as much. Are you going to be OK with that?"

"Well, Declan, I see it this way. First, I just found you and I have no intention of letting you go any time soon. Second, I believe a very wise person recently told me that anything in life worth having requires work. And I just so happen to be a workaholic!" I say with a giggle.

"You're nuts, you know that?" He laughs.

"Yes, I am familiar with my work," I reply.

"So you're OK with it? I mean, we'll be able to see each other on weekends and stuff, but that's pretty much it."

"I know, but we can still talk and text when we have time. Besides, Claire starts back to school in a few weeks, so my weeknights will be spent doing homework, cheer, carpool and PTA." Declan starts to laugh.

"What? Why are you laughing?"

"Because I'm dating June Cleaver!" He can barely get it out, he is laughing so hard.

I sit up and face him. "THE HELL YOU ARE!" I shout as I smack him in the chest. "June Cleaver, my ass!" I grumble as I straddle his lap. "I bet June never did this to Ward!"

I slowly tilt my pelvis back and forth, slightly grinding in his lap. I grab the sides of his head, pull it back and kiss him roughly. I can feel him slowly moving back against me as he moans into my mouth.

"Oh, shit!"

"Mmmmm hmmmmm," I moan back as I continue to grind into him. Pressing my breasts into his chest, I release my lips from his and work my way to his ear. I lightly rim the tip of my tongue around his ear and let out a slow and low moan.

"Oh fuck, Madi, you have to stop," he groans.

"Why, Declan?" I reply, increasing my slow hip rotation.

"Oh God, you have to stop. Please…" he says, almost begging. I nibble and suck my way down his neck.

"Oh Jesus, you're gonna make me…"

"Make you what, Declan?" I whisper in his ear as I bite his earlobe.

"Son of a bitch," he grinds out.

"Say it," I whisper again. "Tell me what you're gonna do, Declan." I flick his ear with the warm, wet tip of my tongue.

"You're gonna make me cum," he says as he clinches his eyes shut.

"I know," I quietly moan into his ear.

I can feel him growing beneath me. "Oh, God," he murmurs as his breathing quickens.

"Do it, Declan." I moan into his ear I grind into him at a faster pace. "Cum for me."

"Madi. Oh God, Madi. Don't stop!" he pants.

"Open your eyes, Declan," I tell him.

His breathing picks up pace as he opens his eyes to find me topless on his lap. I continue to grind my pelvis against his, feeling how hard he is through his jeans. I throw my head back and grab my tits right in front of his face.

"Oh, FUCK! I'm cuming!" he cries out, wrapping his arms around me and pulls me into his chest. I work in slow circles, up and down on his lap, as he moans and groans into my breasts.

As he shudders out the last of his orgasm beneath me, my grinding slows against him.

Through labored breath, he says, "Oh my God. You are amazing."

Putting my lips right next to his ear, I softly whisper, "And that's how you leave it to Beaver," I finish with one more deep thrust of my pelvis against him.

As Declan gasps against me, I can feel his body shaking from the laughter that is now escaping him between pants. "Call me June Cleaver again and see what happens next time!" I say with a glare.

"Madigan Kennedy, you are just too fucking much," he pulls me back so we are facing each other and staring into each other's eyes. "I'm tempted to say it again just to see what happens," he smirks.

I clasp my hands together behind his head and pull him toward me, then lean in and lightly touch my lips to his.

"Beaver may not be able to CUM out and play," I whisper against his lips, then lick them.

"Son of a bitch," he groans. I can feel him getting hard again.

I climb off his lap and let him catch his breath. Sitting next to him I gain my composure, but I think I made my point.

As I turn and face him, I see him staring at me with a very large smile on his face. "What?" I ask.

"I'm glad I came today."

I tilt my head. "Seriously?"

"Hahaha. Well, that too, but I mean that I'm glad I came to see you today."

I smile and kiss him. "I am so glad you came back for me. I thought I lost you last night," I admit quietly.

"Madi, I wasn't going to let you go that easily," he says, rubbing my back.

"Can you stay… tonight?" I ask hesitantly.

"I would love to, but, um, I really should go home for a little bit."

"Oh, OK," I reply quickly.

"No, I mean I need to go home and shower and change my pants, cuz, well… you know," he wiggles his eyebrows at me.

"Hahahaha, oh, right." I blush.

"Can I come back in a little bit?"

"Of course." I smile and kiss him.

"But one question before I head out…" he adds.

"Yeah?"

"Given that we have both professed our deep like for each other, does that mean that I may get to meet Claire someday? When you're ready?" he asks hesitantly.

"I would like that." I smile and nuzzle up into him. My heart feels like it just bottomed out in my chest. He wants to meet my Claire.

Chapter 21

AFTER HE LEAVES, I make the mandatory call to Savannah.

"Hello?" she answers hesitantly.

"Hey. Everything's OK," I reply.

"Oh, thank God. I didn't know how I was going to explain to Luke why you were moving in with us," she says, laughing.

"Gee, thanks. I'm not THAT fragile, am I?"

"Well, I wasn't sure last night. You were a hot mess."

"I was devastated last night, Vannah. Jesus. I didn't know what was going to happen."

"I know, honey, last night was rough. So you guys are really OK? Cuz I told him if he hurt you I was going to cut his balls off," she informs me matter of factly.

"Yeah, we are. He told me about that," I laugh. "He said he is falling in love with me!" I squeal like a giddy teenager.

"Well, DUH! Anyone with eyes knows that boy is in deep over you."

"Well, last night I wasn't so sure. I thought I blew it, V."

"You did what you had to do, Madi. We all understand

why you didn't tell him about Claire right away. Did he understand why? Did you tell him?"

"I did. He got really upset. He started to cry, Vannah. It crushed me."

"Well, honey, imagine how he felt hearing something like that happened to you. He says he's falling in love with you, but I think that boy already fell… and hard!"

"I really like him," I say quietly.

"No, you love him, Madi. We can all see it,"

"I think I do. And it scares the shit out of me. What do I do? I've only known him a few weeks!"

"I know, hun, but just take this one step at a time. You don't have to marry the guy tomorrow or anything. Just see where things go."

"I know, you're right."

"God, I never get tired of hearing you say that," Vannah says with a laugh.

"You're such a bitch," I reply, laughing back at her.

"So when are you going to see him again?" she asks.

"Tonight. He left a little bit ago to go home and get some sleep, shower and change. He's coming back later and we are going to cook dinner together."

"I bet you'll be cooking… in your hoo-ha!" she chirps.

"Nice. On that note, I'm going to go. I need to run to the store."

"Alright, well let me know if you need anything."

"Thanks, V. I love you."

"I love you too, Hooker," she says as she hangs up.

After a quick trip to pick up the essentials for tonight I am back home and getting ready. I have a fresh loaf of bread baking in the oven so I quickly run up and take another shower. I dry my long hair, place a few curls at the ends and pull it up into a low loose bun at the nape of my neck. I put on some makeup to accentuate my features, but not too much—we are just cooking dinner at my house, I'm not working the main room at Tassels & Tata's.

I throw on my long black cotton maxi halter dress and some diamond stud earrings. I don't want him to think I am trying too hard, even though it took me an hour to pick this out. Gotta give him the illusion that I just threw this together for a causal night of dining in, right?

I head downstairs to get some things prepared for him. I light candles around the kitchen and family room and put some soft music on the iPod so it's playing throughout the kitchen. About 15 minutes later, Declan rings the doorbell. I take a deep breath and head towards to the door. I can see him through the window and he looks so good. I smile at him.

"Hi," I say as I swing the door open.

"Hey there, beautiful," he replies with a smile. "These are for you." He hands me a beautiful bouquet of lavender, pink and white roses mixed with pink lilies.

"Oh, Declan, they are gorgeous," I say as he leans down to kiss me.

"Something smells amazing."

"I just took the bread out of the oven," I reply as we walk into the kitchen holding hands.

"You baked bread? Like, from scratch? Hell, you really are June Cleaver," he laughs.

"Of course I did. I made it in my tailored dress and pearls too," I say with a grin.

"Aww, hell. I would like to have seen that." He smirks.

"Do I have to repeat my performance from earlier to

prove I'm not June Cleaver?" I ask with my hands on my hips.

"Ma'am, no ma'am," he says, laughing.

"Well then, I say you quit your talking and kiss me." I stand in front of him and wrap my arms around his waist.

"Gladly." Leaning down, he kisses me. Gently taking his hands and placing them on either side of my face, he tilts my head toward him. "You look amazing, Madi."

"Thank you, so do you." Who knew worn jeans and an untucked plaid button up shirt could be so hot. The man definitely makes the clothes in this case.

He puts his hands on my bare shoulders and caresses up and down my arms. "So, what are we making for dinner? Cuz I already know what I want for dessert," he grins.

"I thought we would have stuffed shells, salad and the bread I made. Does that sound OK?"

"It sounds great. What can I help with?" he asks as he kisses me quickly one more time.

"I'll start the shells. Can you cut up the salad?"

We stand side by side in the kitchen as Declan cuts the vegetables for our salad and I get all of the ingredients for the shell filling. I start to mix the filling together in the bowl with my hands. Declan gives me an odd look.

"What? It's the fastest way to do it and then everything is mixed thoroughly," I say with a grin.

"Oh, I know. I was just thinking of things I could do to you right now, knowing you can't use your hands."

He puts the knife down and wipes his hands on a towel. Coming up behind me, he wraps his arms around my waist and kisses his way down my neck toward my shoulder. I tilt my head to the side, giving him easier access to my sensitive spots.

"You smell so good, Madi," he murmurs between kisses. My hands clench in the bowl of filling, causing it to squirt out between my fingers.

"Are you OK?" he asks with a slight laugh between kisses.

"Mmmm hmmmm," is all I can manage.

Declan brings his hands down my sides and begins to slowly lift up my dress. I lean my head back against his chest as my dress makes its way up around my hips. "I really like this dress, Madi," he says quietly in my ear.

"It's recently become a favorite of mine," I mumble.

His hands move around to the front of me and leisurely slide down towards the thin lace of the panties I am wearing. "I really like these too, Madi." He slowly strokes me through the fabric.

"They have recently become a favorite of mine as well," I mumble again. He lets out a low chuckle as he kisses down my neck. He slides his hand into the front of what are now my soaked pink panties. Gently easing his finger between my wet folds, he begins to stroke up and down.

"Oh my God," I say as I grip the edges of the bowl with my cheese covered hands.

"You are so wet," he moans in my ear. He slides his hand out, takes his finger and slides it in his mouth, sucking on it as he goes.

"Oh God, you don't play fair," I say between pants.

"Life isn't fair, Madi," he answers with a smile as he slides his hand back into my now drenched panties.

"Ughmmph," is all I can manage. I can feel my legs getting weak as he continues to slowly glide his finger up and down my clit. With one smooth motion, he slides one finger inside of me, causing me to inhale sharply. Slowly he adds another finger and begins to draw them in and out at a very leisurely pace.

"Declan, please," I whimper.

"Please what, Madi?" he says as he picks up the pace.

"Oh God, please don't stop!"

My hands come out of the bowl, and with a quick shake I rid my hands of as much filling as I can. One hand grips the counter as the other grasps onto Declan's forearm, holding him in place. I throw my head back against him as my legs begin to shake.

"Come on, Madi. Cum for me," he says with a growl as his thrusting continues.

"Declan! Oh God Oh God Oh God!" I start to shudder in his hands. His free arm wraps around my waist to hold me up. My knees go weak and I start to collapse from the intense orgasm ripping through me.

"That's it, Madi," he moans as he sucks on my neck "Give it to me."

I am out of breath and barely able to stand when Declan is finished. He leans over and kisses me passionately as I try and gain my composure and balance.

"That was so hot, Madi," he says with a smile as he kisses me again.

"I… I…" I stutter as I look around the kitchen in my post orgasmic state. After several minutes he stands me upright, straightens my dress back down and keeps his hands nearby for a balance check.

"Are you ok?" he asks with a shit eating grin on his face.

"I… I..,uh huh," I manage to get out. I look around and see his arm is covered with Ricotta cheese and it's all over the counter. Grinning at me, he turns and starts to wash up in the sink. "So what time shall we eat?" he asks nonchalantly.

"Screw dinner. Let's have dessert!" I announce with a smile once I am finally able to speak in complete sentences.

"Hahahaha. No, we need to eat because I plan on doing that again very soon and you're going to need your energy," he says with an evil grin and an eyebrow raise.

"Can we order a pizza? It will be faster. We could just have salad and bread." I might have sounded a bit too eager as I washed all the stuff off my hands.

"Come on. Let's make dinner," he says, kissing me again. "There will be plenty of time for dessert later. I promise." He releases me and grabs the bottle of wine on the counter. He pours us 2 glasses and starts back cutting up the salad.

I go back to mixing the ingredients for the filling. I will never look at Ricotta cheese the same way again.

We continue our work in the kitchen, talking and laughing, drinking our wine and stopping for the occasional kiss. 'I Won't Give Up' by Jason Mraz comes on over the iPod speaker. Without missing a beat, Declan starts to sing along flawlessly with the song.

He doesn't realize that I have stopped what I am doing to watch him. I am frozen, watching this beautiful man in front of me sing. I had no idea he had such an amazing voice. To hear him sing those words after everything he found out about me in the last 24 hours, and he is still here, standing in my kitchen, brings me to tears.

Looking up, he sees me standing across from him, staring at him with tears rolling down my cheeks. "Oh God, Madi! What happened? Are you OK?" he asks as he comes around to my side of the island. "Are you hurt? Did you cut yourself?" He looks so concerned.

"I'm OK," I say through my sniffles.

"What happened? Why are you crying?" he asks sadly.

"Because you didn't give up," I reply with a smile through my tears.

"What are you talking abo…?" Then it dawns on him. "Oh Madi, baby… I told you I wasn't going to." He wraps his arms around me and pulls me tightly to him.

"That was so beautiful. To hear you sing those words after everything that happened in the last 24 hours, Declan, it was so…" I can't even finish my thought. He pulls me tighter to him and kisses the top of my head.

"It's true, Madi. I fight for what I want. I don't give up." Looking down into my watery eyes, he smiles. I am so overcome with emotions that what quietly comes out of my mouth next surprises both of us.

"Declan. I love you." I turn and press my ear against his heart. I can't look up at him. I can hear his heart pounding over the thunderous roar of my own

"Madi, I…"

"It's OK, Declan. I just needed to… it just came out. I'm sorry."

Declan pulls me away from his chest and looks straight into my eyes. "Madi, don't ever apologize for telling me how you feel. Especially for telling me you love me. That is a gift that I will cherish. Please don't ever take that away from me or apologize."

"I'm sorry," I mumble, looking away.

"Can I finish?" he says, turning my face back towards him. I nod and bite the inside of my bottom lip, looking up at his beautiful face.

"I love you too, Madi," he says as his eyes well up. "I've

known it since the other night on the mountain." He smiles. "To hear you say it to me just now… I can't even tell you what that means to me."

We stand there holding each other for what seems like hours but is only minutes. "Hey, are you OK?" he asks.

I can't speak so I just nod my head against his chest. I feel as though everything is… right. Declan just told me he loves me. I knew we were falling for each other from our conversation earlier this morning, but I had no idea that he actually loved me. I don't know what possessed me to say it to him, but I don't regret it. It's true. I do love him. I've known since last night. I was devastated at the thought of losing him. This was a hard and fast fall.

"Declan?"

"Yeah?"

"How did you know? I mean, the other night…"

"The other night, when we were laying on the blanket watching the stars?"

"Mmm hmm."

"When I looked in your eyes, I saw something that night."

"What?"

"A future. Happiness. Love," he says softly.

"You saw all of that in my eyes?"

"I did. I want to be the person you see when you look at me. I want to see life as you do, with such compassion, contentment, joy. Madi, you are one of the funniest people I have ever met. You find the joy and humor in everything. Your smile and your spirit are infectious." His eyes shine with sincerity.

"Declan, I am a hot mess. How can you say that? I cry because it's Tuesday, I'm a dork of epic proportions, I fall off the treadmill and sing off key, for Christ's sake."

"But you get right back up, Madi. Your compassionate heart and love make you an emotional person. You care… deeply. That's one of the things I love about you. Also, the fact that you sing in public when you really shouldn't," he says laughing.

"Hey. I rocked it. Don't hate."

"Well, that performance is what got me to notice you, so yeah, I guess you did rock it. But the fact that you do it—that you fall off treadmills and get up smiling, you spit food on people and always ask if you have a boog—those are things that make you so fun and so different, Madi. You aren't trying to be someone else or what you think someone wants; you're just… you. Madigan Delaney Banks Kennedy, the funny, beautiful, smart, sexy, quirky, horrible singer who is happy lying on a blanket looking at the stars."

"OK, that sounds more like a list of reasons to run for the hills, Declan, not for loving me," I say, smiling.

"To some, yeah. But for me, it's what makes me happy. I have never met anyone who makes me truly happy, Madi, until that night on the mountain. I was watching you. You were so happy and content, it warmed my heart, and the joy on your face… was real. You didn't need a fancy night out, or to be wined and dined, no spa weekend or shopping spree. You were content wearing Chucks and jeans, eating bread and cheese on a blanket… in the dirt… with me."

"I was with you. That's all I wanted. I LOVED watching the stars with you."

"I know, and it was genuine," he says as he leans down to kiss me. "It was the night I knew I loved you."

"I knew I was in trouble when you handed me that box of

Twinkies on our first date." I grin.

"I had you at Twinkies?" he says, laughing.

"Yes, well that and a few other moments clinched it. I knew I was in trouble with the Twinkies. But when you showed up at work with my favorite drink from Starbucks, I knew I was in deep."

"Haha. Why then?" he asks.

"Because you went out of your way to find out something about me, something I liked. You didn't just make an assumption or get what you thought I might like; you wanted to KNOW what I liked. No one has ever done that for me. You… cared… about me."

"I do care about you, Madi. Why wouldn't I want to know the things you like?"

"It's not that. You could have easily asked me, but you didn't. You went back to the Starbucks where Snatch Von BitchAss works and risked running into her again just to talk to Mark and find out what I liked. You took a pretty big leap there. You could have run into… her."

"True, but you're worth it. And I can handle Snatch Von BitchAss," he smiles. "And?"

"And today. When you said you wanted to meet Claire," I reply as tears well up in my eyes. Again!

"I do want to meet her, Madi. She is a part of you. When you're ready, and only when you're ready, I would love the honor of meeting her."

"See? It's shit like that right there that makes me love you," I say laughing, through some shed tears. "Honestly, Declan, I think I have fallen in love with you about 54 times already. You keep finding things to say or do that blow my socks off and make me fall deeper and deeper. I'm afraid I am going to wake up from this amazing dream and you will be gone."

"It's not a dream, Madi. I'm really here and I'm not going anywhere."

We hug and kiss each other several times before Declan finally declares that not only does he love me, but he's hungry. Laughing, we try and salvage what we can from the now wilted salad and slightly soggy shells. I assemble them quickly and throw them in the oven.

Declan puts the salad in the fridge and grabs our glasses of wine. Taking me by the hand, he walks us into the family room and we sit on the couch together. As we listen to the music being piped into the room, he starts to hum along to the song that's playing.

"Declan, how long have you been singing?"

"A while, I guess. Why?"

"Because you are amazing. Any other hidden talents?"

"Well, I also play guitar and was in a band back home with some of my buddies."

"Seriously?"

He laughs. "Yes, seriously."

"Will you sing something for me?"

"Right now?" He looks nervous.

"You don't have to. It's OK."

"No, I mean I would love to. I just don't know what you want me to sing."

"Whatever you want to. Sing 'Ice Ice Baby' for all I care." I giggle.

He almost chokes on his wine when he starts laughing. "Well, as much as I love me some Vanilla Ice, I'm more of a country guy. I do better with ballads and slower songs."

"When you started to sing in the kitchen, it blew me away."

"I didn't even realize I was singing," he says shyly.

I lean my back up against his chest and cozy into him. He starts to hum and before I know it, he is singing again. He wraps his arms around me and sings Garth Brooks' 'To Make You Feel My Love'. Of course my eyes fill with tears; he has such a beautiful voice. I sit silently and relish this moment with him.

When he is done, he kisses the top of my head and whispers, "I think of you when I hear that song."

"You do?" I ask.

He nods with a smile.

"That is the sweetest thing, thank you." I lift my face upward and gently kiss him.

"I heard a song the other day that reminded me of you too, Declan. 'Smack My Bitch Up' by Prodigy."

He bursts out laughing and takes my wine glass out of my hand and sets it on the coffee table. "I'll smack my bitch up!" he says as he pushes me back onto the couch and hovers over me. Lifting my leg and hiking it up over his hip, he smacks my ass. Hard.

"Ooh, now pull my hair and whisper my name," I say, laughing.

"You are a kinky little thing, aren't you?" he grins.

I put an innocent look on my face. "I have no idea what you're talking about. June Cleaver is all about the missionary."

"Ahh, I bet June likes it dirty with Ward," he says with a growl.

"I bet June makes Ward wear a gag ball and chaps."

"Oh my God, now I'm picturing June in a dominatrix

outfit," he replies, laughing.

"Hey, don't judge. You never know what's under those pearls."

"True. They say it's the quiet ones you have to be careful of."

"That's right. Librarians, stripping nuns and nurses are notorious for being kinky fucks," I say with a giggle.

"You know what? It's really hot when you say fuck," he smirks.

THE TIMER IN the kitchen goes off, telling us dinner is ready. Declan climbs off of me and offers me his hand up. Walking into the kitchen with his arms around my waist, we break apart so I can get the shells out of the oven. I show him where the dishes are and he sets the table for me while I get everything else ready.

As we get ready to sit down and enjoy the meal we made together, he walks behind me and pulls my chair out for me. Then he places the napkin in my lap and pushes me in. So chivalrous.

We sit in comfortable silence and eat, stealing glances and smiles back and forth. When we are done, Declan takes the plates from the table and puts then in the sink while I wrap up the leftover food and put it away. He really knows his way around a kitchen. I'm impressed.

Chapter 22

WORKING TOGETHER AND having a great time we clean the kitchen together, laughing and talking as we go along. As we finish up, Norah Jones' 'Come Away With Me' comes on the iPod.

Putting down his towel, Declan walks toward me with a very serious look on his face and takes me by the hand.

He leads me out of the kitchen and past the family room towards the stairs. As we approach the base of the steps, he scoops me up in his arms and carries me up to my bedroom. The look on his face is intense and full of passion.

As he sets me down next to the bed, he looks at me and smiles a sweet smile. He turns me around so my back is to him.

He reaches up and unties the halter straps from my dress, letting them fall around my neck. Kissing the base of my neck and across my shoulders, he takes the pins out of my hair and lets it fall down my back, pushing it over my left shoulder and leaving my back bare.

As he kisses down my back toward the top of my dress, he slowly starts to peel the fabric from my skin, letting it pool at my feet. He turns me around to face him again. I suddenly feel very self-conscious, standing in front of him so exposed. He has seen me naked before, but for some reason it feels different this time.

His face is full of admiration and passion as he gazes at me. "Madi, you are so beautiful."

I blush and turn my head away.

"Please don't look away," he says, turning my chin toward him slowly. "I want to see you, all of you. You're perfect."

"Declan, my body isn't perfect, I've had a baby," I reply nervously.

"Madi, your body is perfect BECAUSE you've had a baby. Your body gave someone life. There is nothing more beautiful than that,." he stands staring at me, slowly looking up every inch of my almost naked body.

Reaching down, he starts to unbutton his shirt, letting it fall behind him. He pulls his undershirt over his head and takes a step toward me.

I am in awe of his body, so defined and chiseled. He gazes down at me as he slowly undoes his jeans. I reach out and slowly help him pull them down.

We are left standing in front of each other almost bare. I am in my pink lace panties and him in his boxers.

Without a spoken word we both reach for our last article of clothing at the same time, shedding them.

Declan takes another step toward me, so close we are almost touching. Reaching out, he runs his hands through my hair, holding my head gently. Slowly he brings his lips to mine and kisses me with such passion I am almost left breathless.

No more words are spoken. We are communicating through touch.

He lifts me up and lays me flat on the bed. As he hovers over my naked body he leans down and begins to kiss me, so softly and with such love. Using his knee, he slowly parts my legs and settles in between them. Propping himself up by his elbows, he kisses my neck and moves his way down to my breasts. Taking one in his mouth, he gently sucks on my nipple. I let out a soft whimper as I start to writhe under him.

He slowly kisses his way down my belly and kisses the few small scars I have from bearing a child. As he kisses each one, he whispers, "beautiful."

Lowering himself further, he settles between my thighs and lightly runs his tongue up my center. I arch beneath him and moan.

Gently sliding his tongue into my folds, he kisses my hardened clit and carefully sucks it in between his lips.

"Declan," I moan his name breathlessly.

He continues his teasing, bringing me to the brink and then stopping. When I can't take it any longer, Declan raises himself up on his knees and positions himself between my parted thighs. He reaches for a condom in his pants pocket and places it on. Slowly he runs his hard cock up and down between my swollen and sensitive pussy.

As he presses the head of his cock against my opening, I inhale a sharp breath. He slowly enters me, causing that breath to escape me. As he pushes himself completely inside me, he lowers himself down and pulses his hips in a slow, passionate rhythm. He looks into my eyes with such love, I know this isn't just sex. Declan is making love to me.

I'm overcome with emotions. He is so beautiful and he loves me.

No words are spoken as our bodies become one. He gazes lovingly at me and smiles as he kisses me.

I can feel myself building again inside but I don't want this moment to end. I feel so cherished, protected and loved.

He continues his slow thrusting, filling me each time. I can feel him building toward his release. As my orgasm comes closer, I know I can't hold off any longer. I begin to tighten around his hard cock and can feel him pulsing inside of me.

Our eye contact never breaks as we both climax together. At the peak of my orgasm, my eyes fill with tears at the amazing man before me, and the beauty of the moment we just shared. As our bodies continue to ripple with the aftershocks of our passion, Declan leans in and kisses me with reverence and love.

Pulling back, he looks into my eyes and smiles softly. "I love you."

"I love you too," I say as a tiny tear runs from my eye and down the side of my face. I can still feel Declan hard inside of me. I wrap my legs around him and pull him down towards me. I don't want to let him go.

"Are you OK?" he asks as he gently pushes my hair from the side of my face.

"I'm perfect," I reply with a dreamy smile.

"Yes, you are," he kisses the corner of my mouth.

"Make love to me again," I beg with wide, hopeful eyes.

"I intend on making love to you every chance I get, Madi," he says, kissing me again.

As the evening draws to a close, the hours fly by. Declan and I make our way downstairs to the dark kitchen, wrapped in sheets. "Declan?" I ask, standing in a beam of moonlight coming through the window.

"Yeah?"

"I know you can't stay tonight because you're starting the academy tomorrow, but can you stay a little bit longer?" I ask hesitantly, taking a step toward him. "I know that I'm not really going to get to see you much during the week now and…"

"Madi, stop," he says softly. I stop walking and immediately go silent.

"You look so beautiful right now. Please don't move," he says, taking a few steps closer to me. "I want to remember this sight. The light behind you… you wrapped in that sheet. You look like an angel."

He smiles. In the dark kitchen, I can feel myself blush as I look down at the floor. As he takes another few steps closer I am suddenly nervous.

"Dance with me?" he asks.

"Here? Now? There isn't any music."

"Yes there is. Listen." He takes me in his arms.

As we slowly start to sway, Declan begins to softly sing. I can't quite make out the lyrics, but it doesn't matter, I am lost in the moment. He finishes his song but we continue to dance together in the silence. I don't want to break our contact because I know he will have to leave soon. I want to savor this moment with him.

"Madi?"

"Hmmmm?" I say with my head pressed against his chest.

"I was hoping you would ask me to stay tonight. I brought a bag of clothes for tomorrow. I left them in the truck." He leans down and kisses the top of my head.

Jolting my face up towards his, I let out a squeal that would rival a 13 year old girl seeing Justin Bieber. I leap into his arms and wrap my legs around him.

"You did?"

"Yeah," he replies, laughing.

"Well then I say we… well, you… go get your bag and hurry back in."

"Yes, ma'am," he says as he kisses me.

"Hey, you have a nice view from up here!" I say, looking around the kitchen.

"I sure do." He wiggles his eyebrows, looking down at my half naked body before putting me down.

Declan wraps the sheet around him more tightly and heads out to his truck to grab his bag. He seems to be taking a bit longer than I would have thought. As he comes back inside, he's laughing.

"What's so funny?"

"I just met one of your neighbors."

"YOU WHAT?" I shriek.

"Hehe. One of your neighbors was out walking his dog. We chatted." He takes the bottle of water I hand him.

"Seriously? This shit only happens to me. Was it a guy with a small white mop-ish looking dog?"

"Yep. I believe his name is Allen." He smiles smugly.

"And what did you and Allen talk about?"

"Just that it was a lovely night out, not too hot. Perfect sheet weather." He laughs.

"Oh my God. He is going to tell all the neighbors I'm some sort of whore who has men roaming the streets at midnight in a toga. Ugh."

"It's all good, Madi. I introduced myself and told him he

would be seeing more of me around—clothed, of course. I told him that I'm your boyfriend."

"Oh. Boyfriend. I like that part. Say it again," I plead as I wrap my arms around his waist.

"Boy. Friend," he slowly enunciates.

"That's like ear porn right there. It gives me chills," I laugh.

"I'll give you chills," he replies as he lifts me up into his arms and walks us toward the stairs.

Taking me upstairs, Declan lays me on the bed and climbs in next to me. As we curl up in each other's arms, I feel so content and happy. We lay awake for hours, talking, and before I know it it's almost 2:30 in the morning. Declan has to report to the Academy at 8am. We finally nod off, snuggled together.

When the alarm on his cell phone goes off at 7:00, he quietly sneaks out of bed and jumps in the shower. When he finishes getting ready, he comes back up to the bedroom and leaves one of the pink flowers that he brought last night on the pillow next to me with a note attached.

M,

I didn't want to wake you, you look so beautiful.

I will call you tonight to let you know how the first day went.

I'll be thinking about you.

XO,

D

P.S—Yep, you snore!

P.S.S—I love you.

When I wake and find the note on the pillow—well, more accurately, under the right side of my face—I am sad to see that I missed seeing him off. I read the note again and again before I finally roll over and go back to sleep. Apparently, copious amounts of sex can wear you out. Who knew! I hope Declan does OK today and isn't too tired. I will feel horrible if he doesn't do well because he didn't get enough sleep.

Around 10am I finally drag myself out of bed and take a long hot shower. I find another note on the kitchen counter with a Starbucks gift card.

Go have coffee with the girls, on me.
XO,
D

Well, he doesn't have to tell me twice. I have so much to tell them. I send out a message to Savannah, Elise, Grace, Lynn and Taylor.

Chapter 23

-GIRLS, STARBUCKS 11AM?? Who's in? Declan's treat! Woot Woot!-

Grace: *I'm in!*

Vannah: *I'm there*

Taylor: *I work for a living, slacker! Have fun*

Elise: *Count me in.*

Lynn: *Coffee + the girls = I'M THERE*

As I pull into the Starbucks, I am suddenly filled with panic. In my post euphoric state, I forgot that Snatch Von BitchAss works here. I may need to find another Starbucks. Ugh.

I see that Grace's and Lynn's cars are already here. I walk

in to find them sitting at a table talking. I look around to see if she is here. No sign of her yet. Phew.

"Hey girlies! How are you?" I call out. Vannah is walking in the door behind me.

"HOOKERS!" she shouts across the store. I'm sure the mother to the toddler appreciated it based on the look she gave Savannah.

"Oh, my bad. Sorry," she says with a shoulder shrug to the woman.

"Hey, have you guys seen Tiffani with an i?" I ask.

"No, not yet," Grace replies.

"We better not, either. I will cut a bitch if I see her," Vannah pipes up.

"I am so pissed at what that asshole did the other night. I swear to God I wanted to kick her ass," Lynn adds. As we are talking, Elise walks in. We are so excited to see her, we never get to hang out anymore.

"Hey! OK, who are we kicking the ass of and why? I mean, I'm down, I just wanna know the severity of said ass kicking that we are planning."

"Let's go get our drinks and I will fill you all in," I reply with a grin.

"Madi got laid," Savannah says bluntly.

"Jesus, V. Shut up."

"It's true. Look at her. It's written all over your face. You don't have a poker face, Madi, or even a 'poke her' face, for that matter." She is so pleased with herself.

As we start to gather back at the table with our drinks, I see Mark come out from the back. "Hey, ladies, how are you doing today?" he asks.

"Great/Good/Fine Thanks/Awesome!" We all answer

our own sentiment in unison. "How are you?" I ask him.

"Pretty good, aside from people strolling in late," he says as he motions toward the door.

The only person that could make me simultaneously vomit in my mouth and want to commit heinous acts of violence at the same time is walking in.

"Uh oh. Problem child, is she?" Grace asks.

"To say the least," he answers. "She's always late, on her phone texting, or being rude to the customers. I think she might be on her way out. I just have to get enough documentation to cover my ass. She looks like the type to cause trouble if she got fired."

"Oh you have no idea," Lynn pipes up.

As Tiffani with an i walks past the table, she smiles and puts on her plastic happy face. "Hello Mark, sorry I'm late," she says as she scowls at me. Seeing the look she gave me, Mark raises his eyebrows.

"Umm, what was that?"

"She hates Madi," Savannah blurts out.

"Vannah!"

"Well, it's true, Madi. Jesus, we all witnessed it."

"What happened? Did she do something here that I need to know about?"

"No, Mark. It was at a club the other night. She was just causing some trouble, but it's over." I smile.

"OK, if you're sure. Well, if you guys need anything you let me know."

"Will do. Thanks, Mark."

"Yeah, I wouldn't ask her for anything. She'd poison you just for spite," Grace interjects.

"She'll get what's coming to her," Savannah says with an

evil grin. I'm a little scared myself and it wasn't even directed at me.

"What the hell did I miss?" Elise asks. We sit down and Savannah gives her the Cliff's Notes version of the past few weeks.

"Madi saw Declan. Declan is HOT. Madi made an ass out of herself in front of Declan. Several times. Declan is Madi's personal trainer. Declan and Madi went out for breakfast. Declan is 30. Madi is not. Declan asked Madi out for a real date. Madi and Declan played slap and tickle. Declan and Madi went on another date. Declan and Madi like each other. We went clubbing. Tiffani with an i saw Madi and Declan at the club together. Tiffani with an i is Declan's ex-girlfriend. Tiffani with an i freaked the fuck out and told Declan about Claire. Madi had not. Declan took off upset. Madi was sad. Declan showed up at Madi's to talk. Declan and Madi made up. Madi and Declan played slap and tickle again. Declan and Madi are OK now and are dating.

"There, I think I filled her in," Vannah finishes, slightly out of breath.

"Declan and Madi said they loved each other," I add quietly.

A very loud, collective "WHAT!" comes from all the girls at the table. I smile as they crowd around me for the third degree.

As I fill them in on the basics of our confessions, I couldn't help but notice that Tiffani with an i is at the counter watching us. Apparently Grace noticed too, because she felt this was the perfect moment to aim her sights and fire.

"OH MY GOD, MADI! DECLAN TOLD YOU HE LOVED YOU? I AM SO HAPPY FOR YOU TWO!"

The very loud clatter of something breakable hitting the floor comes from the counter, quickly followed by the feeling of hot iron pokers being seared into my flesh from behind.

"Mark, I need to take a break." I hear her walk around from behind the counter.

"Tiffani, you just got here," he says, more than a little pissed.

"I know. It's personal. I'll be back." She walks outside and promptly picks up her cell phone.

"Ooh, BURN!" Savannah says.

"Burn? What is this, 1985?" Grace remarks.

I feel sick. Did she poison me? Oh no, wait, she wasn't here when I ordered. "I don't have a good feeling about this," I say to the girls.

"Nothing is going to happen, Madi. It will be OK," Elise reassures me.

"Yeah, we'll kick her ass if she does anything," Savannah chimes in.

"Well, the good news is that she has no more ammo on me. She already dropped the big bomb for me," I reply with a shoulder shrug. "I guess you're right."

She comes back in a few minutes later, looking more pissed than when she left. Her eyes are red like she's been crying. She couldn't have been crying, though—harpy shrews don't have souls, and to feel emotion you must have one, so clearly this is a bad case of allergies.

As Tiffani with an i walks past our table, the look she gives me is a bit frightening. I am not a confrontational person by any means, but there is something about her that makes me want to claw her face off and feed it to my dogs.

"Maybe we should go. I have things to get done before I

work tomorrow night." I have a very uneasy feeling. Did she just go outside to call Declan? I'm sure he didn't answer since he's busy with orientation for the academy right now, but I doubt she knows that. Did she call her Pussy Posse to come to Starbucks and shank us in the parking lot?

As we get up and make our way to the door, I can feel her watching me with her dagger eyes. A sudden burst of confidence and balls the size of grapefruits grabs me. I stop in the doorway, turn and lock eyes with her, and slowly mouth the words 'He loves ME' with the added smug smile.

As I turn back around to walk out, I throw my hand straight up in the air, high overhead, and give Tiffani with an i the one fingered salute. Yep, she's number one in my book! I am deafened by the loud screeches and hoots from the girls who are cracking up as we walk to our cars. "Madi, I have never been more proud to call you my friend," Savannah says as she embraces me in a tight, awkward hug.

As I make my way to my car I feel sick again. Maybe I shouldn't have pushed her buttons. There is something about Snatch Von BitchAss that bothers me.

Aside from being Declan's ex, she gives me a bad vibe. Maybe I should start my car remotely and have someone taste test my food. Andy, perhaps?

My drive home is filled with thoughts of different ways I can surprise Declan. I'm not going to get to see him much this week with his orientation at the academy and me working the next few days. When I get home, I have a message on my voicemail from my dad.

"Hey, Kiddo, Mom and I wanted to know if we could stay at the cabin a few extra days with Claire. Someone bought the place down the road and they have 2 little girls about Claire's age. She's been having a blast playing with them and wants to stay a few more days. Give us a call and let us know if it's OK. If not, well, too bad. We want to stay a few more days. (He laughs.) We love you. Bye." I love that my dad still calls me kiddo even though I'm 40. It makes me smile.

I call my dad back and let him know it's fine if they stay longer. I wish I had gotten to talk to Claire but she was out for a nature walk with my mom. He promises to have her call me tonight.

Claire loves going to the cabin and spending time with my parents. This will give me the weekend to figure out what I am going to do about introducing Claire and Declan to each other.

Claire has no delusions about Andy and me. She knows that we loved each other once but were better as friends. We split when she was so young, she doesn't remember us together. I wish I shared that same ability. However, the thought of introducing them is terrifying for me. What if she doesn't like him? What if they don't get along? What if they do? Right, OK, those are the calming thoughts I need.

After pacing around the house like a caged, bored jungle cat, I decide to call Savannah and see if she wants to go to the mall. I'm in the mood to shop. This should be a red flag for me. This is where my 'Danger! Danger! Will Robinson' alarm should sound, but it doesn't. Instead, my Amex lets a soft whimper escape—it knows it's going to hurt.

90 minutes later Savannah, Lynn and I are at the mall, bouncing from store to store.

"So, what do you guys think? Should I buy some hot lingerie and surprise Declan Saturday morning with breakfast, wearing it?"

"Ooh, hell yeah!" Savannah says. "Men love slutty lingerie, I should know." She laughs. Sudden flashes of her as a stripper go through my head. Ugh. Run away! I love her, but the thought of her booty popping in some old guy's face wearing a school girl outfit gives me the dry heaves.

We head into a rather racy lingerie store and flip through the racks. Lynn busts out laughing and holds up an outfit. "Holy hell, Madi! I found it!"

Lynn lifts up what I believe is supposed to be an inmate costume of the slutty variety. It appears to be a black and white striped G-string with an inmate number of 696969 stamped across the front of the tiny panel, and a push up bra that says "Department of Erections" on one side.

"OH MY GOD! You HAVE to get it!" Savannah screams and rips it from Lynn's hands. Running up the counter she throws it down and tells the lady to ring it up.

"Savannah, I was thinking something more like this," I say, holding up a black bustier with garter belts. "You know, sexy with a hint of slutty," I smile.

"OK, well, you can buy that crap if you want, but this is going home with you today, even if I have to pay for it."

"You are not buying me lingerie, Vannah," I roll my eyes.

"Bitch, please. I have no problem buying you sex clothes. I look at this as my version of 'Big Brothers Big Sisters'. You know, mentoring those who need it. I am your slutty big sister." she busts out laughing. "I shall mentor you in the art of being a sex kitten."

"Kitten? Isn't the accurate term for me Cougar?" I gag.

"Eww. Ick. No. You are so not a cougar, Madi," Lynn replies.

"Hells no, you're not a cougar. A cougar is some overly

tanned, fake boob, long glitter nails, bedazzled in jewelry, wearing sweats with the word JUICY across the ass, 3 inches of makeup to hide the fact that she has skin like an alligator, carrying some huge leather purse that has a large sparkly cross on it. And her name is like Vicki or something. And she sounds like she smokes 5 packs a day. That's a cougar."

"Wow. That is oddly specific, Savannah," I say with a laugh.

"Oh, and she lives in Boca! You... well... you're not a cougar. You're more of a... sexy, pygmy marmoset," she says with a sincere smile.

"The fuck? I am not a pygmy marmoset, you asshole."

"Haha. Hear me out. You're cute and little, like a pygmy marmoset. Have you seen one of those things? Landon was learning about them at school and first thing I thought of was you. Those things are so frickin adorable. They look sweet, like you."

"Could have been worse. She could have called you a sexy sloth," Lynn says, laughing.

"You're a dick," I huff. I storm up to the checkout, throwing the black lace bustier on the counter along with some crotchless panties. I'll show YOU sexy pigmy marmoset. "Throw that in too!" I snap, pointing to the Department Of Erections outfit.

"Hell yeah! Madi is joining the PENILE system!" Savannah shouts.

"SHUT UP!" I whip my head around at the two bitches standing behind me.

As I sulk out of the store, we decide to hit a few more places before we go our separate ways.

I choose a few new tops and a pair of insanely cute but

ridiculously expensive jeans. We have spent most of the afternoon walking around the mall, laughing and talking. I forgot how much fun it can be to just shop with your girlfriends. No children having to pee, needing food or water, or anything. Jesus, they are so needy. Feed me, Mommy! I need water! Blah Blah Blah. GHAW! You ate yesterday, psssh!

When I look at my watch, I see it's getting close to 5. Declan should be headed home soon. I can't wait to hear all about his first day. The girls and I say our goodbyes and head to our cars.

On my drive home, Declan calls me.

"Hello?"

"Hey there, beautiful. How are you?"

"Better now. How are you? How was your orientation?"

"Better now? What happened? Are you OK?"

"I'm fine. I just missed talking to you today. I didn't get to say goodbye this morning and wish you luck."

"I'm sorry, but you looked so cute all snuggled up, I didn't want to wake you."

"You're very sweet to me," I say, smiling. "So how was it?" I ask again.

"Awesome. It's going to be tough, but I'm excited to get started."

"So what did you learn today?"

"Learn?" he laughs. "Nothing today. We just did all our paperwork, took our physicals, did assessments, and went over all the academy rules. Pretty boring, actually. Tomorrow starts some of the fun."

"That's so exciting. I'm so proud of you," I reply with a big smile.

"Thanks, baby. That means a lot to me," I know he's grinning.

"Well, it's true! You are making your dream come true. Not everyone can say that."

"Well, I am definitely living the dream right now."

"I'm sorry I kept you up so late last night. Were you OK today?"

"Don't apologize, I'm a big boy. I could have gone to sleep, but I couldn't pass up lying with you and talking all night. That was… what do you say? Amazeballs?" he laughs.

"It was amazeballs, wasn't it?" I laugh.

"But I am pretty beat. I'm going to go home, take a shower, call my mom, eat something and go to bed. Tomorrow we start at it pretty hard core."

"I'll miss you," I say quietly.

"Oh, baby. I'll miss you too."

"Well you be safe driving home and get some rest, OK?"

"I will. Can I call you tomorrow? You're working, right?"

"Of course you can. Yeah, I work the next 3 days."

"OK, I will call you tomorrow before you leave for work."

"OK. Deal."

"Madi?"

"Yeah?"

"I love you." I can hear him grin.

"I love you, too." It feels so natural to say it to him.

"Bye, baby."

"Bye."

WHEN I GET home, I bring my naughty lingerie out and decide to actually try it on. I was too pissed in the store to do it. I walk out of my bathroom in the slutty inmate get up and immediately start laughing at the sight before me. I look ridiculous, but I get why guys like this crap. It has done wonders for my boobs. I think it's the vertical stripes. They make objects look larger than they are.

Next, I put on the black lace corset and thigh highs with the garter belts. WOW—I thought that other thing made my boobs look big. I look like a porn star in this thing. My tits look awesome! I may never take this off. I may wear it under my scrubs tomorrow night. Damn!

I put everything away and decide to wear the black one on Saturday morning when I surprise Declan at his place with breakfast.

Tuesday morning rolls around and I decide to go to the gym. I haven't been in a few days. Taylor is going to kill me. When I walk in I hear the scoff come from behind the counter.

"Well, well, well. Look what the smitten kitten drug in," she smiles.

"Good morning, my friend."

"You certainly look better than you did the last time I saw you," she smiles wider.

"Yeah, things are good now."

"So I hear. Savannah filled me in. So everything is OK? He knows all about Claire?"

"Yep, we talked it all out the next morning."

"And apparently you both admitted you love each other?" she asks with raised brows.

"Yeah," I say with a big smile.

"I'm happy for you guys. I think you're going to be good for each other."

"You do? I didn't think you would."

"Why? You know I love you and just want you to be happy. Why wouldn't I want you guys together?"

"I don't know. You're always so rational. I would have thought you wouldn't think a guy 10 years younger than me would be good. And telling each other we love one another so soon… I just…"

"You just nothing. I don't believe love has a time line. When I met Garrett, I knew on our first date that I was going to marry him. Declan is a good guy, Madi, and I knew from day one he was head over heels for you."

"You did?"

"Yeah, it was SO obvious. He kept asking me all kinds of questions about you that day you got busted singing. I knew he liked you."

"How?"

"Well, he wasn't asking me to sign you up for a record contract now, was he? Why else would he ask? He wanted to get to know you."

"What else did he ask?" I ask a little too giddily.

"Just the basics. What your name was, if you were married, how well I knew you. I told him your name was Madi, that you were married once but were single and that I knew you all too well," she replies with a laugh.

"Oh."

"After your little tumble that day, he seemed worried about you and kept asking me if I had heard from you, if you were OK."

"He did?" I'm shocked.

"Yep. Then, when I blackmailed you into training, he saw your name on the PT list and asked if he could be your trainer. Who am I to stand in the way of budding young love?" She grins and bats her eyelashes.

"I knew it! I knew you blackmailed me into it for a reason."

"I was going to pair you guys up together anyway just to see what happened, but when he asked I ran with it. And now look!" She clasps her well-manicured hands together. "Listen, when I saw the way he looked at you that day you were singing, I knew there was something there. Most of us were covering our ears or turning the volume up on our headphones, but he didn't. He just stopped what he was doing and watched you. That's not normal. I got a feeling in my gut, like I did when I knew that Garrett was the one. I knew you guys would be good together."

"Well, I guess I need to thank you then."

"No, no thanks necessary. I didn't really do anything. Declan beat me to it by asking if he could be your trainer. I just bought the gym that brought you two together," she winks.

"Thank you for buying a gym, getting hit in the head and coming into the ER for stitches so we could meet and become friends, and then talking me into joining your gym so I could meet Declan," I say, laughing as I hug her.

"It was nothing, really," she shrugs.

I decide to walk on the treadmill I was using when I got caught singing, reflecting on where it all happened. I send Declan a quick text message for him to see when he gets out of training tonight.

-I hope U had a gr8 day 2day. I luv and miss U. XO-

He will love that, talking bingo to him.

Heading back home an hour later, I take a quick nap before work. When I wake up, I feel refreshed and start to get ready for my very long evening ahead. My bright side is that I should be getting a call from Declan soon.

As I am finishing my hair and makeup, the phone rings. Oh, that must be Declan. I run and grab the phone but it says Unknown Caller. I choose not to answer it. A minute later it tells me I have a voicemail.

"You better watch your back, you little cunt." And the line disconnects.

In shock, I hang up and put the phone down. It had to be Tiffani with an i. She is the only person who would have it out for me. But how did she get my number? It didn't sound like her, though; there were no harpy shrew tones. It was a deeper voice. Maybe one of her friends. I'm not worried about my safety, but as a mother my first thought is for Claire. I'm so glad she is at my parents' cabin.

A few minutes later the phone rings and I jump. It's Declan. Thank God.

"Hello?"

"Hey, baby. How are you?"

"I'm OK. How are you?" I reply.

"I'm great. Are you OK? You don't sound right," Declan asks, concerned.

"I'm fine," I answer, trying not to freak out.

"Madi, talk to me. What's going on?"

"Nothing, I just got a weird phone call. Everything is fine," I say, trying to calm him.

"What kind of call?"

"Just a strange message. It's OK. So, tell me about your day?" I ask, overly chipper.

His tone is different. I can tell he's worried, but he doesn't want me to know about it. "It was great. How was yours?"

"It was good. I went to the gym and walked on the treadmill."

"You didn't sing or fall, did you?" I can hear him laughing.

"NO. I was actually walking on the same treadmill that I was on the day you caught me singing. I sent you a text while I was there. Didn't you get it?"

"No. When did you send it?"

"Earlier. No big deal. Maybe the reception was bad in the gym."

"What did it say?"

"Just that I hope you had a good day and that I loved and missed you. But I typed it in Declan Bingo," I giggle

"Declan Bingo? Is that like Pig Latin?" he chuckles.

"Something like that."

"Madi, you don't sound right. What's going on?"

"Nothing. I'm fine, Declan. I just miss you."

"I know, baby, I miss you too. When is Claire coming back from your parents' cabin?"

"I'm not sure yet, maybe early next week. Why?"

"I want to see you this weekend. How about Saturday afternoon? Maybe we can go for a ride on my bike and have lunch?"

"I would love that!"

"OK. Well, I know you have to get ready for work. I'm going to go home and shower and study."

"Alright, well you have fun with that," I say, laughing.

"I hope you have a wonderful night, Madi."

"Thank you, I will. I got to talk to you so I'm good. I love you."

"I love you too, baby. Talk to you tomorrow?"

"Absolutely. And Declan, be careful, OK?"

"I will, Madi. I love you," I can still hear the questioning tone in his voice.

"Love you too."

Chapter 24

PULLING INTO WORK, I am suddenly sick to my stomach. What if that was Tiffani with an i or one of her cronies? If they got my cell number, they could easily find out where I work or live.

As I walk through the parking lot, I feel vulnerable and fight the urge to constantly look over my shoulder. Once I'm safely inside the hospital, I relax.

I shouldn't read too much into it, right? It was an idle threat by a bimbo. I'm sure she can't even spell the word idle.

The night goes by pretty quickly with the usual less than glamorous tasks we nurses do—wiping noses and asses, cleaning off blood and God knows what else from people. But I do love my job. When the morning comes, I hear my phone beep in my pocket. It's a text from Declan.

-Just wanted to tell U I <3 U XO—

I reply.—*I <3 U 2. XO XO XO—*

Several seconds later, the text is returned undeliverable. That's odd. Maybe the satellite is having issues. I'll send it again later.

When 7am comes around and shift change is complete, Savannah and I walk out together to our cars. She notices that I am leery as we walk out.

"What's wrong with you? Why are you constantly looking around?" she asks.

"Nothing."

"Bullshit. What's going on?" she stops walking.

"It's nothing, Vannah. Let's just go."

"Madi, who is following you?"

"No one. OK, listen. Please don't say anything to the other girls, but last night I got a strange message on my phone." I pull out my cell and play the message for Savannah.

"Who was that? Was that Snatch VonB?" she asks with a shocked look.

"I don't know. It doesn't sound like her, but I can't think of anyone else who would say that to me."

"Does Declan know?"

"NO! And I don't want him to. He doesn't need to worry, he's got a lot going on right now. I'm sure everything is fine. I'm just being paranoid. I don't want Declan to freak out. He needs to concentrate on training."

"Madi, you need to tell him," Savannah urges as we start walking again.

"I will. Maybe this weekend. I'm going to surprise him Saturday morning with breakfast, and then he wants to go for a ride on the bike and have lunch."

"OK, but promise me you'll tell him."

"I will. I promise," I say with a weak smile.

When I get home, I pull into the garage and let out a sigh of relief. I feel safe in my home. Between the alarm system and the two hounds from hell, I'm good.

I run upstairs, take a shower and throw on a t-shirt and panties. I'm not really hungry this morning so I decide to head to bed. Climbing into bed, I hit retry on the text message to Declan, and it still doesn't go through. That's odd. I will have to ask him when I talk to him later tonight. I drift off to sleep a short time later.

When I wake up, its 4:00 in the afternoon. I don't usually sleep that long. I must have been tired today.

Being paranoid will do that to a person.

I head down to the kitchen and pull out some of the leftover shells Declan and I made the other night. Suddenly, I am hungry for more than food. Insert evil horny laugh here. Boy, he is in for it Saturday morning when I see him. Now that my hoo-ha has been awakened, she is like a hungry bear after hibernation.

I quickly eat and run upstairs to get ready. Throwing on my signature black scrubs, I pull my hair up into a high ponytail and put on my makeup. I head to my jewelry tray and put on my earrings and watch. I try to keep my accessories to a minimum at work and usually just wear the diamond stud earrings the girls bought me for my 40th birthday and the watch my parents bought for me when I graduated from nursing school. I have seen one too many nurses have an earring ripped out by a flailing patient. No thanks.

I am sentimental when it comes to jewelry; I don't wear a lot of it, unless the occasion calls for it. The pieces I do wear on a daily basis mean something to me and were given to me by someone I love.

I head back down stairs and hear my phone ringing. Right on time. Declan is calling as soon as he leaves the academy.

"Hey there, hot stuff," I answer.

"Well hey there yourself. How are you today?" he asks.

"I'm good. How was your day?"

"Great, now that I'm talking to you. You must have been busy this morning at work."

"No, not really. Why?"

"Oh, ok. Just surprised I didn't hear back from ya."

"I replied but it came back, maybe the network was having an issue," I shrug to myself.

"Maybe. I'm excited for Saturday," he adds.

"Me too. I can't wait to see you."

"Oh, baby, me too. I miss you."

"I miss you, too. I need a Declan hug," I say, giggling.

"What's a Declan hug?" he asks with a slight laugh.

"I don't know. Just the way you look down at me, then wrap your arms around and pull me into you so we are touching so closely. It's nice." I can hear him smile and chuckle.

"You give good hug," I add.

"I give good hug?"

"Yeah, you kind of do."

"Well, be prepared for a hug fest on Saturday when I see you."

"OK!" I answer an in overly eager tone.

"Alright. You need to get going to work."

"I know. I'm glad you called," I say shyly.

"Me too."

"I love you, Declan."

"I love you too, Madi."

We say our goodbyes.

When I arrive at work a little while later, I am surprised to see Savannah already there. As I walk into the ER, I am beckoned over with a hand wave by Grace. She pulls me into Triage 3.

"Why didn't you tell anyone about that phone call?" Grace asks sternly.

"SAVANNAH!"

"I'm sorry, Madi, but when I told Luke he said I needed to tell someone at work about it, just in case."

"So when I tell you not to tell ANYONE, that means rush home and tell your husband?" I reply angrily, with my hands on my hips.

"Shut up, Madi," Grace interjects. "She was right to tell someone. You know that we have ways of protecting you here."

"Grace, I am not afraid of her or whoever it was. She is a stupid bimbo who is just trying to scare me away from Declan, and it's not going to work."

"I understand that, and right now I want to rip her fucking face off. But we have to take steps here at work to keep you safe. I'm not talking to you as a friend right now, Madi, I'm talking as your boss. Number one. From now on when you leave at the end of your shift, you do not leave alone and you go with security. They can take you out on a golf cart to your car. Second, when you get in every night you need to text me or call the security patrol and have them meet you at your car. This is non-optional, Madi. Do you understand?" Grace says very seriously.

Feeling like a scolded child, I nod.

"It's for your own safety, Madi," Savannah pipes up.

"Don't talk to me," I turn and walk out of the triage bay. Not only did I just get lectured by my boss, I now feel like a child who can't take care of herself.

I am so pissed at Savannah for telling Luke and Grace. I know she did it to protect me, but it pisses me off that she did.

The rest of the night is a very quiet one for the three of us. Normally when there is downtime we laugh and joke. Tonight I keep myself busy so there is no downtime for me. I am so angry I can't see straight.

At 6:00 am, Grace asks if some of us want to head out a bit early. The ER is quiet and I am exhausted from all the busy work I have been doing all night. She gives me the OK, so I call the security desk and have someone bring a golf cart around.

"I'll walk with you, Madi," Savannah says as I wait by the doors for my ride.

"I have an escort, thanks. Have a good day," I reply, staring straight ahead.

"Madi, please don't be mad at me. I had to tell someone. What if something happened to you? What about Claire? I wouldn't be able to live with myself if something happened to you because I kept quiet. You can be pissed at me, but deep down you know I did the right thing," Savannah says, choking back tears as she walks away.

Security pulls up a few moments later. I hop on the seat next to the driver and tell him where I'm parked.

As I get into my car, he gives me a nod and pulls away. I see Savannah almost at her truck. I start the car and drive around. Pulling up alongside of her, I roll my window down.

"I know you did the right thing, Savannah. I'm just pissed

at the situation, OK?"

"I only did it because I love you."

I nod. "I know, I love you too." I roll up the window and pull away.

Could today suck anymore? I haven't heard from Declan yet, I got reprimanded by my boss at work over a potential stalker threat, I'm pissed at one of my best friends, and to answer my original question… yes, today can suck more. I just broke a damn nail. My perfect French manicure is now mangled and gnarled by the hideousness of a broken middle fingernail. Well, at least it's an opportune break. I can flip people off and just tell them I was showing them my broken nail. Could work.

I walk into the house and toss my purse and bag on the counter. The noisy greeting from Zoe and Athena makes me smile. They are always so happy to see me even when I've had a shitty day. I put some toast in the toaster and pick up my cell phone.

No messages from Declan. He should be on his way to the academy. Maybe I will give him a quick call to tell him I love him. Talking to him always makes me feel better. The phone rings once and a message appears on my screen.

This number has been blocked at the request of the subscriber. Message 1436A

What? I hit his number again. Same message. What does that mean? Blocked?

I head over to the computer and pull up the internet. I go to Google and type the error message in. Right before my eyes, Google informs me that my phone number has been blocked by the other party so no calls or messages will go through. I don't understand. Why would he do that?

I stare at the screen, unable to comprehend why Declan would block me. I can't even call him to ask why. I start to cry as I thump my head down on the desk in front of me. Why would Declan block me? Everything was fine last night. What happened?

I sit at the desk and cry for several minutes when my phone starts to ring, scaring the hell out of me.

On the screen I see Declan's name. Why would he call me if he blocked me? I don't understand. I am so hurt, why would he do that? I clear my throat and answer.

"Hello?" I say quickly. I don't want him to know I've been crying.

"Hey, baby. How are you?"

"Fine."

"Are you still at work? I didn't think you would answer. I was going to leave you a message for you to hear when you left."

"No, I'm home already. They let some of us leave early because it was slow."

"What's wrong baby? Are you OK?" he asks.

"No. Why did you block me?" I ask sadly as the tears start to well up again.

"What are you talking about?"

"You blocked me from your phone so I can't call or text you. Why?" I sniffle trying to hold back the tears.

"Madi, I didn't block you," he sounds upset.

"I tried to call you today when I got home from the shitty fucking day I had and a message came on saying that the call was blocked at the request of the subscriber. I looked it up online and it told me that you blocked my number from incoming calls and text messages."

"Madi, baby, I never blocked you. Why would I do that?"

"I don't know," I sob.

"Son of a bitch!" he yells.

"What?" I ask, panicked.

"It was Tiffani. I'll call you back," he hangs up.

What does he mean, it was Tiffani?

I sit down at the island, trying to understand what he meant by that. Moments later there is a knock at the door. Walking toward it, I see it's Declan.

"Hi," I say through watery eyes, swinging the door open. He looks pissed off.

He steps inside and pulls me into a tight Declan hug.

"I called the phone company. Someone logged into my account and blocked your number from my account so I couldn't get any calls or text messages from you. The only person who could have done that was Tiffani."

"I don't understand. How could she do that?"

"When we were dating, I bought her a cell phone and added her to my plan because she couldn't get one on her own. She knew the password to the account. She must have logged in, looked at my call history, figured out which number was yours and blocked it. She likes to play games. She thinks that doing this will get me to call her."

"Oh God, Declan. I was so worried that you were upset with me for something. I couldn't imagine why you would just block me with no explanation."

"No, the only person who is blocked on there now is her. No more calls or messages. The phone company fixed it and gave me a new logon and password so she can't access it. I'm sorry she upset you, baby," he says, still hugging me.

"I guess that explains why my messages weren't going through yesterday."

"Yep, it sure does. Listen, I can't stay, I'm going to be late. But I wasn't far away so I wanted to come and tell you what happened and give you good hug," he says, smiling.

"Oh, God. You have no idea how much I need that hug today," I sigh.

He leans down and embraces me in his arms, pulling me to him. I'm pretty sure I moaned.

"I love you, Madi," he murmurs as he kisses my forehead.

"I love you, too." I look up dreamily at him. "Have a good day." I kiss him.

Closing the door, I watch him through the window as he gets in his truck. Man, he looked hot in his academy issued clothes. He was in navy blue workout pants, a fitted navy 'Police Academy' shirt and had a black baseball hat on backwards.

I think I'm going to start calling him Campbell's. He is Mmm mmmm good.

I make my way upstairs to shower and get some sleep before my last shift of the week.

When it's time to get up, I go through my usual routine to get ready. A little after 5:00, I am sitting in the kitchen eating dinner and catching up on my social media when my cell rings. Like clockwork, it's Declan.

"Hello?" I answer.

"Hey, baby. How are you?"

"I'm good. How are you?" I reply.

"Great! What are you doing?"

"Eating dinner and Facebooking."

"Ooh, dinner. What are you having?"

"Soup. I had a craving for soup today," I giggle to myself.

"Are you excited about Saturday? Just one more day and a wake up."

"Oh my God, I am so excited. I knew I missed you, but seeing you for those few minutes this morning reminded me how much."

"I know, baby, me too. I wanted to scoop you up in my arms and drag you upstairs and have my wicked way with you this morning." He's smiling, I can tell.

"Oh please, don't tease me!"

"You think I'm teasing? Then you don't know me very well. I wanted to rip those black scrubs off and take a dirty shower with you," I can tell he's smiling, and now I am too.

"Stop it," I whine.

"Haha. What's wrong?" Like he doesn't know.

"I have to leave for work soon. Don't," I say sternly, which means nothing to him.

"Does the thought of me ripping off your scrubs and carrying you into a hot, wet, naked shower with me upset you in some way?" He is smiling so big right now.

"STOP. IT. I haven't had had an orgasm in 2 days. This isn't fair," I growl.

"2 days? What the fuck? I haven't touched you in 4!" he sounds pissed.

"Relax, Declan. Sometimes a girl's gotta take things into her own hands. But good to know where we stand on the jealousy thing," I laugh.

"Wait, what? Did you just tell me that you…?"

"Mmmm hmmmm," I purr before he can finish.

"Fuck. What time do you leave for work? I can be there in 12 minutes."

"Nope." I laugh. "You'll have to wait until Saturday."

"Aww, man," he pouts. If he wasn't driving, I would think he just kicked the dirt with his shoe like a little kid.

"Good things come to those who wait," I reply in a patronizing tone.

"Man, the thought of you doing that… ghaaa… makes me so hard, Madi. That's not fair," he whines.

"Well, at least you can go home and do something about it. I'm sitting here in my scrubs all ready to go to work. I can't."

"Oh, the hell you can't! You need to take your other hand right now and put it down the front of your pants for me," he says.

"Ha. Calm down, Declan, you're driving. How will you explain that to the responding officers? I was listening to my girlfriend play with herself over the phone and drove into a tree? No, I don't think so."

"Let me just tell you, if they've got hot girlfriends and wives, they would totally get it and probably give me a medal or something for getting you to do it." He laughs.

"Oh, I didn't say I wouldn't do it. Just not right now." There is silence on the other end. "Declan?"

"I'm sorry. Declan just died and went to heaven because his girlfriend is too good to be true. In lieu of flowers, please make a donation in his name to The Wildlife Fund. They are working hard to save all of the tall trees being ravaged by hot beavers," he laughs.

I pull a Savannah, spitting soup out of my mouth all over the counter, and start coughing.

"Are you OK?" he asks, still laughing.

"Oh my God! I can't believe you just said that!" I bust out laughing as I get up to get a towel.

I can hear him still laughing on the other end of the phone. "I couldn't resist. I learned from the best."

"Ahh, you have snatched the pebble from my hand, young one," I say in my best Kung Fu voice.

"God, I love you," he sighs. "More and more every day." I can hear the smile in his voice.

"I love you too, Grasshopper."

"Well, I'm home, and let me tell ya, it was hard—pun intended—not to drive straight to your house and have my way with you. Or at the very least, watch you have your way with yourself. Man all mighty." I can hear him opening his front door and setting his keys down.

"Oh, come on. It's not that exciting, is it? Geez."

"Are you kidding me? The thought of YOU, doing THAT? Off the charts hot!" he says.

"Wow, I never knew that was such a big deal to a guy. We do it all the time, and any woman who says she doesn't is a big fat liar who is dead from the waist down."

"Sooo, how often do you do it?" he asks quietly.

"Hahaha, as often as I need to. Sometimes every day, or every few days. Whenever the mood strikes me."

"That's so hot," he says in a low voice.

"Well, since we are sharing, how often do you? And don't lie and tell me you don't," I say, giggling.

"Every fucking chance I get," He laughs. "But now that I have you, a lot less often."

"When did you, last?" Now I turn shy.

"About 2 minutes ago."

"Declan! Come on, answer. I told you it was 2 days ago for me."

"What if I said I was doing it right now?"

"What?" I squeak.

"What if I told you that the second I walked in my front door I reached into my sweats and started stroking myself?"

"Really?" My pitch goes even higher.

"Yeah. The thought of you playing with yourself got me all kinds of revved up, Madi."

"Holy hell, that's hot," I say with a giggle.

"Did you just giggle?" He laughs.

"Yeah, I did."

"So, does the thought of me stroking myself turn you on?"

"The thought of you doing anything turns me on. But this, well… yeah, that's kind of panty soaking."

"Are you wet?" he asks.

"Mmmm hmmm."

"Reach down. Feel how wet you are for me, Madi." He sounds a little breathy. "When you do it, do you use your hand or do you have… toys?"

"Both."

"Oh shit. How wet are you, Madi? Tell me," he begs.

"So wet, Declan. God, I wish you were here. I wish it was your fingers, not mine," I moan.

"Oh God, Madi, keep talking." He exhales harshly.

"I want to feel your hands on me, softly stroking my clit, teasing me." I'm panting.

"Fuck, Madi. Keep talking, you're gonna make me cum. Taste yourself. Please take your fingers out and suck on them."

I've never had phone sex before. This is so hot! I do as I'm told and give an extra slurp sound for his benefit.

"Oh Jesus, Madi. I'm gonna cum. Do it again."

I follow his instructions and start to stroke myself again for Declan. I moan into the phone as the pleasure inside me builds.

"Oh Declan, you feel so good," I whisper.

"Do it, Madi. Make yourself cum. I want to hear you."

"Oh God, yes. Keep talking, Declan. Tell me what to do."

"Slide your fingers inside of you, then pull them out and suck on them for me, baby."

"Ahhhhh, yes." I make a louder sucking noise on my fingers.

"Oh yeah. That's right, Madi. Suck 'em." I hear him panting out his orders, but I can tell he is holding back.

"I want you to suck my clit, Declan."

"OH FUUUUUUUCK!" he groans out, and I can tell he found his release.

I continue to moan and pant into the phone as I tease myself to the brink. Hearing him cum brought me right to the verge, and with a few swipes of my fingers I am pushed over the edge. "Oh God… Declan. Yesss." I whimper and pant into the phone, almost dropping it.

After several seconds of silence, I can hear Declan stirring on the other end of the phone.

"Hey, are you OK?" he asks, sounding very relaxed.

"Mmmm hmmmm," I murmur. "You?" I ask softly.

"I'm great. Thank you."

"Why are you thanking me?" I giggle.

"Because that was amazing, Madi."

"It was pretty amazing." I feel so relaxed. After the day from hell yesterday and the thought of going into to work tonight, I was a bit stressed out, I guess. That was the perfect release.

"You surprise me at every turn, baby," he says with a smile.

"You ain't seen nothin yet, cowboy," I laugh.

"Bring it on!" I can hear his grin from ear to ear.

In my post orgasmic glow, I look up at the clock and realize I'm supposed to be pulling into the parking lot of the hospital right now. "OH SHIT! I gotta go! I'm gonna be late for work."

"Oh God, I'm sorry. Please drive safe, OK?"

"I will. I love you!"

"I love you too," he says, and I hang up.

Chapter 25

AS I BOLT from my car to the ER I am met with an unhappy Grace who is looking at her watch and back at me. "Where have you been? I was worried sick. I thought something happened to you."

"I'm sorry. I got stuck on the phone and lost track of time," I answer with a slight grin.

"Did you have security escort you in? NO, you didn't, did you?" she says abruptly

"No. Look, I'm sorry. I didn't have time to wait for them to get there. I was late. Besides, as fast as I just ran to get here, no boogie monsters could have caught me unless they had wings," I reply, smiling.

Grace is not.

"It's not funny, Madi. You need to take this seriously. If you want to take chances on your own time, that's fine, but when you pull into this parking lot you are on MY time and follow MY rules. Got it?" she says sternly.

"Yes, Dr. Kelly. I've got it. Are we through? I have charts

to review," I say abruptly with a raised eyebrow.

"Yes, we are," she turns on her heel and walks away.

Savannah comes to me. "Hey, are you OK? What was that about?"

"Grace is pissed at me for being late and for not calling security to escort me in."

"You were only a few minutes late. I'm late on a daily basis and she doesn't say anything to me."

"I don't know. Hey. I'm sorry about yesterday, Vannah. I was just overwhelmed, and…"

"It's OK. You don't have to apologize. I get it. I know why you were mad, I just hope you understood why I did it."

"I do. I'm sorry," I say hugging her in the middle of the ER.

A few hours later, Grace comes back to the unit bearing several Starbucks cups and an apologetic face.

"Umm. So listen. I'm not good with this I'm sorry shit, so here's the deal. These drinks represent my feelings. Can we be done?" she hands me my favorite chai latte, on the side of the cup it says

'I'm sorry, I love you,' with a smiley face.

Savannah's has a smiley face and a heart.

"Oh come here, you big softy!" I say, grabbing Grace and pulling her into a hug.

"Ugh, God! Get off me, you big carpet muncher!" she groans as she wiggles out of my embrace.

"Only your carpet, Grace!" I shout as she walks away.

All is right in the world again.

The night goes pretty smoothly. No real drama, which is a nice change from last night. As our shift winds down, I am so relieved that I have the next few days off. I can't wait to surprise Declan tomorrow morning.

On my drive home, I consider what I should bring. I'm thinking croissants, strawberries, cream, champagne, orange juice and his favorite Starbucks should be good. I don't plan on eating much anyway. Hehe. When I pull into the grocery store parking lot, I send him a quick text.

–Today and a wake up until I get to see you again XO–

*–Counting down the hours. XO–*he replies.

I run in and grab the things I need for tomorrow. Heading home, I am filled with such excitement. This feels like a first date all over again. Before I know it, the day has whizzed by and Declan is calling me on his way home from the academy.

"Hello?"

"Hey, baby! How are you?"

"I am fan-frickin-tastic. How are you?"

"I am so beat, but good."

"Did you have a rough day?"

"Yeah, we did some pretty intense stuff today."

"Are you OK?" I ask.

"Oh yeah. I'm fine, just tired. But I am looking forward to seeing you tomorrow," he says happily.

"Oh God, me too. I have missed you so much."

"I know, baby. I'm sorry. This is going to suck for the next 5 months," he growls.

"It will be OK. We will just have to make the most of the time we do have together," I reply in my most convincing voice.

"Oh, I intend to."

"Is that so?" I inquire.

"Oh hell yeah. I am going to enjoy every precious moment I have with you."

"I haven't stopped thinking about you all day," I tell him.

"Oh God, Madi. You have been on my mind every minute. Last night? Oh Jesus, last night was so hot. I haven't been able to get that out of my head since."

"You need to focus, mister. I don't want you failing the academy, and I would feel guilty for the rest of my life if I crushed your dream."

"Well, maybe I would have to find a new dream then. Maybe I could make a living off of laying around and pleasing you all day." He laughs.

"Oh honey, if I could afford to hire you for that, trust me. It would be a done deal."

"I would do it for free, ya know."

"I would let you do it for free, ya know," I answer.

"I want to see you," he says quietly.

"I want to see you, too."

"I could come over now for a little bit. We wouldn't have to wait until tomorrow." Oh, God. I want him to come over so badly, but I have this whole thing planned for tomorrow and I'm so excited about it.

"I know, and I really want you to, but…"

"Arrgh! No… no buts!" he says, laughing. "You could come here?"

"Patience, my love. Patience. Tomorrow will be here before you know it. Get a good night's sleep, wake up refreshed, and then we will go for a ride on your bike and have lunch somewhere."

"Why do you have to be so strong-willed? How come you

can't just cave in and let me come over?" he says with a chuckle.

"Because I have a surprise for you." I smile through the phone.

"Ooh. I love surprises. Well, at least the good kind. Not the Crying Game kind of surprises," he adds.

"Ha. No, nothing like that. It's a good surprise, I promise. And with that, I am going to let you go so you can shower and eat and get some sleep. I have some things to do for tomorrow."

"Oh, there are things to do? Niiice!"

"I love you, Declan."

"I love you too, Madi. I will see you tomorrow."

"Night."

"Good night, baby."

Before I know it, it's time for me to go to bed. I have been busy all day cleaning, doing laundry, waxing, shaving, buffing and polishing. I get the lingerie ready, and decide I will wear loose jeans and a long white button-up to hide the secret beneath it. I don't want him to see any of it until I am ready to unleash the beast on him.

I jump into my bed and fall asleep quickly. The faster I can get to sleep, the faster tomorrow will be here and I can go surprise Declan. I'm like a kid on Christmas Eve waiting for Santa. Except I'm a horny woman waiting to ravage her boyfriend.

My alarm sounds at 6am. I jump out of bed and start the shower.

After getting ready, I head down to make sure everything is packed. I have all the essentials stowed in my basket. I even brought a blanket so we can have a living room picnic on his floor. Goofy, I know, but it will be fun. We can't go on a real picnic with me dressed in black lacy things so his condo will have to do.

I put all the stuff in the back of my car, then check my hair and makeup one more time. I drive to Declan's house and I'm overcome by butterflies in my stomach. What if he thinks this is stupid? Oh right, that's when I rip off the white shirt and flash him my lacy tata's. That should distract him long enough to make him forget all about the picnic fail.

As I round the corner into his condo complex, I am all smiles. I am just 2 turns away from my silly surprise. As I turn the last corner, I see a car driving toward me.

It slows as it approaches me.

Looking at it, the driver seems familiar. As I slow down to wait for the car, I can see Declan standing in his doorway wearing just his workout shorts, no shirt. He is leaning against the door frame.

Looking back at the car approaching me, I now see that it's Tiffani with an i. Slowing alongside me, she smiles, waves and mouths 'I fucked him'.

She drives past me and extends her arm out the window, flipping me off.

I slam on the brakes and look back up at Declan. He's still standing in his doorway, half dressed. I look up in my rearview mirror at her car and then back at Declan several more times. He knows I saw her. I can see his mouth yell the word 'SHIT' as he runs back inside his condo to grab a shirt and his keys. He runs back out and jumps in his truck.

Before he can get in his truck, I am already backing up and turning around.

I have to get out of here.

I can't breathe.

I peel out of his complex and start to cry as I head down the road.

The gate to his complex closes behind me, so I have a few seconds lead on him. I'm sure he is making a beeline for my house, assuming that's where I will go.

But I can't right now. I can't go home. I head in the direction of Savannah and Luke's.

My phone is on the seat next to me and it starts to ring. I look over at the screen. It's Declan. I hit ignore.

It rings again and again. Each time I hit ignore, sending it to voicemail.

Several minutes later I pull up in front of Savannah's. I text her that I am out front and need to talk. I don't want to knock and wake Luke or the boys up. She texts me back and tells me to come in, the door is open. Walking in, I find her in the kitchen making breakfast for everyone.

"Hey there! You're up earl… What the fuck happened? LUUUUKE!" Savannah yells after she sees my face.

"I just saw Tiffani with an i leaving Declan's condo," I manage to get out between dry heaves.

"WHAT? She was leaving his condo? This morning?"

"Yes. She slowed her car down as I was pulling in, mouthed that she just fucked him, then laughed and took off. What am I gonna do, Vannah?" I sob.

"Well, I mean… I don't know," she looks stunned. "Where was Declan during all of this?"

"Standing in his doorway half naked. He just had shorts on. He saw me and came after me."

"He followed you? Is he outside? LUKE! Get your knife, we're going dick hunting!"

"No, the gate to his complex closed behind me before he could get there. I had a head start so I came here. I'm sure he went to my house. But I just couldn't. I couldn't go there, Vannah."

"No, honey, you did the right thing coming here. Do you want some tea?" she offers with a pathetic smile, not really knowing what to say or do.

I nod mutely.

Savannah makes us some tea and sits down with me. I've stopped crying. Now I am just sitting in stunned silence.

"I can't do this," I say flatly.

"What do you mean? I thought you loved him."

"I do, Savannah, but I can't do this. I can't handle the thought of him cheating on me. I can't go through that again. It broke me with Andy. I can't go through it with Declan. I don't know if I will survive it," I reply, staring blankly out her window.

"Then maybe you need to go talk to him, honey. Find out what happened. Just don't make any rash decisions until you talk to him."

We sit in silence for what seems like days, then Savannah speaks. "What do you want to do, sweets? Do you want to call him? Do you want me to take you home? What can I do to help?"

"I wanna go to Vegas," I mumble, still staring out her window.

"You want to what?" she questions, surprised.

"I want to go to Vegas. Can we go to Vegas?" I ask, turning to look at her.

"Well, OK. Sure. When, honey?"

"Now. I want to go now. Can you call the girls?" I can't

seem to rid myself of the blank stare on my face.

"Well, ummm, OK. Let me see who I can round up. You sit tight. I'll be right back."

Savannah leaves me alone in her kitchen. I get up and dig my phone out of my purse. I have missed 9 calls, 4 voicemails and 3 text messages, all from Declan, in the last 30 minutes.

Message #1: "Madi, please wait. Don't leave! FUCK!" I can hear the panic in his voice and the door to his truck slam. This must have been as he was getting in his truck to follow me.

Message #2: "Madi, it's not what you think. Please, baby, just pull over and wait for me so we can talk."

Message #3: "I'm outside your house. You're not answering the door. Please come to the door. I need to talk to you."

Message #4: "You didn't come home. I'm here, I'm waiting for you. I love you."

Text #1: *Madi, please stop!*

Text #2: *It's not what you think.*

Text #3: *I love you. I'm here, waiting for you.*

Savannah comes back a few minutes later to find me at her table, holding my cell phone with tears rolling down my face, but I'm not actually crying.

"Did he call you?" she asks.

I nod. "9 times. 4 messages. 3 texts," I reply in a monotone.

"Are you sure you want to go to Vegas, Madi?"

I nod again.

"OK. Well, I just called the girls. They are all in. I also called Rachel and Lilly, I hope that's OK. They are going to fly in and meet us tonight."

"When do we leave?"

"I don't know yet, honey. Luke is booking our stuff right now, OK?"

"OK," I answer numbly.

"You need to talk to him," she says hesitantly. "You can't just run away. You need to talk to him before you go."

I nod. "Text me the info on our flight and when I need to be ready, OK?" I reply, standing to leave.

"I will. Please be safe driving home. Promise me you'll listen to him," she says, hugging me.

AS I PULL on to my street, I can see Declan's truck parked in front of my house.

Turning into the driveway, I see him sitting on the front porch, waiting for me.

He stands as I get out of the car and rushes towards me.

"Madi, please. Let me explain," he looks crushed, his eyes red from crying.

I walk toward him, still numb. I can't look at him. I sit down on the front porch. He sits down next to me.

"Madi, baby. Nothing happened with Tiffani. You have to believe me," he begs.

I stare straight ahead, emotionless.

"Why was she there?" I ask in a hushed tone.

"I have no idea. I'd just gotten up. I was laying on the

couch watching TV when someone knocked on the door. I thought it was you. I got excited and opened the door. When I saw it was her, I froze."

"What did she want?" I manage to squeak out.

"She was trying to convince me that I should take her back. That she could make me happy and that things would be different this time. I told her she needed to leave. She got upset and asked me why."

He kneels in front of me, on one knee, taking my hands in his. "Madi, look at me."

As my eyes find his, the tears begin to roll out uncontrollably. I start to wring the corner of my bottom lip between my teeth.

"I told her that I am in love with you and nothing she could say or do would change that," his eyes plead for me to believe him.

"I love you Madi, you know that," he says, our eyes still locked.

"And?" I ask softly

"And nothin'. She got mad and started yelling at me. Telling me she was the best thing that ever happened to me and that no one will ever make me feel like she did. I told her she was right. No one will ever use me and make me feel like a chump again. She slapped me, got in her car, and left."

I nod.

"When she drove past me she…" I start to choke up. "She said she fucked you."

"NOTHING HAPPENED, Madi! You have to believe me!" He pulls my hands toward his heart, his tortured face inches from mine.

"I do, Declan, but…"

"No. No but!" he says sternly.

"Declan, I… the thought of her touching you," I get choked up at the thought "of what could have happened, it makes me physically ill."

"But nothing happened, Madi," he pleads, his eyes filling with tears. "Baby, you have to believe me."

"I do," I say as I begin to cry. "But, I… I just need some time to think."

"What do you mean? Either you believe me or you don't. What is there to think about?" he asks.

"I don't know, I just…"

"Please don't shut me out, Madi," he begs.

"I'm not shutting you out, Declan. I just need some time to think about things. I love you. Too much," I pause, choking up. "The thought of losing you… I can't. Seeing her leave your place today brought back all of the insecurities I have—about you and I, our age, our differences—and I was thrust right back into the face of infidelity like I was with Andy. It crushed me when Andy cheated on me, Declan. I don't know if I would recover if you did. And that scares me. It scares me that I am so in love with you that I may not survive if you ever left me."

"Goddamnit! I'm not Andy, Madi!" he says angrily. "I wouldn't cheat on you. I wouldn't risk what we have for anything," he says earnestly.

"I just need a few days, Declan. It's for the best. Plus, I think it would be good to give Tiffani some time to cool off. I don't want her to do anything stupid."

"What do you mean?"

Taking a deep breath, I decide now is the time to tell him.

"I got a phone call on Tuesday night."

"From her?" he asks.

"I don't know. I didn't answer, it said Unknown Caller. They left a voicemail."

"What did they say?"

"They said I had better watch my back and called me a little cunt."

"Are you kidding? Why the hell didn't you tell me, Madi? Seriously?" he's pissed.

I pick up my phone and start to play the message on speaker phone.

"That's not her voice, but I'm pretty sure I know who it is," Declan says through clenched teeth.

"Who?"

"One of her friends. Mary. She was always makin' trouble. She would fill Tiffani's head with stupid ideas, most of which she acted on. I'm sure she put her up to it."

"Should I be worried? I mean, they have extra security for me at work now because of this."

"WHAT?" he asks, upset.

"They're making me ride with a security guard to and from my car every day. Grace was worried."

"You told Grace, but not me?" The look of hurt in his eyes cuts through me.

"No, Declan. Savannah badgered it out of me the night it happened. I asked her not to tell anyone but she told Luke and Grace."

"Has anything else happened?"

"No." I shake my head.

Several moments of silence pass between us.

"So you need a few days to think. How does this work exactly?" he asks

"I don't know Declan, I just need to get away for a few days. Clear my head and think about things."

"Where are you going?" he asks softly

"Vegas. The girls and I are just going for the weekend."

"Right. And the party capital of the world is the perfect place to reflect on our relationship?" the rudeness in his tone makes me flinch. "Got it." he nods

"Declan, it's not like that."

"No. It is, Madi. It's exactly like that. You and your girls are going to Vegas for the weekend, leaving me here to sit and worry about our relationship."

"Should I be worried?" I ask.

"I don't know. You tell me. You're the one who needs to 'get away and think'," he replies, using air quotes and a sarcastic tone.

"You know what? You can be pissed off if you want. All I asked for was a few days to think. You can make your own assumptions on what that means. I have to go pack," I stand up and walk towards the front door.

"Don't do anything you might regret, Madi," he replies coldly, his back still to me.

Pausing with my hand on the door knob, I look back over my shoulder, take in a slow breath and reply softly "Right back at ya, big guy."

Epilogue

THE CLICK OF the door sends a chill down my spine. I can hear his footsteps as he stomps down the steps of my porch, away from my house. Leaving.

The sound of an engine roaring and tires squealing are the last thing I hear from Declan.

Its Luke's truck that now occupies the spot out front of my house, the same spot Declan's did a short time ago.

"Hey hun. Are you ready to go?" Savannah asks with a kind face

I nod and attempt a smile, it's forced and it's obvious.

"Someone drag racing on your street Madi? What's with the skid marks?" Luke asks with a laugh at his skid mark comment.

"Those are from Declan. Earlier," I answer softly

He nods slowly in reply

"Thanks for taking care of the dogs for me Luke. I appreciate it," I say

"No worries babe, I got this," he winks

"Luke are you flirting with Madi? It's because you saw her tits isn't it?" Savannah asks in mock disgust

"Yep, you got me," he replies putting his hands in the air in surrender.

"I knew it! I knew there was something going on between you two," Grace says shaking her head

"Wait? When did Luke see Madi's tits?" Lynn asks confused

"Long story. My girls aren't nearly as spectacular as yours Savannah. Granted mine aren't paid for like Tatianna and Trixie there," I say motioning back and forth at her huge boobs "But I've never had any complaints," I smile

The idle chit chat continues all the way to the airport. I know everyone is trying to avoid the 6'6" Crimson Tide shaped elephant in the room, so to speak, and I love them for it. But I can't help but think about him… in every thought.

Should I have left?

Should I have stayed to talk it out?

Can I overcome my insecurities and let Declan love me?

Acknowledgements

There are so many people I'd like to thank. First I'd like to thank the Academy for this prestigious award…

Sorry, wrong speech. I need to save that for the Hollywood blockbuster based on the books.

This wouldn't be possible without the following people.

Starbucks for the amazing work they do in caffeine. You truly do Gods work.

Dr. Pepper and the makers there of. Also, fine work in the caffeine. I blame you for my new addiction and addition to my waist size.

My amazing parents who remained anonymous in the book to protect their identity and not embarrass them further because their only child wrote a smut book.

Your undying and unwavering support means the world to me. I could not have done it without you.

My daughter Brynlie who sacrificed many board game nights and "Mommy, Look at me's" so I could meet deadlines and let creative juices flow. I love you

Brynlie Belle. (We did it!)

The real life Zoe and Athena who have learned to stretch their bladders so I could finish my thoughts before they had to go out. Thank you for all the asshole kisses. If this goes NYT I'll let you on the furniture.

Aaron Ford, Tamra Wade, Emily Gibbs, Tom Cavness, Sarah Cox and Rachel Topp. Thank you from the bottom of my heart or your generosity.

Uber babe Heather McNeal for her amazing work on the cover. You turned a pussy and her play thing into a true work of art. I heart you a latte!

My amazing editor Trish Kuper, AKA T-Kup. Thank you for not charging me by the comma.

Here,,,,,,,, Just in case I forgot a few.

And last but not least, the real life character in my life.

To Linda (Grace), Yvonne (Taylor), Amy (Lynn), Jessica (Elise) and of course, Jennifer (Savannah)… without all of you and our real life events, mishaps, inappropriate conversations and shenanigans the book would have been far less entertaining.

You truly have written the story of my life. I am forever grateful for your support, laughter, tears and friendship.

I love you all more than any words can say.

~Stephanie

About the Author

Stephanie L Macy was born and raised in Arizona and still lives there today. Why she has stayed for 41 summers in Satan's arm pit remains a mystery. She currently resides in a suburb of Phoenix with her biological daughter and two adopted girls of the 4 legged canine variety. Yes, that is a lot of estrogen in one house.

She attended the University of Get a job you have bills to pay. For some unknown reason she thought that a career in healthcare was the way to go and spends her days stabbing people with needles for money.

In her free time… well she doesn't really have free time, she is a single mother who works full time. She hasn't had free time since November of 2004, I believe it was a Sunday.

She is an avid reader thanks to EL James and all Fifty Shades of her Grey. Enjoys the works of romantic fiction which let's face it, is just a classy way of saying Mommy Porn.

Stephanie never imagined that she would write a book much less publish one. She can barely write a check.

She sincerely thanks you for purchasing her book and supporting her on this amazing journey.

If you downloaded a pirated copy of this book then Stephanie thinks you're a jerk and hopes you drop your E-Reader.

Connect with SL Macy

Facebook: https://www.facebook.com/SLMacyAuthor
Twitter: https://twitter.com/SLMacy
Email: slmacyauthor@gmail.com

Made in the USA
Lexington, KY
22 May 2015